Why Natasha?

A Natasha McMorales Mystery

C S Thompson

Why Natasha?

Published in the U.S. by:

CSThompsonBooks.com
Bristol, TN 37620

ISBN 978-0-9794116-4-9

Although the major characters are all fictional and any resemblance to a real person is accidental and unintentional, many of the places are real and the people one would find there are real as well. Those places are:

In the Bristol Area: Blackbird Bakery, Eats on 5th, Ellis' of Abingdon, King College, Manna Bagel, Scotty Wades, State Street, Virginia Intermont College, Meadowview

Beyond Bristol: Florence, Montepulciano, Positano, and Rome, Italy; Chicago, Naperville, and Lombard, Illinois.

Special thanks to:

Craig and Mary for editorial support

Brandon, Craig, Karen, Matt, Sarah and Tommy for contributions to plot and character.

Abby, Barb, Gayle and Myra for encouragement.

Dianna, Aireal, Hannah, Lacey, Sarah, Tiffany and Wesley for technical assistance.

Katie, Emily and Alexa for inspiring Nattie in the first place.

Barb for tolerating an absentee husband.

PROLOGUE

There should have been a sound--she knew that much--but she was also aware that not hearing anything was curious. It was as if she was watching someone else from a detached distance. Then a voice followed by an explosion of white light. Then all was darkness.

Her next awareness was of lying on her back and of the intense throbbing in her lips. She tried unsuccessfully to lift her head. The failure to lift herself refocused her awareness to the dull pain in the back of her head and how hard it was to breathe. She laid her head back and just tried to move her lip, which had the effect of doubling the pain.

"Just lie still," a calm male voice said.

She squinted, then closed her eyes, then opened them as wide as she could in an attempt to get the face behind the voice into focus.

"You're ok," the voice said.

"What happened?" Nattie asked as the man's face came into view.

"As near as I could tell you were sucker punched." The voice was impassive, professional. "You never saw it coming. He walked up to you, said something, and then bam. You didn't lift your arms; you didn't flinch; you didn't protect yourself at all."

Nattie noticed that he was in a blue uniform. He was a policeman.

"My partner and I saw the whole thing. We were parked right over there."

Turning her head to look in the direction where he pointed made Nattie wince. Her neck was stiff. She labored to take a long deep breathe and began to sit up.

"Are you sure you're ready to do that missy?" the policeman asked, but seeing that she was not to be dissuaded he put his left hand under her right arm and supported her neck with his right. "Just go slow," he encouraged.

Once she was upright, Nattie bent her head forward and fought off dizziness. She touched her lips. She could not tell if they were swollen yet but she knew they would be. Her front teeth felt loose against her tongue.

"Do you know who hit you?"

Lifting her head Nattie gazed across the parking lot outside her office. After a prolonged consideration she slowly turned to face the officer, who was still squatting next to her. "I don't think I do."

"That's okay," he said, "we'll know who he is soon enough. My partner caught him as he ran around the front of your building."

"Already?"

Laughing more heartily, the officer said, "He wasn't the brightest assailant we've ever had to catch. He attacked you right in front of us and then when he tried to make his escape he ran straight toward us."

How nice for you, thought Nattie.

"Are you sure you didn't recognize him? It looked like he said something to you just before he hit you."

"He did." she remembered. "He asked me my name."

CHAPTER 1

NATTIE

"Peace and goodwill," Nattie announced as she crested the State Street hill on Monday morning. Immediately she touched her lip. Although it had been nearly a week since she had been punched in her parking lot, pronouncing words that begin with the letter "p" still hurt.

On Wednesday she had driven to the Opryland Hotel in Nashville and on Thursday and Friday she attended a review course in preparation for a private investigation agency licensure exam on Saturday. She returned to Bristol late Saturday night and enjoyed the solitude of being home on Sunday without anyone knowing she was back.

The timing of the trip to Nashville was a blessing for her. Staying in Bristol would have required endless questions about her fat lip. Having no answers for those questions would have been embarrassing enough without the added pressure of her profession. She could picture the comments:"You say you don't know who hit you or why?--Too bad you don't know a private investigator." In Nashville, if one of the other private investigators were to ask, "in the line of duty" would have been an acceptable explanation.

She was already a licensed private investigator but this license would qualify her to own and operate her own agency. Passing the agency exam had been Nattie's main concern for the last five days; but now that she was home in Bristol, finding out who attacked her moved to the top of the To-Do list. She did not see herself as a crusader defending women against men. In spite of knowing that women are just as capable of villainy as men, she still had a slight fantasy that the inaugural case of her new agency, assuming that she passed the exam, would be to find justice for a victimized woman. *I just wish it wasn't me*, she thought.

On State Street, two blocks east of the "Bristol: A Good Place to Live" sign, is a hill. Atop of that hill is a panoramic view overlooking downtown Bristol with the "knobs" in the background to the west. The knobs were not exactly mountains, but if she was squinting she could envision herself looking over the hillside surrounding Assisi, Italy, the home of Saint Francis.

Nattie's affection for Saint Francis was not born from a Catholic upbringing. Her parents went to a Lutheran church on those occasions when they went to church at all. It was her mother, Ingrid, who had first been enamored with the founder of the Franciscan order. Ingrid had a small plastic statue of Saint Francis on her dashboard and was fond of telling stories about him to her children. When Nattie was eleven, Ingrid married Lionel O'Brien, who considered Ingrid's plastic statue to be a form of "idol worship," so she threw the statue, a DVD of "Brother Sun, Sister Moon," and two biographies of Saint Francis away. Nattie retrieved it all and the very first thing Nattie did when she bought her first car was to place that same plastic Saint Francis statue in the middle of her dashboard.

If traffic on State Street was thin, as it often was early in the morning, she could lean over to the middle of her front seat and include the statue in view of the city and hillside. She could then imitate Francis himself welcoming the Sun to a new day in the hills of Assisi, "peace and goodwill."

The scene observed from behind Saint Francis was her favorite view of the city. She did not have this visual experience as often as she would have liked because it needed daylight and sparse traffic, which meant early in the morning. When she started her morning this way she knew it would be a good day.

Natalie "Nattie" Miriam Moreland slid into her usual parking spot in the lot outside her office. As usual she was the first car there. Not a big surprise for seven thirty on a Monday morning. Her Private Investigator office had a side entrance leading directly to the parking lot which allowed her clients to enter with some anonymity. The front entrance facing State Street would have been better advertising, but it would not have allowed much privacy.

She had been gone nearly a week and could see already that the sign painter had worked on her door. *Good*, Nattie thought, slinging her bag over her left shoulder. She transferred her keys to her right hand and headed for the door. But something she noticed stopped her in mid-stride. The key to her office door froze in time just six inches from its home. She could not believe what she was looking at on the glass door to her office.

Natasha McMorales
Private Investigator

Nattie almost knew that she would eventually find this very funny. Almost, but not quite. What she did know was that someone got her name wrong. Her name, the name she had written on a work order exactly as she wanted it

4

painted on her door. The name she had written on the work order her receptionist had downloaded from the Ace Sign Company. The name on the check that the Ace "policy" required before they would start to work. The name she had pointed at and said aloud to her receptionist before she left town six days ago. The name she wanted on her door was her name, Natalie Moreland.

Her eyes blinked then opened wider as she lowered her right hand and let the key dangle. She realized that it really could be Ace's fault, but a screw-up like this had Kevin's fingerprints all over it.

"Why Natasha?" she asked out loud without expecting an answer. Then her eyes narrowed and her breathing became very deep and very slow. In spite of knowing that it was 7:30 in the morning and that Kevin, her receptionist, her little brother, had never come to work before lunch on Mondays, she still looked for him in the parking lot. When they were kids and Kevin knew he had done something that would tick her off, he would always hide somewhere to gauge her first reaction from a safe distance. She was sure he was watching from somewhere now.

"Are you Ms McMorales?" shouted a man from across the intersection.

The shout startled her. Maybe it was because this was the first time she had returned to the scene where she was attacked. Nattie was surprised by how much the shout startled her. She just looked at the shouter, a man she did not recognize. *If you don't know the rules of the game it's not wise to roll the dice.* So she stood there, non-committal about her name, and watched the shouter wait for traffic to thin enough to cross the street.

He was bald, middle-aged, maybe a healthy 50 or a 40 with some hard miles. He was dressed in spotless white painter's pants, a white tee-shirt, also spotless, and a blue sports coat. He carried two cups of coffee from Java J's as he tiptoed through traffic toward her.

"You are Natasha McMorales" the shouter stated, "I just knew it when I saw you." His smile was big, too big for Bristol, Tennessee, where the standard operating procedure for smiling was to show the upper teeth and occasionally the upper and lower teeth on one side of the mouth or the other. But this tiptoeing middle-aged man wearing a sport-jacket and painter pants was showing every tooth he had.

He held out a cup of coffee in his right hand, "Your office manager told me you drink decaf with splenda." Then he nodded as if to say, "Go ahead; take it."

"Do you mean Kevin?" Nattie asked as she pointed her thumb back over her shoulder toward the door behind her while thinking, *My idiot brother?*

"Si, Kevin." Mister Tip-toe frowned, retracting the coffee cup. "Did he play a joke on me?"

Nattie stepped forward and reached for the decaf coffee, "I'm sorry for acting so rude. I don't usually think of Kevin as my office manager." She shrugged. "He's my brother."

Mister Tip-toe's gigantic smile returned as he released his gift into her hand.

"Thank you," she said, as she took a sip through the plastic lid. It burned her over-sensitive upper lip, but she added, "This is perfect."

Placing all five fingertips of his right hand on the middle of his chest, the man announced, "I am Oliver Ruggaliano"; and after bowing slightly, he added, "Please call me Ollie."

"Hello, Ollie," she said as she shifted the keys to her left pinky finger and offered her right hand to shake, "I'm Nattie."

Ollie moved his coffee to his left hand, then after drying his right hand on his right butt cheek he shook her hand enthusiastically. "Nattie! It is a good name, a good American name." His teeth disappeared and he knitted his brow, "Natasha is a beautiful name, though, a dignified name, important."

"Why is the name Natasha important?"

"I need to hire a detective who has--" He paused. "--European sensitivity."

"European sensitivity?"

"I must explain," Ollie said, "but it is a long story and you have just gotten here. I will come back later when we both have time."

She was tempted to tell him that "Nattie" is American for "Natalie," not "Natasha," but with the "European sensitivity'" comment the game just got more confusing. "Let me go inside and check my calendar."

Ollie held her coffee while she slid the key into the lock of the door. "I was gone all last week," she explained.

His "I know" froze her for the second time that morning. She lifted her head and made eye contact with her own reflection in the glass door. *Did you hear what I heard?* she asked herself silently.

It was not fear that Nattie felt, although she was aware that several alarms had rung in the last few minutes. Then again, maybe the awareness of alarms being rung was how she felt fear. Setting the questions of emotional intelligence aside she decided to keep Ollie in front of her and with his hands full until she was within easy reach of one of the guns she kept in her office. The gun she normally kept holstered at the small of her back was still locked in the glove compartment of her Subaru. Pulling the door open with her left hand she ushered him in with her right hand.

"After you," Ollie said politely.

"I appreciate that, Ollie," she said pleasantly, "but I have the door and you have your hands full so please, go ahead."

He tried giving the coffee to her, but she said, "You hold the coffee and I'll get the lights."

Ollie half-bowed again and then stepped through the door into the unlit waiting room. Nattie followed him through the door and flipped on the light switch which was to her left. With the lights on she turned toward Ollie only to watch him set off another alarm in her head.

The waiting room had a large frumpy couch, upholstered with a heavy dark green fabric that reminded many folks of an L.L.Bean dog blanket. The couch was along the short wall to the right of the door, which made the wall crowded enough to offend even marginally sensitive tastes. But aesthetics was not why Nattie wanted the couch there. Her real reason was because she wanted the end table to be just inside the door.

It was a plain end table and it usually held a disorganized pile of odd and unrelated magazines; *People*, *Gold Digest*, *Southern Living*, and *Sojourners*. But the real importance of the plain end table was the spring loaded hidden drawer that held one of the two guns she kept in her office.

What was alarming Nattie at the moment was that Ollie was now standing next to and facing the end-table. After he put her coffee on top of an old *People* magazine proclaiming Mel Gibson as the sexiest man alive, he slid his hand under the lip of the top and sprung the secret drawer open, which immediately thudded against the wall.

Nothing about this scene was acceptable to Nattie. Ollie knew way too much about her for her comfort, which was par for the course when Kevin was involved. Also, Ollie had a very European name and an interest in "European sensitivity," whatever that was, but his accent sounded more like he was from New England than Italy. And the secret hidden drawer, which normally missed hitting the wall by half an inch, was not where it had been last week. And worse yet, it was most certainly not a secret hidden from this oddly dressed tip-toeing man who now smiled warmly gesturing at the gun in the drawer with a hand motion that would have made Vanna White proud.

Nattie did not know whether to leave the gun be or put it in the holster and clip it on her belt at the small of her back. Ollie made the decision for her by stepping backwards to the middle of the room and giving her the "go ahead; take it" nod again. As Ollie turned his back to Nattie to look at a framed poster replica of "The Birth of Venus," Nattie put the gun in the right pocket of her jacket and closed the drawer.

"I love this," Ollie said, pointing at the poster. "Who was the artist again?"

"Botticelli," Nattie said as she looked for her calendar on Kevin's desk. Her calendar/appointment book should have been locked in the middle drawer of his desk, but it was not there. She finally found it left open in the middle of his desk. All it took to find it was to remove the stack of Sudoku puzzles Kevin had left half finished. Apparently this was part of his work week while she was gone.

"I think this painting is in Venice." Ollie said from the chest high counter on the other side of Kevin's desk.

"Actually, it's in Florence," Nattie said apologetically. She did not want to sound arrogant or make Ollie feel bad for being wrong but she did feel some satisfaction in knowing where the Botticelli hung. She knew the name of the museum in Florence too, the Uffizi. It felt good to know the name of the museum. It would not have felt good to say it.

"Ah yes, Florence," Ollie smiled, "They say that the 'Birth of Venus' kicked off the Renaissance. Do you think that's true--Nattie?"

Nattie had been stooping over the desk but stood up and looked at Ollie square in the face. As a private investigator she had trained herself to avoid making hasty judgments. When confronted with a situation in which she did not know the rules, her strategy was to slow down the rolling of the dice. With people she used a different metaphor. She envisioned gathering puzzle pieces, and her strategy was to slow down picturing the finished puzzle until enough puzzle pieces had been gathered. Slowing down was the common denominator in both metaphors.

The puzzle pieces Nattie had already gathered about Ollie so far were the oddest collection of personal facts she had ever encountered. And her collection was only fifteen minutes old.

"I don't know if it started the Renaissance or not, but the art history teacher I went to Florence with said it was." Nattie pointed back at him with her chin and asked, "Are you interested in art history?"

"A little," Ollie replied, "My mother's family is from Tuscany. She loved everything Tuscan and passed that on to me."

"Have you been to Toscana, Ollie?"

"Toscana!" Ollie repeated, "You say Tuscany like an Italian--Toscana"

"That brings me to another question Ollie. What do you mean by the term 'European sensitivity?'" asked Nattie.

"I don't really know what it means either. I told the man who was here last week that I need a detective who knew about Italy and Italians. He told me that you were famous for your European sensitivity." Ollie showed all his teeth again and pointed at the appointment book Nattie held. "But that is a long story for another time." Then he looked out the window and added, "I am a bit late for work so if you would not mind checking your schedule I'll be on my way."

"Of course." She opened the calendar and placed it on the desk. She ran her finger across the Monday column out of habit as her schedule was completely free all day. The puzzle pieces she collected so far confused her a bit and piqued her curiosity. What she knew, from what she observed so far, was that there was not much she knew. At least she knew she was no longer afraid, but she did not quite know why.

What Nattie did know for sure was that before she would talk to Ollie again she was going to talk to her brother. She wanted a piece of Kevin's hide. "How about one o'clock today?" she said to Ollie, "Right after lunch."

Ollie squinted and clinched his teeth, "I'm afraid I cannot come so close to lunchtime." He pointed out the window, "I am the chef at Michelangelo's across the street."

Michelangelo's was a fairly new restaurant to Bristol. She ate there for lunch almost every week and almost always ordered their Tomato Florentine soup and a Greek salad. Ollie had not been there two weeks ago.

"How about three o'clock then?"

"Three o'clock is perfect. Thanks," he said and started for the door.

"One question before you go, please," she blurted out.

Both Ollie's hands were poised to push the door open but he stopped and turned his head toward her.

The question Nattie most wanted answered was how he came to know about the secret drawer and the hidden gun. But she wanted to talk to Kevin before she asked Ollie about that. So she asked her second question instead. "How did you know that I was gone last week?"

Ollie smiled that big smile again and said, "I knew you were gone last week because I'm the one who painted your door last week."

CHAPTER 2

NATHAN

Nattie opened the blinds on the window facing Michelangelo's and watched Ollie trot across the parking lot. He did not tip-toe across the street this time; *Tip-toeing is just for dancing with cars*, Nattie thought, *at least for those with a European sensitivity*.

"I'll see you at 3:00, Mr. Rugga-whatever-your-name-is," she said out loud, watching Ollie disappear from sight. Then she surveyed her office manager's/brother's desk and thought, *Lucky for you, Mr. Renaissance man, the freak collection that is my life has a vacancy for a tip-toeing chef.*

"I have to hand it to you Nat, you never cease to amaze me," Nathan Moreland, Nattie's ex-husband, said as he sauntered across the waiting room floor like he owned the place.

'I've got to put a bell on that door,' Nattie thought as she realized she had not noticed his entry. "Nathan, how nice of you to drop by--unannounced--again. It is so inconsiderate when people tie up my phone lines by calling first, don't you think?"

Nathan was always a good looking man; tall, athletic, with a surfer tan and GQ taste in clothes. But it was the smile that made her weak in the knees. It was a crooked smile and he had big teeth, big white teeth. Smoking was the only vice he had refrained from as far as she could tell, and his teeth showed it.

As usual her sarcasm was lost on him, or at least her sarcasm failed to keep his big crooked smile from coming closer and closer. He was acting as if it was perfectly natural for him to kiss her. The closer he got the more she found herself wanting him to keep coming closer.

Just before he could kiss her Nattie put her left hand on his chest and leaned away. "Eight o'clock in the morning is kind of early for you, isn't it, Nathan?"

He did not answer. He did not keep coming, but he did not lean back either. He did continue to smile, though, and she wondered if he was enjoying the awkwardness of her position. He was never aggressive. Charm and insensitivity were his strategies.

His eyes moved down to her lip, "What happened?"

"Bar fight," she answered. "Three guys attacked me with baseball bats--one got away."

Nathan rolled his eyes and stepped back.

"What did you mean when you said I never cease to amaze you?"

"That new name you chose, Nat." Chuckling he stepped back and turned his face toward the door. "*Natasha McMorales*—Why Natasha? It is from Bullwinkle, right?" He did not look at her to see if she intended to answer.

Nattie did not have an answer. Nor did she expect him to wait for one. She had witnessed this scene before. He was amusing himself with his cleverness. All he wanted from her was to be his audience. They would still be married today if only she could have accepted as her calling being his audience. And the real tragedy was that she could have made being his audience her calling if only he had been a grown-up.

"And 'McMorales'--what kind of name is that? Is it even possible?" He had maneuvered to the middle of the waiting room with his arms out to either side, emphasizing his point. "I mean it, is it even remotely possible? It's like--it's like--ah--"

"Mohammad Chang," she volunteered.

Nathan got still and looked at her like a five-year-old who was telling a joke and she just ruined it.

"That name," she said, rolling her right hand over several times to stress that she was trying to explain. "McMorales is like two ethnic names that don't go together. Like--" she stopped rolling her hand and extended her hand forward imploring Nathan to speak.

"Like Moses Chang. I know. I got it," he said with a sneer.

Nattie forced a smile, "What else should a girl with mousy blonde hair and vanilla ice cream complexion call herself?"

After pausing she tried again, "Don't you think I could pull off being a dark, brooding Irish woman with a preference for tacos?"

Nathan looked at her like she was speaking Swahili.

Nattie took a deep breath and a long look out of the window. "Here's the deal. I was in Nashville last week. I thought with me gone it would be a good time to get your uncle's name off the door. It was supposed to say, 'Nattie Moreland, Private Investigator.'" She pointed at the door. "I have no idea how *that* happened."

"Kevin?" Nathan asked.

"Probably." She liked that he knew her family. He had always been very tolerant and very sweet about her family.

"I'm sure Kevin has a good story to explain it," observed Nathan as he ran his finger across one of Kevin's Sudoku puzzles. Then, as if he had lost track of their conversation he asked, "Did you make coffee yet?"

"No," she answered, "but Manna Bagel is open."

He nodded, "Why were you in Nashville?"

"License stuff for the agency."

Nathan frowned, "I thought you got your P.I.'s license a while ago."

"That was my personal private investigator's license, and it was a year ago. This was a different license. It allows me to have my own agency."

Licensure was a touchy subject between them. Eight years ago, when Nattie was twenty and did not return to Freedom University in Kingsport, Tennessee, for her junior year, she began working for Nathan's uncle Hiram as a receptionist. Hiram Moreland was the only private investigator in Bristol for years, specializing in insurance fraud. Almost immediately, Hiram began to encourage Nattie to get her private investigator's license. "You are a natural," he had told her. "You are so easy to talk to that people just open up to you." So, with his constant prodding she began a home study course she found online while she did more and more of the office interviewing.

Two years later her position as the favored child, the heir apparent of the Hiram Moreland Agency, all but disappeared with the arrival of Hiram's nephew, Nathan. Nathan was older, he had an MBA, and he was family. For the next year she continued to function as receptionist and chief interviewer while she kept her home study program going at a steady pace toward getting her license. She believed that the agency would eventually have three private investigators and they would hire someone else to be the receptionist. She told herself not to notice that while she studied at home, Hiram insisted that Nathan study at the office during work hours.

What Nattie did notice was Nathan's attention. He was the most attractive man who ever gave her the time of day. Nattie tended to be suspicious about the attention she got from attractive men because she was convinced that she was plain and slightly frumpy. Nathan told her she looked like Kristen Bell; but rather than receive a compliment, her automatic response was to discredit it. She told him, "I'm a short wise-cracking blonde detective," which was the character Kristen Bell portrayed in *Veronica Mars*. Kristen Bell was also quite attractive, an attribute Nattie could not allow for herself. She did recognize the similarity between them but if pressed Nattie would refer to herself as 'someone who looks like she could be Kristen's sister.'

Nathan was confident, charming, and intelligent; and she fell in love with him. He was fun to be with, and he was not going to need her to take care of him. At least that is what she remembered thinking then.

Nattie was twenty-three when she and Nathan married, he was twenty-seven. Everyone was happy, even her mother and stepfather who were constantly disappointed with her for not sharing their conservative Christian view of the world. Nathan, much to their approval, spoke fluent Fundamentalism.

Within a year of their wedding it became clear to Nattie that the public Nathan, articulate and confident, was a carefully cultivated and maintained façade. The façade covered an immature, self-indulgent, pugnacious adolescent. She had married Peter Pan. The discovery was a grave disappointment, but she bore the burden resolutely, more as a parent than as a wife. This she could do with her eyes closed. After all, she had been parenting everyone else in her life for as long as she could remember. Her solace was that at least she had not married an alcoholic, as her mother had.

Nathan had seemed threatened by her private investigator's skills, so she stopped pursuing her own license in spite of having finished seven of the eight home study segments. Neither Nathan nor Hiram mentioned it. Nattie never mentioned it either as she unconsciously implemented the "keep the peace at all costs" strategy.

Nathan mismanaged their finances: late fees, overdrafts, credit card debt. So she took control of the check book and the budget. She could keep everything together as long as he went to work and was nice to her. When he failed his first attempt to pass the licensure exam she hid the results from Hiram. When Nathan told Hiram that he had missed the exam because she was sick, she held her tongue.

So Nattie pushed and prodded him through the study program and got him licensed six months later. She could and did protect him from most dangers of adult responsibility, but she could not protect him from himself. With the exam behind him, more was expected of him at the office. He was not prepared for adult responsibility and as his confidence weakened, he turned more and more to alcohol for courage or comfort or whatever it was that alcoholics looked for at the bottom of a bottle. Nattie was deprived of even that solace. She was more like her mother than she cared to admit.

Their unspoken marital contract required her to be the grown up, to see to all the details, and to make him look good. All he had to do was cooperate, but his fatal flaw was simply that he could not tolerate negative feedback. Although Nattie was an Olympic champion at never giving negative feedback, his need for some kind of correction was growing rapidly. She tried encouraging him to cut back on his drinking, but he shrugged her off. She tried pleading, but he accused her of legalism. When he got his first DUI, she told him to get help and he promised he would. But he never did, and when his second DUI cost him his private investigator's license, she told him to move out until he got sober. He moved out, and two weeks later he filed for divorce and left the Hiram Moreland Private Investigation Agency.

Nattie passed the licensure exam and was licensed four months after Nathan lost his. And now he asked her about it as if it were not a forbidden topic for them.

"Agency license?" he repeated.

"In the state of Tennessee a licensed private investigator with less than one year's experience must work in a licensed agency," she explained.

Nathan nodded in understanding, "That's why you kept Uncle Hi's name on the door."

She nodded.

"You needed his license"

"I needed his agency license," she corrected.

"And now you have your own."

"*Si.*"

"And that's why you changed the name on the door."

"*Si.*" Then, as if a switch had been flipped, the charming, Nathan with the giant grin was back, "So you changed your name to Natasha to court all the Eastern European business in the Tri-Cities."

"Don't minimize it, thank you." she said, grateful for the transition from serious to sophomoric. "I'm after all the business from Central America and the British Isles, too."

His charming grin disappeared, and he looked at her as he had looked at her when they first got involved.

Nattie turned her head toward the window. If she kept looking at him she was going to want him to kiss her. She did not want to want him to kiss her. It would not be safe.

"I miss you," he said softly.

Sighing, she confessed, "I miss you too." She did not look back.

"I really blew it, didn't I Nattie?" He balked, as if he was poised to step toward her if she gave him the slightest encouragement.

He was difficult to resist, but rescuing him from his messes was not her job anymore and not because she quit. He fired her. But it took all the self control she had to watch him in pain and keep quiet.

"The past is the past, Nathan," she said softly. "Today has enough trouble of its own."

When he failed to respond, she asked, "Were you just stopping by or was there something specific you had on your mind?"

"Oh yeah." He withdrew an envelope from the inside pocket of his sports coat, "Uncle Hi sent this to you."

The envelope had no stamp or address on it, only her name, Natalie. Hiram was the only one who still called her "Natalie."

She held it up. "He sent this to me. Why do you have it?"

"It's Uncle Hi's way to force me to come see you. Not that I need a push." He shuffled his feet, looking like an embarrassed little boy. "Do you know what it is?" he asked.

"Do you?"

Holding his hands up defensively he said, "I didn't look--I promise."

"I sent him a check before I left for Nashville. It's probably a thank you."

"A check for what?"

"A check for the agency. After Hiram's heart attack he had to stop working, so he let me keep the agency open. I needed his license to do it, so we made a deal. That was the final check I sent last week."

"You paid off the debt *before* you got the agency license?" Nathan's tone conveyed disapproval.

Nattie just shrugged.

"You were never short on confidence, were you, Nattie." He ran his hand through his hair, "I'd have needed three tries to pass."

You have no idea how short on confidence I am, she thought. Out loud she said, "When you are out of choices--"

"What does that mean, Nat?" he asked, interrupting her.

"It means I'm out of money and this business has to succeed right now or I join the Coast Guard."

"Well, for heaven's sake Nat, why'd you send that money to Uncle Hiram. He'd have let you wait. All you'd have to do was--" he paused and pointed at her, "That's it isn't it, you would have had to ask for help."

Nattie just stared at him.

"Seriously, Nat, what are you going to do?" Then his eyebrows went up, "I could always come back and help you get some of that insurance fraud work Uncle Hi used to do."

The one really marketable skill Nathan felt confident with was his ability to schmooze. He could hob-nob with the rich and powerful. It was a skill Hiram needed since his agency was no longer the only one in town. Other agencies were courting insurance companies for their fraud work, and Hiram needed to compete. When he did show up for work, Nathan could always schmooze.

"Thanks for the offer Nathan, but that's not the kind of work I want to do anymore."

"No problem Nattie." He came towards her. She allowed him to put his arms around her. "Just know that if you need me I'm here."

It felt good to hug him, "Thank you Nathan, I know you mean that." She believed he meant it, too; she just did not believe he could live up to it. Not yet anyway. "If it gets bad enough, I can always hit Ingrid up for some of the trust money."

"Let's hope it never gets that bad," he said sarcastically. Nathan was one of the few people who felt comfortable joking about Natalie's mother, Ingrid.

Ingrid's parents had a small farm on the southeastern side of Johnson City. It was never much of a farm, but became quite valuable when developers started growing the city in that direction. They sold several parcels of land and went from farmers with a subsistence farm to millionaires with a garden over night. When her parents and only sibling all died in the same car accident, Ingrid became quite wealthy. There was more than enough money to educate Nattie and Kevin and provide each of them with a handsome nest-egg to start life with, but Ingrid's second husband, Lionel O'Brien, thought it would make them lazy. The tendency for Ingrid to repeat whatever Lionel said as if it were her own thought was a constant source of embarrassment and dismay for Nattie. When they were married, Nathan had once suggested that Nattie ask her mother for some help with a dental bill for an abscessed tooth. Nattie's response was, "Not unless Chicken Little herself fell from the sky."

"Let's hope not," she agreed and broke the hug. Turning toward the phone at Kevin's desk, she added, "I'm hoping some of those calls will be some new business."

Taking a few steps toward the door Nathan said, "I can take a hint Nattie. I hope at least one of those calls is from that international market you're aiming at these days."

Nattie just smiled slightly. He had always found himself more amusing than she did.

"Keep the faith, Natasha," he said sarcastically as he left, but he caught himself and in a more tender tone he added, "It could happen."

Nattie watched him through the window as he got into his car. He still moved his body like an athlete. There were other things he was good at before he became an alcoholic. She watched him drive off until he was out of sight.

Nattie looked across the parking lot at Michelangelo's and said, "You're right about that, Nathan; you never know when it could happen. Sometimes the international market walks right up to you in your parking lot."

CHAPTER 3

ZOE

Sitting down Nattie turned her attention to the envelope she still held in her hand. Kevin's chair was in position to receive her, but not because she had given it any thought. The thank you note she had expected from Hiram was not in the envelope. Instead, the envelope contained the last two checks she sent Hiram paying off the agency. Each check had been cut in half.

She poured the contents of the envelope onto the desk and put the check pieces together as if they were a puzzle. As if she needed to see them together to believe it. One check was for $2,000 and the other for $4,000.

With this money Hiram Moreland had relieved her of the financial pressure she had felt just moments before. The agency was making just enough money each month to cover expenses, pay her bills, and pay off her debt to Hiram. Now that the debt was paid, the agency could start showing a nice profit, but not this month because she had not worked in a week, the calendar for this week was pretty thin, and next week included a trip to Chicago for a wedding she had to go to. Hiram had come through for her in a big way, and with great timing.

"You big old lovable bastard," she said out loud, tearing open the envelope. She hoped he had put a note inside. He had. It said, 'Congrats from a fan.'

"Excuse me, please." The voice was soft, almost timid, but so unexpected that it startled Nattie.

"Oh my goodness," Nattie said clutching the empty envelope to her chest. Being startled by someone who had not been noticed was un-nerving for anyone. For a private investigator it was also embarrassing, and it seemed to happen too often for her comfort.

"I'm sorry dear." The woman with the soft voice said, "Are you going to be all right?"

"I'm fine; I was just startled." Natalie put the check pieces back in the envelope and stood up.

"I'm here to see Mr. McMorales. Are you his secretary?"

The woman with the soft voice could not have looked less threatening. Nattie put her age in the early fifties, slightly overweight, brown hair, hazel eyes, very fair complexion, and the wide-eyed look of someone expecting to be shocked--or maybe amused. And in spite of the timid voice and non-threatening appearance, this was the second time in a matter of minutes that she said something that startled Nattie.

"I'm sorry; did you say 'Mister McMorales'?"

"Yes," the woman said, "Mister McMorales. This is his office, isn't it?"

"I see," Nattie said holding her palm against her forehead. "This is a Private Investigation Agency. It used to be the Hiram Moreland Agency and now it's mine."

"Oh dear," the woman grinned and a twinkle came to her eye. "I was pretty sure Natasha was a woman's name but the man who was here last week gave me the impression that--" She did not finish her thought. "My name is Zoe," she offered her hand, "and I take it you are Natasha."

Natalie shook Zoe's hand, which had a surprisingly firm grip, "Please call me Nattie, And may I call you Zoe?"

Zoe nodded.

"Is there a private investigation matter I can help you with Zoe?"

"There is, but it is delicate and I want to talk to you first before I give you any details."

"That's understandable," Nattie said as she glanced into her office to see if it was presentable. "We can talk in here."

"I have the two hundred dollar consultation fee." Zoe rifled through her oversized purse and withdrew a bank drive-through envelope. "I assume cash is ok?"

"Cash is fine, Zoe, but we don't have a consultation fee." She ushered Zoe into her office, "If after we talk and I think I can help I'll be delighted to take the two hundred dollars as a retainer."

"Plus seventy-five dollars an hour."

Nodding, Nattie added, "Plus expenses."

Nattie's office was furnished with everything Hiram left behind when he retired. Nearly empty bookshelves were placed against the far wall and a wooden desk facing two upholstered chairs occupied the middle of the room. There were no paintings on the wall or any other artwork, knick-knacks, or embellishments. Kevin referred to it as "stylishly undecorated."

Zoe sat in one of the upholstered chairs and placed her purse by her feet.

After taking a notebook and pen from her desk Nattie sat in the other upholstered chair and asked, "Do you mind if I take notes while we talk?"

"I don't mind," Zoe said. "Where would you like me to start?"

"You can start anywhere you wish, but sometimes it is easier for me to listen to the details if I know what you want me to do first."

"I want you to prove my husband is having an affair."

"Okay, that's clear enough. Now tell me, what makes you think your husband is having an affair, Zoe?"

"Well, Natasha," Zoe scooted forward to the edge of her chair, "I believe my husband is having an affair because he disappears every Tuesday and every Thursday afternoon."

Nattie scooted forward in her chair. "If it's that predictable, then I should be able to just follow him and find out where he's going. I could probably try it this Thursday. And please, Zoe, call me 'Nattie.'"

"Oh, I already know where he's going."

Nattie did not try to hide her confusion, "You already know where he's going?"

"I followed him last Thursday. He went to a horse barn, you know, a stable where they teach people how to ride."

Looking Zoe in the eye, Nattie realized that it was her turn to talk, "I don't suppose you believe he's taking lessons."

Zoe closed her eyes and shook her head slowly. "He is afraid of horses. I mean, *seriously* afraid. Besides I sat there watching for nearly an hour and they never left the barn. If they were riding they'd have left the barn, don't you think so?"

"They?"

"The woman he went into the barn with," Zoe snorted. "More like the *girl* he went in the barn with. A twenty-year-old cheerleader with a Barbie body and bright red hair."

"You've seen the other woman, then."

Zoe nodded.

"Have you seen them--"

"Together?" Zoe finished Nattie's question. "No."

"You want me to find out what's going on in the barn?"

"I do and I'm sure that will be a simple matter for a private detective with your experience, but I need to make sure of what will happen with the information once you have it."

"My license does not allow me to conceal a criminal act, but--"

"Oh I can't imagine that you'll discover a crime, Natasha, I mean, Nattie, I'm sure it will just be garden variety sin."

"If there's not a crime involved, then you have both my license and my word that any information I discover while on the clock for you is your sole property."

"And you don't keep a record for yourself?"

"I will turn everything I have over to you when we are done."

"Thank you. I didn't mean to doubt you or insult you. It's just that this is sensitive and I've never done anything like this before. I knew I would know if I could trust you when we talked face to face, Na--" she paused. "Would you mind terribly if I called you by your given name. I have an aunt, a cousin, and a close friend named 'Nattie.'"

"Does that mean you are hiring me?"

"I think so," Zoe answered with a single nod of her head for punctuation.

Nattie grinned, "Good. Then you can call me anything you want." She adjusted her pen and notebook, "Would you like to give me the particulars?"

"My husband is Paul Lancaster. Does that name mean anything to you?"

"No; should it?"

"It's just good that you don't know him. We're from Abingdon, but I didn't want to talk to anyone from Abingdon."

"Is that because a private investigator from Abingdon might know him?"

"Everyone in Abingdon knows Paul. We can't go out for dinner without stopping at every table as we cross the room. He's the senior pastor of the largest independent church in the region."

Nattie wrote 'Paul Lancaster,' 'Abingdon,' and 'Senior Pastor-Independent church' in her notebook.

"I'm not trying to protect his image, mind you. But if he's guilty and not repentant, there will be a lot of people hurt. Everyone he's ministered to or counseled, the people who look up to him, who trust him--all of them would be devastated." Zoe looked down at her hands, "Whatever happens, I want to make sure we do what is best for his congregation."

"Certainly." Then leaning forward Nattie asked, "Are you planning on giving him a chance to repent? To reconcile?

"I'm plenty angry, if that's what you mean. Last Thursday my first instinct was to wait until he went to sleep and then cut off his hoo-hoo. But vengeance isn't what I want."

Nattie sat back. Zoe no longer sounded so timid.

"I want you to verify what he's doing. Then I'm going to confront him without letting him know I have proof. If he's honest with me and repents, then of course I want reconciliation."

"And if he's not forthright?"

"That's when I'll bring out the proof."

"That sounds like a good plan," observed Nattie. "Do you want me to get started this week?"

Zoe picked up her purse and once again withdrew the drive-through bank envelope with the two hundred dollars in cash. She handed it to Nattie. "Here is the retainer. I will have to call you with the directions to that horse barn. I hid them in a book I knew he'd never open, and I'm afraid I went off this morning without it."

"Thank you." Nattie took the envelope. "I'll wait to hear from you and then I'll go out there and find out what I can."

Standing up, Zoe asked, "When will you let me know what you find out?"

"I'll call you as soon as I have something to say," Nattie answered, as she put her notes and the envelope on her desk, "but please feel free to call us anytime you'd like."

Zoe nodded, shook Nattie's hand again, and headed for the door. Before leaving she stopped and, turning toward Nattie, said, "Thank you, Natasha."

CHAPTER 4

KEVIN

Nattie's jaw dropped open and her right index finger shot forward in a gesture that meant "wait just a minute" in any language, but Zoe had already gone. Nattie had given Zoe permission to use her given name--which was apparently becoming Natasha. She thought about checking her driver's license. *Maybe I am Natasha.*

The phone rang. Up until now her standard phone greeting had been, "Hiram Moreland, Private Investigators; this is Nattie, how can I help you?" That greeting was no longer appropriate, but she had not thought through a new one yet. She found herself answering, "Natasha Moreland!"

"That was great. I always wanted to call you 'Natasha.'"

"Kevin?"

"But it's 'McMorales' not 'Moreland.'"

"Kevin!" This time she sounded like the mom from *Home Alone.*

"But don't worry about that. It is a hard name to say but that's the point, isn't it." "Kevin, where are you?"

"If people have to work hard to say your name, they will be more likely to remember it. Not bad, hungh?"

"We're going to have to talk about that name, Kevin. But right now I need to get some air. Are you at the Blackbird Bakery?"

"Not on Monday, Sis; they're closed. I'm at Manna Bagel. Are you coming down?"

"Yeah, order me an Earlybird with sausage on an onion bagel." An "Earlybird" was the breakfast special at Manna Bagel. The bagel/coffee shop was two blocks from Nattie's office, not far enough to be much exercise but far enough to refresh her.

"You got it," Kevin said before he hung up.

Kevin was sitting by himself against the right wall reading. He noticed Nattie approaching his table and directed her toward the counter with his finger. "I told Joe you were on the way, so he's keeping it warm for you."

"Morning, Nattie," said Joe Bell, the Rabbi of the Lion of Judah Messianic Church which owned Manna Bagel. As he put an empty coffee cup and a paper bag on the counter he added, "Your brother ordered you an everything bagel, but I made it with an onion bagel like you like it, but I can change that if you want me to."

"No, the onion bagel was what I wanted. Thanks, Joe."

"No problem Nattie."

"Kevin didn't pay for this did he?"

Joe smiled.

"I didn't think so." Nattie shook her head, "Do me a favor Joe will you?"

"Just ask."

"Hold the check until we go. Kevin has owed me breakfast for a couple of weeks now."

Joe smiled and attached the bill to the side of the cash register with a magnet.

After serving herself coffee Nattie sat down across from her brother. Pointing at the book he was reading she asked, "Are you enjoying that?" *Among His Personal Effects* was written by John McDonald, the King College professor she had gotten close to in a literature course while studying abroad one summer. She had given Kevin a signed copy for Christmas.

"I am." He put a Hershey wrapper in it as a bookmark and said, "It's so cool that it's kind of written in Scottish."

"What?"

"It seems like it is English, but then there are different words--like--" He opened the book and thumbed back from his bookmark. When he stopped he pointed his finger at a word he had underlined. "What's that mean?"

Nattie had to move his finger to see the word, "Bairn?"

"Yeah, 'Bairn.'"

"Can't you tell what it means by the sentence?" Nattie asked.

"Well sure. It means 'baby.' But it's cool that it's like a different language."

"Scotland is a different country."

"Hey, congratulations on passing the agency license thing," Kevin said, changing the subject.

"Don't congratulate me yet, we don't know if I passed that exam," she pointed out, a bit irritated. In her head she knew he meant that he believed in her, but it still felt like pressure to perform. A pressure she felt even as a little girl. Whether they meant it or not her family did not have permission to fail, which loaded any and every performance with the threat of criticism and sometimes even rejection.

"Well, they emailed some forms to the office on Friday," Kevin explained, "I assumed you passed."

"They could not have gotten it processed that fast."

"Sure they could. It was on a computer wasn't it?"

"Yes, but the exam was on Saturday. What were the forms about?"

Oblivious to her question Kevin asked, "Did you see the door?" and then continued without waiting for an answer. "I think he did a great job. Did you meet Ollie?"

"He seems very nice, Kevin. And the door is beautiful, but," she reached across the table with both hands and held his face so he would have to look at her, "What were you thinking?"

He stared at her with that 'I know you caught me but aren't I cute' expression he had perfected as a child.

"Natasha? Why Natasha?"

"We could change it," he said sheepishly.

"Oh, we are going to change it; but the only two cases I have right now both think I'm Natasha, so we will leave it be for a few days. I need to understand how all my clients came to believe that I am Natasha McMorales before I make a bigger mess trying to fix it."

"I can explain it." Kevin shrugged. "It was kismet."

"Spare me the romantic spin, Kevin."

Kevin saluted her. "Just the facts. Right, Sarge?"

Her mouth was full so she answered by rolling her finger indicating he should continue.

"You see," he pointed at her finger, "that's why Teddy Small called you Natasha."

"Teddy Small." She swallowed hard. "Wasn't that your best friend in grade school?"

"That's him. He had a crush on you but you scared him when you acted like a drill sergeant."

"Who?" she asked innocently. "Me?"

"We called you Natasha when you weren't around. 'Watch out, Natasha could be watching,' or 'Natasha will torture your family.' It was from the Bullwinkle and Rocky show. Someone told me that there were a lot of drug references in that show, but I never noticed. I think it was a pothead who told me that. Did you ever notice how it is usually potheads who see pot references all over the place?"

"Focus Kevin," she said waving her hand. "Just stick to the name on the door."

"I called the sign painter first thing Monday morning. Just like you told me."

"By first thing, do you mean sometime after ten o'clock?"

"Do you want me to focus or not?"

Nattie rolled her eyes and had another bite of her breakfast bagel.

"Anyway, they were supposed to come on Tuesday but they would have charged us twenty-five dollars to scrape the old sign off so I told them to put the work order on hold and I started scraping it myself."

"You did that? Thanks for taking the initiative." Her tone was sincere.

Kevin grinned and bowed his head.

"So what happened?"

"Well I'd scraped some of the door and the phone would ring. Then I'd come back and scrape some more and the phone would ring again. By the time I went home Monday my arm was really sore. I didn't finish scraping but I only left a little bit." He rubbed his right forearm, "I was going to finish scraping on Tuesday."

"What *exactly* was the little bit you left on the door on Monday when your arm was sore?"

"The bottom line, 'Private Investigator,' was still there. Everything else was gone except pieces of your name."

Nattie's eyes sharpened on him. She knew he was nearing the part of his explanation that she had been looking for from the beginning.

"The only thing that was left of your first name was the first three letters."

"Nat."

"Yeah. And the 'M' for Miriam was still there but only 'Mor' was left of Moreland."

"So it said 'Nat M. Mor.'"

He nodded.

"Well that makes perfect sense then."

"Come on Nattie," Kevin looked serious, "sarcasm is bad for your soul."

"I'm sorry," she said sarcastically.

"Really, I'm just trying to take care of you."

"I know you are." She rubbed the top of his hand. "Keep going."

"When I got to the office on Tuesday morning there was a guy there staring at the door."

"Ollie?"

Kevin nodded. "We talked about a ton of things. He's really into cooking and he knows a lot about art and travel. He seemed to be in love will all things Italian. He even said he wanted to hire a detective with a 'European sensitivity.'"

"That's interesting, Kevin." Nattie leaned forward. "He used that phrase with me and when I asked him what it meant he said he got it from you." She leaned back. "Did you tell him that I'm famous for my European sensitivity?"

"Maybe." Kevin answered sheepishly.

Nattie closed her eyes and shook her head back and forth slowly before saying, "Go on about the name."

"Well," he continued, "when Ollie asked me what your first name is, I looked at the 'Nat' on the door and 'Natasha' just came to my mind."

"Because it sounds more European?"

"Well it does." Kevin said with a shrug that meant "what else could I have done?"

"And the name 'Natasha' came to mind because Teddy Small called me that in grade school."

He shrugged again. "It was in my head."

"And the 'McMorales'?"

"When Ollie heard your name was 'Natasha,' he said, 'Ah-Eastern Europe.' I didn't know if that was good or bad so I had to think of something for your last name that wasn't Eastern."

"And?"

"And I had been reading this book with all the Scottish stuff in it so I just turned the 'M' for 'Miriam' into a 'Mc'."

"And the 'Morales'?"

"I know." Kevin made a face that said, "I just bit into a lemon." "That was bad, I panicked."

"You took a Spanish name and made it Scottish."

"I couldn't think of a Scottish name that starts with 'Mor.'"

"So McMorales just popped out?"

"It just popped out," Kevin agreed with a look on his face like he was reporting something amazing that he happened to witness.

"And Ollie bought that someone would be named 'Natasha McMorales'?"

"He seemed to."

"That's unbelievable." Nattie said, "And I was hired by a woman this morning who is convinced my name is 'Natasha.'"

"Oh you met Zoe? She's real nice. I told her how great you are. She came by the office Friday afternoon looking for a private detective who would be discreet. She wouldn't leave her name or phone number, but I told her that you'd be in on Monday morning. I knew once she talked to you she'd feel comfortable."

"Really, Kevin?" Nattie raised one eyebrow. "Zoe seems to have gotten the impression that I'm a man."

"I don't know about that--" he paused, "--but maybe she got that idea when I called you 'Sarge'."

"Sarge?"

"Yeah." He flinched. "She asked when you'd be back and I may have said 'the Sarge will be in on Monday.'"

Nattie put both palms flat on the table and leaning forward she slowly said, "but 'Natasha McMorales' is not a believable name."

"That's the beauty of it. It's a hard name to get your head around, but once you do you'll remember it forever. That's why it is so good for marketing a business."

She sat back. "Okay, that was weird."

"What?"

"What you said about that name being good for business."

"So you like it?"

"I didn't say that, but I don't hate it so much anymore."

"Well we had to do something to make up for that bad publicity."

Flinching her eyebrows Nattie asked, "What bad publicity?"

Leaning over Kevin retrieved a backpack from under his seat and withdrew a folded piece of newsprint. "Read that," he told her as he handed her the paper.

Nattie looked at the headline of the story Kevin had circled in red. "Private Investigator Attacked in Her Own Parking Lot" was written in bold letters across the top of the page 3 story. According to Twila Pearce, a new reporter at the *Bristol Herald Courier*, her attacker was the disgruntled spouse of a client the agency had been hired to follow. Jefferson Sadwell, Nattie's assailant, had objected to having his affair with another woman discovered and reported to his wife.

Pointing at the story Kevin said, "That's why I think you should enroll in some kind of self defense class or something."

"I know," she sighed. Improving her ability to defend herself made perfect sense but it was just not a priority for her.

"And that's also why you needed a public relations boost. So please, Nattie, don't change the name before you have a chance to see how it does."

"We don't have to change it now, but the State of Tennessee is going to require us to register the agency pretty soon and that will settle that."

Kevin stood up quickly, "Want to head back to the office?"

"Yep," Then she pointed toward the counter, "as soon as you pay for my breakfast."

"No problem." Then after padding his hands around his pockets he asked, "Can I borrow a ten?"

So much for that plan, she thought as she handed him a ten-dollar bill.

Kevin leaned on the table, "As far as the State of Tennessee wanting the agency name goes, they asked for it last Friday when they emailed us at the office." He snapped the bill from her fingers. "It's already settled."

CHAPTER 5

OLLIE'S CONTRACT

"What is it?" Nattie asked, looking at the dessert that suddenly appeared in the middle of her desk.

"What is it?" Ollie said emphatically as he threw up his hands. Then he turned and looked at Kevin, who was standing in the doorway to Natalie's office. "What is it!" he repeated, this time toward Kevin.

Kevin licked powdered sugar from his upper lip. Taking a bite of what looked like the same dessert on Nattie's desk, he grinned back at Ollie.

Ollie seemed pleased by Kevin's appreciation and, turning his attention back on Nattie, leaned over the desk and handed her a fork.

"No more talking," he declared. "You eat."

Natalie picked up the plate and studied the cake on it more closely. It appeared to be a pound cake with a layer of powdered sugar on top. She took a small piece on her fork, but before eating it glanced at Ollie again.

Ollie pointed at the cake and then rolled his hand over several times.

Due to her highly developed European sensitivity, Nattie knew immediately that Ollie wanted her to hurry up. She smiled and offered the bite toward him as if she were making a toast with champagne. Then she tried the bite not knowing what to expect beyond sweet.

The bite was amazing. The cake itself was denser than pound cake and tasted of hazelnuts and poppy seeds. Above the cake was a layer of lemon curd that she had not noticed before since it was covered with a light coating of the powdered sugar.

"This is remarkable!" She said as she pointed her fork at the cake. She took a bigger bite and closed her eyes as she savored it

Ollie giggled, watching Nattie savor his cake delighted him tremendously, 'You like?" he asked knowing the answer.

"Did you make this, Ollie?"

"*Si*, I made it."

"It's delicious. Did you have the same thing as I did, Kev?"

At the moment in which Nattie asked her brother the question neither she nor Ollie could see his face. Kevin was holding the plate in front of his face like a mask. When he lowered it there was a small touch of lemon curd on the tip of his nose.

"It is my version of Italian lemon cake," Ollie proclaimed. "I am--" he paused and waited for their attention. It was as if he were announcing royalty. "I am--a pastry chef."

"You certainly are," noted Nattie.

"*Valisimo*," Kevin bellowed with his best Italian accent.

Ollie looked oddly serious and gently said, "I don't think you mean '*valisimo*.' '*Belisimo*' means very beautiful. You probably mean '*bonisimo*.' '*Bonisimo*' means very good."

"I think he means both," said Nattie, as she savored another bite.

"Thanks," Ollie said to Kevin.

"No problem, man. I'm just telling the truth," Kevin crossed the room and took the empty plate and fork from Natalie's hand. "I'll just clean these up while you two talk."

"Please have a seat, Mr. Ruggaliano," Nattie said, after Kevin cleared her dish.

"No--please--call me 'Ollie.'"

"Ok, Ollie, what can we do for you?"

Ollie stood up and took his wallet from his back pocket. He fumbled through the bill section for a moment and retrieved a photograph, which he handed to Nattie. "That is Adelle."

Nattie looked at the picture. Adelle appeared to be in her late thirties, medium length brown hair, olive skin, dark eyes. Nattie knew that most people would react to Adelle's expression as stoic, harsh, or cold, but to Nattie she just looked uncomfortable.

"She's my--" Ollie paused. "Addie was my fiancée."

Nattie set the photograph down and waited.

"We were going to be married this summer," Ollie explained, "but she disappeared."

"She disappeared?"

"She did not go in to work one day," Ollie explained, "and that was very much not like her. So I went to her apartment." Shrugging he added, "She was gone."

"Did she leave a note?"

"Nothing."

"Have you heard from her? Email? Text? Anything?"

"Nothing."

"Ok then," Nattie said, "tell me about her family."

Ollie did not know much about Adelle's family because she did not talk about her family much beyond occasional references to something her mother would do or say. He knew she went to King College in Bristol, Tennessee, and that her family lived close enough that she could go home on weekends. He said, "I think her father has some kind of business because he wanted her to keep the books." Most of what Ollie could share was what kinds of foods she liked, what kinds of books she read, and what kinds of music she listened to. He clearly had considerable knowledge about her current preferences but very little of her history and family. In other words, he knew almost nothing that would be useful in finding her.

Nattie took a long, slow breath. It was her custom to let people tell their stories the way they wanted without asking too many questions. She was a natural listener. People could talk to her. This was especially true of people who felt victimized or disenfranchised. Hiram once told her, 'you get more information than an FBI interrogator because you don't judge and you don't push.' He first noticed this quality in her when he saw how the wives of his clients would open up to her. That is also when he began letting her do more of the initial interviewing.

But later, when Nattie began working for herself Hiram had added, "If you don't push a little you will find a great deal of time slipping through your fingers." Nattie realized this was likely one of those times when she was going to need to push.

"I assume you want us to find Adelle. Is that correct?"

"Si." Ollie said, scooting forward on his chair. "I want you to find her for me."

"What will you do when we find her?"

"I will ask her--'Why did you leave me?'" With that Ollie looked straight into Nattie's eyes.

She recognized the look on his face. He was not hiding anything, which was important to her. He was looking for something in her eyes, be it judgment, scorn, or condescension. He just confessed that he had been left by this fiancée. Surely that hurt. But it was embarrassing too. Also, it might be embarrassing to admit you are still hanging on to someone who left you.

"I want to understand why she left. Why she said nothing. I thought we were happy. One day we went out to buy a suit for me. It was her idea. I don't care about a suit." He touched the fingertips on his left hand as he talked, "First the suit, then a shirt, and a tie, and then the socks. These were for me, but they were for her. You understand?"

Nattie nodded.

"It was a good night. We bought clothes for me, shoes for her. We laughed. We went out to eat, Chinese food. She likes Chinese food. We laughed together all night long. We watched her favorite movie, *Sweet Home Alabama*. She would always laugh when the scene about the bologna cake came on. She thought it was funny that I didn't know what bologna cake is." His eyes were focused elsewhere while he enjoyed the memory. "I still don't know what it is." He sighed, "And then the next day she disappeared."

"Do you think something happened to her?"

"What could have happened?" Ollie asked, "She packed her things and left."

"And you came here because you think she came here?"

"This was her home. I didn't know where else to look."

"You have sure gone to a lot of trouble to find her--"

"What do you mean 'a lot of trouble'?" Ollie interrupted.

"I mean you have left your home, your job, your life to come here and find her. Are you sure all you want to do is ask her why she left?"

"Coming here is no trouble for me. I work in a business run by my family. We own restaurants around Chicago. So I am in no trouble to stay for a while. I have enough money and my job is secure. I just need an answer so I can continue with my life."

"Are you hoping to--" Nattie struggled for words, "--to talk her into coming home with you?"

"No," he answered solemnly.

"Really?"

"She had a reason to leave; of that I am sure. Maybe I will understand her reason. Maybe I won't. But," he added in a louder voice, "I will never understand why she left no word. She owed me at least the effort of a lie."

"That is reasonable."

"So you will help me?"

"I am willing to help you put this behind you so that you can continue with your life, Ollie."

"*Molto buono*," he said excitedly.

"But--" Nattie held up her index finger to slow him down. "--have you considered that she might not want to be found."

"*Si*, this is why I need you, a private investigator."

"And if we find her she may not want to talk to you. Have you considered that?"

"That is ok. I don't need to see her. I don't even need to know where she is. I just want her to know she cannot get away with treating me this way. We made love and plans and promises with each other, and then she left without an explanation."

Nattie pondered this a moment before asking, "So if I ask her and she tells me why she left, that will be enough?"

"No," Ollie said and then looking down to the left he bobbed his head slightly as if he were trying to shake a word loose. "I need a --"

"Recording?"

"*Sì*, a recording."

"So if I can record her answering your questions that will be enough?"

"*Sì*." He looked directly at her again, barely breathing, and waited.

"I will help you, but I need much more information."

He only heard "I will--" before he stood and repeated, "*Molto buono.*"

CHAPTER 6

DR. BUTMAN

Nattie thought it curious that Oliver Ruggaliano would move from Chicago and set up life in Bristol, Tennessee in order to track down a woman who jilted him. He was changing his entire life to find a woman who showed no inclination toward making direct contact with him. Maybe he thought he could just slide into town, open the phone book, and find Adelle Quinlin's phone number waiting for him. But moving his life to Bristol in order to get to a Bristol phone book was a tad bit unnecessary. And then, why had he not turned to a professional investigator from the very beginning? Why was it so important to try it himself first? Why was it important enough to justify uprooting his life? And now that he had hired a professional, why was he sticking around Bristol? Why not go home to Chicago and the family business? Nattie knew these questions were irrelevant to her contract with Ollie. But the questions still bothered her, and she wondered if the answers to them might become necessary before this was all over and done with.

Nattie was deliberately cautious about how her contract with Ollie was worded. She made sure that she was under no obligation to do anything other than find Adelle Quinlin, give her an envelope, and record her response for her client. Agreeing to turn Adelle's whereabouts over to Ollie was not ever going to be part of the deal unless he answered most of those questions. Maybe it would have been acceptable to another investigator, but not Nattie. And it was certainly not acceptable with a client's telling as shaky a story as this one.

Ollie could not find the Quinlin home. King College was bound by FERPA restrictions, which protected the confidentiality of students regarding their grades and transcripts, and therefore could not release to him any information about a student. Apparently the Bristol phone book was no help in locating them either. *How can Ollie be expected to know what to do next? Is he a trained professional? No. Is it my fault that I know what to do next? Is it my fault that it is easy for me to do?* A familiar inner voice accused Nattie: "You don't deserve this." It was a message that reappeared anytime she did not over-earn whatever she received.

I am a licensed professional investigator, she thought. *This is the kind of work we do.* She pictured herself wearing a ten-gallon cowboy hat and moseying up to a bar where all the other licensed professional investigators drank and told stories about close calls and loose women. The image made her shiver, but at least shivering had the desirable effect of erasing the picture. *Focus,* she told herself. *I have the resources to make this an easy task. It is what professionals do. Ollie Ruggliano does not care about the monsters in my head, he wants results and he is willing to pay for those results. He could care less if getting the results he wants is easy for me.*

Locating Adelle Quinlin's family would be easy if her old contacts at King College still remembered her. It could be as simple as making a phone call.

"Benjamin Butman speaking" The voice was attached to the chair of the foreign language department at King College. He led the study-abroad program she had attended one summer. Nattie was not a King College student, but used him as an adviser during her sophomore year at Freedom University. Her own adviser never seemed to have enough time for her, but Dr. Butman always did. It was not long before she called him first whenever she had a question about her academic career.

"Doctor Butman, this is Natalie Moreland. I'm surprised that I caught you in."

"Nattie." He sounded genuinely glad to hear from her. "How delightful to hear your voice. How have you been?"

A knot formed in her throat. The question had caught her off guard, but she knew she should have expected it as soon as she heard it. "I'm doing well now. I don't know if you had heard that Nathan and I are divorced?"

"No, I sure didn't."

"It's been about a year now."

"I'm real sorry to hear that, Nattie. How are you doing?"

"The good days far outweigh the bad ones now, but overall I'm doing pretty well. Nathan and I are still friends and we see each other often."

"Are you still working together?"

"A bit. Nathan's uncle has retired and Nathan is no longer with the agency, but he still has contacts in the insurance industry that we will need so it is good to have a friendly relationship with him." She was not convinced that she would ever need to make use of his contacts; but as long as it was a remote possibility, she could keep that door open in good faith. "The agency is all mine now. In fact it was just last week that I passed the licensure exam so I could head my own agency."

"Well congratulations, Nattie. I'm sure you will be a great success. If I ever hear of anyone who needs an investigator, I'll sure send them your way. How is it going so far?"

"Since you asked, I'll tell you that in the very first moments of having my own agency I was hit with a pretty big bombshell." She paused and grinned. "And it was partially your fault."

"Oh my!" Benjamin said dramatically.

Nattie laughed and explained how she had become Natasha McMorales and the part John McDonald's book had played in how she was named.

"Some authors aspire to writing something that is merely life-changing for folks, but how many authors can boast of writing a name-changing novel?"

"Not many in my neighborhood."

"Nor mine." Benjamin said, "An author tried to move into my neighborhood last month, but we were able to get a petition together just in time to block it."

"Close call."

"I'll say." He cleared his throat and asked, "So, Nattie, what can I do for you?"

"Are you free for lunch?"

"I'm always ready for lunch, but free is another thing altogether."

"Great." She exclaimed, "How about Eats on Moore Street at 11:30?"

"Make it 11:45 and it's a date."

Eats on Moore Street was a restaurant that had its roots in barbeque. The owner, Mark Canty, began by catering picnics and other outdoor gatherings out of a portable barbeque pit he could pull behind a pickup truck. Before he opened Eats of Moore Street--the catering business was a side job. His primary job was with the Post Office. He had been the Butmans' mailman at one time. The menu was small, but the country style food was great. Customers could order one of three main dishes and two sides to go with it. Most customers had a favorite they always ordered. Benjamin Butman had the jerk chicken, collard greens with vinegar, and soup beans. Nattie had the meatloaf, coleslaw, and black beans. They both had corn bread and water with lemon.

As Nattie expected, when the check came the waitress placed it in front of the man at the table. But she was ready and was able to grab it before he could. He looked genuinely disappointed; letting others do for him was not his best skill.

"You don't have to do that," he said with a serious tone, "I was just kidding about not being free."

"Oh I know that," she said. "But I'm actually on the clock right now."

"I didn't think this was just a lunch."

"Was I that transparent?" she asked.

"Couldn't it be that I'm just that perceptive?"

"Of course."

"I do have sharply honed deduction skills," he chuckled.

Nattie grit her teeth.

"So you are investigating something now."

"I am."

"Is it me?" he asked.

"Is it you?" She laughed, "Of course not."

Putting his hand on his chest he sighed dramatically, "Well then, as long as I'm not in trouble, how can I help?"

"I'm looking for a former student by the name of Adelle Quinlin."

"Is Addie okay?"

"I'm just trying to find her. She went missing from her job in Chicago about two months ago, but as far as I know there was no foul play. She could be at home enjoying herself with her family right now for all we know."

"Meadowview," he said.

"Meadowview?" Nattie was hopeful that she had just discovered where to look.

"Meadowview," he repeated, "she could be in Meadowview. It's where she's from. Why are you looking for her? Is she in trouble or something?"

"No, she's not in trouble. She's part of another investigation that she probably doesn't even know about it. I just need to find her and ask her a couple of questions and that will be the end of it."

He took a folded piece of paper and a pen from his shirt pocket and began to write. "I'll have to track down her folks' phone number but I can give her a call this afternoon and see if she is around."

"No, please don't do that," Nattie said with what she hoped was not too much urgency. "I can get their number from information. Besides, if she did not come home, then it would be better not to unduly alarm her parents."

"Are you sure?"

"I am." Nattie said, "But thank you for the offer. And thank you for being someone that I could always count on."

Blushing, he replied, "You are welcome, but I did not do anything."

"You remembered that she's from Meadowview, Virginia. Most professors wouldn't remember her name, but you remember where her parents live. That's not only amazing, but it's all I need."

He shrugged, a bit embarrassed by the flattery, "I'm just glad I remembered." He tucked his note and pen back in his pocket, "And I think I know why I just remembered her family so well."

She waited.

"Do you remember when you first told me about your family, Nattie?"

Nattie nodded that she did. He had been the first (and only) person she had talked to when she lost her residence assistant's position and could not afford to return to college. Benjamin Butman had offered to talk to her family about financially supporting her education. He knew that they could have easily afforded to pay her tuition. It was her problem to solve, and he could not understand why she would not let him try to fix it. But his solution of appealing to her family for help would have created problems she preferred to avoid, even it if meant postponing college.

"Your reaction to my offer to talk to your parents about your tuition was almost identical to her reaction to me for virtually the same thing. I remember thinking at the time how much you reminded me of Addie Quinlin."

CHAPTER 7

THE QUINLINS

Meadowview, Virginia, is a small town half an hour north of Bristol. At least it took Nattie half an hour to make the trip up Route 81 to exit 25. It took another fifteen minutes to find the Quinlin homestead just past the downtown area. The farmsteads of Meadowview were all well kept. Rolling hills were spotted with livestock and bordered with white fences. Traditional farmhouses with large wrap-around porches and traditional red barns were the norm, as were the open barn-shaped structures where tobacco was bundled and hung to dry. The Quinlin place was different; it had no tobacco structure and their barn was a sheet metal garage with over-sized doors. But the house itself matched the other houses Nattie had seen as she drove.

"We don't know where she is because she doesn't want us to know where she is." James Quinlin said definitively from the doorway. He took up most of the opening with his 6'5" frame, which was probably more slender than athletic when he was younger. Advancing age had plumped him up in the mid-section of his body and his cheeks, but not his arms and legs. Nattie guessed he probably looked a bit like a dumpling when he was not agitated. He was probably agitated quite often.

That was Nattie's first impression of the man. He was responding to a question she had asked his wife. The question, "Do you know where your daughter is?" may have been a touchy one for his wife but she did not need his protection. His intrusion into their conversation was more an act of entitlement than protection or concern.

His pale blue eyes glared at her as she pondered how to respond. His face was red and his chin jutted forward defiantly punctuating his claim that they did not know where Adelle was. It all seemed to say, "I dare you to challenge me."

"I don't mean your daughter any harm, Mr. Quinlin," Nattie said with as soothing a voice as she could muster, while she thought to herself, *I'll bet you can be a bully when you don't get your way.*

"This is Nattie Moreland, James." Adelle's mother, Alma, explained, standing up and inserting herself between her husband and Nattie. "She's a nice girl and she went to King College like Adelle did."

James Quinlin towered over his wife, still drying his hands on a small towel.

"So you know Addie, then?" he asked, more suspiciously than inquisitively.

He handed the towel to Alma without looking at her.

Taking the towel and meticulously folding it, Alma explained, "She is much younger than Addie, James. But her favorite professor is the same one Adelle liked so much."

Nattie had told Alma earlier that she had gotten their location from Benjamin Butman, that he was one of her favorite professors. Alma had mistakenly assumed that this meant Nattie had attended King College herself. Nattie decided to let the error slide.

Ignoring what Alma said, James kept his focus on Nattie. The jutting chin, red cheeks, and glaring eyes were replaced by suspiciousness. "Why are you looking for my daughter, Ms. Moreland?"

"I'm a private investigator," Nattie took a business card from her bag and handed it to him.

"And what is your interest in my daughter?" he repeated, taking the card and putting it in his shirt pocket without looking at it.

"I've been hired by her former employer to find her and simply ask her a few questions. Revealing her whereabouts is not part of my contract with them."

His face shifted into a sneer as he turned from Nattie to his wife. "Do you believe this?" It was not a question.

"Mr. Quinlin," Nattie began, but he interrupted her by jerking his head toward her again and holding up a finger.

"First of all, Ms. Moreland, or whatever, your real name is," he said with the rolling rhythm of sarcasm, "it is completely misleading to say 'her employer' when it was really her fiancé who hired you."

"Mr. Ruggaliano was her fiancé and he is who hired me. But I am being paid by the Ruggaliano Corporation."

The smacking sound he made with his tongue communicated quite clearly how much that distinction mattered to him.

"But it is the broken engagement that is surely driving his interest in hiring me." Nattie admitted.

"Well thank you for that," he said sarcastically.

"I understand your concern, Mr. Quinlin. I really do."

"Do you?"

"Absolutely. Your daughter left a job and an engagement without explanation. I don't know why she did not communicate when she left, but it was clearly her choice." She paused and looked directly at Alma and then at James.

Neither spoke. Alma was sitting in her glider with her hands folded over the towel in her lap. James kept his focus fixed on Nattie but his expression had changed once again, this time to a blank poker face.

"If she is frightened or hurt or confused, and she has chosen to handle it by leaving and breaking communication, then her choice should be respected."

"Exactly!" He said smiling victoriously.

"I have every intention to respect her right to break her engagement, to leave her job, and to remain hidden from the Ruggaliano family. But I do need to ask her some questions."

He sneered and made the smacking noise again.

"Look," Nattie said sharply, "protecting women from bullies is precisely what my life is about." She stood up and poked the air with her finger. "I'm going to make contact with her and I'm going to ask her questions for my client. It's my job. And if she does not want anyone to know where she is after that, then mark my words, Mr. Quinlin, no one will ever, or could ever, find her through me."

James Quinlin was quiet. His face had turned red again and his eyes had become slits.

Alma Quinlin, on the other hand, looked paler as she stared at her husband. Her eyes were wide open and she was holding her breath. Apparently it was taboo to speak to James Quinlin assertively.

Noticing each of the reactions, Nattie guessed that they were in uncharted waters. *He is re-assessing his opinion of me and she is expecting an explosion.*

"Look," Nattie said to Addie's mother in a calmer voice, "I don't need to find her." She turned to Addie's father as she spread her arms apart in a non-threatening open posture, "I really don't."

Nattie sat back down on her glider. Leaning forward, she pleaded, "All I really need is to talk to her. You can give her my phone number and she can call me from a disposable, untraceable cell phone if she wants."

Neither Quinlin responded, but the explosion no longer seemed inevitable.

"Would you at least give Adelle the information?" Nattie asked, as she held eye contact first with the father and then the mother. "You know, Addie may be feeling overwhelmed or hopeless right now. It is possible that if I could talk to her she would use the opportunity to say some things she is otherwise fearful to say. She has a right to be heard in all of this."

Nattie watched the couple look at each other and waited. There was something, maybe several things that they knew, but were not saying out loud in front of her. It was the kind of eye contact that was loaded with references that could only come from a long history.

Nattie leaned back in her glider, "What harm could come from giving Adelle the choice?"

James sighed, "What you ask is fair, Ms. Moreland, and we will give Adelle the choice when she makes contact." He looked at Alma before adding, "But you must understand that it may be a long time before she makes contact with us."

Nattie leaned forward in her glider again.

"That Omar Rugg fellow broke her heart. When she showed up here she was a mess." He turned to Alma. "Wasn't she, honey?"

Alma nodded.

"I just knew he would come after her. And believe me--" He pounded his fist in his hand. "--I wish he'd show up here. But he isn't going to be man enough to do that. So," he paused and looked at his wife with a curious expression on his face.

Nattie wondered if he was waiting for Alma to finish his sentence.

"So," he continued speaking when it became apparent that Alma was not going to, "I told her to get away from here for a good while. And I told her not to call or write unless it was life or death. I just wanted to protect my daughter."

Nattie knew he was lying. In the corner of her eye, she saw Alma flinch, but she would have known he was lying anyway. He had sounded defensive and uncertain. Counterattack was his preferred defensive posture, not confession. Uncertainty may be more familiar to James Quinlin, but he would more likely bluff rather than confess his uncertainty. He had looked to Alma before he confessed, but had avoided looking at her after speaking.

It was not unusual to lie to a private investigator. Knowing that was part of Nattie's job. What was more curious to Nattie was whatever was going on between the two of them. *Is he protecting Addie from Ollie? Or is he protecting himself from me? Or-- is he protecting himself from his wife?* Nattie glanced at Alma, who was watching her husband closely while he continued to avoid looking at her.

I think I'll let these two have a moment alone to let this ferment, she decided. Standing, she asked, "Would you mind if I use your bathroom? I had a big coffee while I drove up here."

Alma nodded and walked Nattie to the door, explaining where the bathroom was.

As Nattie entered the Quinlin home she noticed James was seating himself in the glider she had just left. She guessed that she had two, maybe three

42

minutes alone in their home. She glanced up the stairway and continued on. It would have been nice to see if she could find Addie's bedroom, especially if Addie were in it. But she did not have enough time, nor did she want to explain why she went upstairs if she got caught. The bathroom was through the kitchen so her search for, she knew not what, would be limited to these two rooms. A quick scan of grandchildren art on the refrigerator revealed nothing. The wall phone had an empty notepad mounted next to it. There was nothing written on the notepad, but she took the top sheet anyway. Shading it later might reveal a note written with a heavy hand. A missing blank sheet from the notepad would never be missed anyway.

The trash can in the bathroom was empty. Nattie flushed the toilet and ran water in the sink to legitimize her trip to the bathroom.

Nattie had expected the waste basket under the kitchen sink to be empty too but it was not. The plastic container was lined with a brown paper grocery bag which was common. The plastic grocery bag sitting loosely inside the paper bag was not common. Nattie lifted the plastic bag, which contained coffee grounds, egg shells, and some banana peels. This was normal kitchen garbage, wet and prone to odor if left too long. Under the plastic bag the paper bag held mostly dry garbage, empty dry goods boxes, and plastic vitamin bottles, none of it wet as kitchen garbage should be. Tucked along one side of the paper bag was a two month old copy of *National Geographic*. In the magazine were two letters sticking up like bookmarks. Nattie removed the letters. The first letter had a return address from Paula Busch of San Francisco. The second letter was from Adelle. She put it in her pocket, returned the first letter to its place in the magazine, and returned everything else to its previous place under the kitchen sink.

"I don't want to have to run the shower for half an hour every time I shave." As James finished speaking he sat back, turning his attention to Nattie's return to the front porch.

He laughed. It was a hearty laugh. He was obviously in a better frame of mind. "I suppose that sounded a little strange," he said.

Nattie looked at Alma. She was smiling warmly. They looked playful.

"That didn't sound strange at all." She winked at Alma. "I shave in the shower too. It doesn't take me half an hour, though, but then again I'm not nearly as tall as you are."

This brought another roar of laughter from James and a snicker from Alma. Nattie could not tell if Alma's amusement was the result of listening to Nattie or watching James.

"So, Ms. Moreland."

"Please call me 'Nattie.'"

"Ok, Nattie." He nodded. "Did you get enough hot water in the bathroom?"

"I thought it was fine, but I don't wash with real hot water anyway."

Alma quickly turned her head toward Nattie with a quizzical look on her face.

Ignoring Alma's reaction Nattie inquired, "Why do you ask?"

James explained that they had remodeled the master bathroom and changed from a standard water heater to a continuous water heater. "It's great for when you're in the shower and someone starts the dishwasher or one of the grandkids flushes the toilet. The water gets hot as it comes in the house, so once you get hot water you won't run out." He tipped his head toward Alma. "But neither she nor her plumber warned me that I'd have to drain all the water out of the plumbing before I'd have any hot water."

"So now you have to shave in the shower." Nattie smirked playfully at James. Alma's sudden sullenness was unnerving, but this was not the time to deal with that.

"It has been nice to meet you both," she continued with a studied cheerfulness. And I hope you can find a way to give Adelle my phone numbers. I did give you my card didn't I?"

James patted his shirt pocket and feeling the card there he said, "Sure."

Then he remembered he had not yet looked at the card.

Nattie watched him read the card. She watched his eyebrows slowly come together and realized what he was about to say.

"Are you Nattie Moreland?" he asked, "Or are you Natasha McMorales?"

CHAPTER 8

NEWSOME FARM

"Hello, Natasha, this is your office calling."

"Kevin!" Nattie said sternly toward the cell phone mounted on her dashboard. She was traveling south on Route 81 and needed both hands as she was being passed by a tractor-trailer going faster than she was going.

"Yeah, Sis?" responded Kevin with an innocent tone that Nattie found annoying.

"Why are you talking like that?"

Kevin stuck with the innocent tone, "I just think saying, 'this is you office calling' sounds more professional than saying, 'this is your idiot brother calling.'"

Nattie rolled her eyes. Referring to himself as an idiot was his way of keeping her from confronting him about anything else. It was a deflection technique she would have been vulnerable to if he had not already used it on her thousands of times.

"Did you just roll your eyes, Natasha?" he asked.

"Please don't call me that, Kevin," she said through clinched teeth.

"I just don't want you to have eye strain, Sis. You know your eyes are very important, the window to the soul. I think Gandhi said that."

"What do you want, Kevin?"

"And now I'll bet your teeth are clinched. Are you stressed?"

I am now, she said to herself.

"I bet you have a death grip on your steering wheel too."

She had not noticed her grip, but he was right. That irritated her, too. "Kevin, I can't exactly talk right now. I'm doing 75 on Route 81 heading back to Bristol."

"Great. I'm glad I caught you. Zoe Lancaster just called with directions to that stable."

"Oh, good."

"Well, it's off the Damascus exit on the north side of Abingdon. I thought you'd want to check it out while it was on the way."

Nattie got off Route 81 at Exit 19 and followed Kevin's directions. Three minutes later, she parked along the road in front of a sign that read:

Newsome Farm
Stables for Horses,
Lessons for People

"Great directions, Kevin. It was good thinking to catch me so I could do this on the way."

"No problem, Sis. I'll make you an appointment for a deep muscle massage for your stress."

Nattie flinched. She preferred to make her own decisions about when she needed help. She would have preferred that he offer to do it rather than tell her he was going to do it. But he was right and she had already gotten through one wave of irritation. There was nothing to be gained by getting irritated again.

"Thank you, Kevin. I'd appreciate that."

"No problem, Natasha." He hung up.

Nattie slowly released her exaggerated grip on her steering wheel. *Serenity now*, she thought, remembering the stress episode of Seinfeld. *Serenity now.*

A dark blue Grand Marquis drove past her and turned through the gate into the Newsome place. Nattie watched it drive up the tree-lined gravel drive, past a large colonial farmhouse, and park outside of a large barn next to a fire-engine red Mustang convertible. There were no other vehicles in the parking lot.

Zoe Lancaster's husband, Paul, drove a dark blue Grand Marquis but this was Wednesday. Zoe had said he came here on Tuesdays and Thursdays. He was not supposed to be here today.

This can't be him, Nattie thought. *That kind of luck only happens in the cheap detective novels.*

She watched a tall, thin, balding man emerge from the car. He walked over to the Mustang and glanced inside. He stood up and looked toward the barn, then the house, and then the barn again.

Nattie took a small set of binoculars from her glove compartment for a closer look at the man's face. She had not expected him to be here, so she had not brought the photo that Zoe had given her; but if her memory was correct this was Paul Lancaster.

Her camera bag was easy to reach from the floor of the back seat. She carried a palm-sized digital camera in her bag; but at this distance, some one hundred yards, she would need the larger camera with its zoom lens.

Before Nattie got her camera ready a young red-haired woman walked from the barn and slung a backpack from her left shoulder into the backseat of the

Mustang. Other than the heavy socks and work boots, the redhead was dressed like a Hooters' waitress. Nattie did not need to use the zoom to see that the redhead was also built like a Hooter's waitress.

"It figures," she said under her breath.

Paul and the redhead were obviously glad to see each other, but they kept their distance out in the parking lot. After greeting each other for a moment, Paul held up a finger. The redhead waited as he turned and took a small gift bag from the back seat of his car. She looked inside the bag and then held it against her chest as she rotated her shoulders seductively.

Oh please, thought Nattie. *Give--me--a--break*.

Then the redhead stood on her toes and kissed Paul on the cheek. He had to lean forward because of the difference in their height. As he leaned forward, his right arm reached out as if he were going to embrace her but he caught himself. It was broad daylight after all.

The redhead stepped away from Paul. Then she took a half step toward the barn. She held out her right hand inviting him to join her in the barn.

"Time to pay for the gift, right, Cookie?" Nattie whispered to no one.

Paul took her hand and they walked into the barn. Nattie continued to take pictures until they were out of sight.

The counter on her camera told Nattie that she had taken twenty-seven pictures. It was more than enough. She got everything she needed.

Not a bad day, Nattie thought.

She did not finish getting her camera put away before Nattie's feelings of satisfaction were disrupted by a tap on her window. The tap startled her, making Nattie jump and clutch at her chest with her right hand as if that would help her start breathing again.

"Can I help you?" The face attached to the voice was of an older woman. Glasses. No make-up. Long grey hair clipped up in the back. The voice was warm, the accent more southern than usual for the area, and the expression was pleasant.

"I'm Nancy Newsome," she said as Nattie rolled down her window. "This is my place. Can I help you with something?"

Nattie had to think quickly. She had not heard Nancy Newsome approach which was not particularly professional. Hiram Moreland had warned her more than once to be careful on stakeouts, "When you get too focused on what is in front of you, you can't help but lose awareness of what is behind you." Now she had to explain why she was sitting there with a camera in her lap.

"I'm sorry," Nattie said as she stepped out of the car, being deliberate about not trying to hide her camera. "I was exploring the area and when I saw your sign, I was kind of interested in lessons but I couldn't find a pen so I took a picture of it to get the phone number." She lifted the camera up. "I hope you don't mind."

Nancy touched Nattie's shoulder with a mock push. "Oh my goodness, no. You can take all the pictures you want to, honey. I'm just glad you are ok. I saw you sitting there and I was afraid you were hurt or something."

"That's very nice of you."

Nancy smiled, "I'm delighted you found us. Would you like me to show you around the place?" She took Nattie by the arm, "Come on--you can bring your camera."

Nattie wondered how long her luck was going to hold out as she put the camera strap around her neck.

Nancy covered the history of the Newsome Farmstead as they strolled arm-in-arm up the gravel driveway toward the barn. It was originally a "Gentlemen's Farm" which meant it did not need to make a profit. Her husband's grandfather bought the place after he sold an invention of "some kind of mining tool." Her husband's father added the barn and the horses.

Nancy Newsome's husband--she called him 'Butch'-- taught history at Emory and Henry. "Before he died three years ago he was a Benjamin Franklin authority. Did you know that Ben Franklin discovered the Gulf Stream?"

Nattie wanted to say, "I did not know," but she did not have time to respond before she heard footsteps on the gravel behind her.

"Good to see you Mrs. Newsome." It was a man's voice.

"Pastor Lancaster." Nancy called out, "Are you in a hurry?"

"It's Wednesday," he said as he trotted to his car. He nodded and smiled at Nattie then turning toward Nancy as he opened his car door she added, "You are welcome to join us for Wednesday evening service whenever you care to."

"I just might show up sometime," Nancy said as she maneuvered Nattie out of the way.

"Anytime," he said as he shut the door.

"He's a Baptist minister," Nancy whispered, as if she were telling a secret. "He's very nice, but we're Methodists. He just won't let it alone." She waved as he passed.

"Is that your truck at the road Momma?" The redhead had emerged from the barn.

"It is," answered Nancy, "We've been walking and talking. This is Nattie and she's thinking about taking some riding lessons."

"That's great," said the redhead as she walked from the barn door to shake Nattie's hand.

"This is my daughter, Kendra." Nancy told Nattie, "She runs the stable."

Kendra's handshake was firm. Her hands were calloused and there were small bruises and cuts on both knees. Kendra might possess the body of a Hooter's waitress, but she used it like a farmhand.

"Did you get the full tour of the place?" asked Kendra as she stood next to her mom. "That usually includes a brief history of the Newsome family."

Nancy scowled. Kendra stuck out her tongue. "I bet you told her about the Gulf Stream, didn't you, Momma?"

Kendra did not wait for her mother to answer before turning to Nattie, "Do you want to see the barn?"

Nattie used the old look-at-your-watch-as-if-she-was-late-for-something ploy. "Could I take a rain check on that? I'm afraid I'm late for a dinner engagement."

"No problem," said Kendra with a wave of her hand, "Come on, I'll walk you to your car." She turned to Nancy, "I'll get your truck, Momma. The keys are still in the ignition, aren't they?"

"Probably," admitted Nancy. "Good to meet you, Nattie. You call us when you are ready for lessons. Kendra is the best. Ask her any questions you want."

Nattie's first thought was, 'I wonder how your daughter would respond to Zoe Lancaster if she could ask any questions she wanted.'

Nattie waved at Nancy and said, "Good to meet you too."

As they walked toward the gate, Kendra asked, "So do you have any questions about riding lessons?"

The best cover stories were mostly true. The truth had a tendency to sound true, and the more truth there is in the story the easier it is to remember later. So Nattie's questions about taking riding lessons were entirely true if she were, in fact, interested in riding.

"I've never been comfortable around horses. Is it true that horses can sense fear?" Nattie asked

"They can definitely tell the difference between a tentative rider and a confident one."

"That makes me a pretty hopeless case then."

"Not at all Nattie. All we have to do is teach you how to be confident with horses. I do it all the time. We start by getting you used to the barn, the stalls, and the smells, then grooming. By the time you are comfortable grooming a horse sitting on top of one is easy. When we get you in the saddle you would be ready."

"I'm afraid I'm already too old, Kendra." This statement was conveniently completely true.

"I have a client who is a lot older than you, and he was so afraid of horses you could see his hand tremble if he patted one on the side." Kendra shook her head. "He had hidden it from his wife for years. She liked to ride, but he made up all kinds of stories to avoid going with her. He could never tell her the truth."

"And he took lessons from you so he could ride with his wife?"

"Yeah," Kendra exclaimed, "I guess the guilt finally got to him. He wanted to take her riding on their anniversary." Kendra laughed, "He even got a pearl necklace for me to hide on the trail for her."

"And it worked?" Nattie wondered.

"I'll say it worked. He rides great now."

"Was his wife surprised?"

"We'll find out tomorrow." Kendra answered then she pointed over her shoulder at the barn, "He brought me the necklace to hide just before you got here."

CHAPTER 9

ALMA QUINLIN

When Nattie got back to the office that night, it was empty. Kevin was gone, but had left two notes on the desk. The first note told her about a massage he scheduled for her on Thursday morning. That worked out well for her since she was flying to Chicago on Friday for a wedding on Sunday and a rehearsal on Saturday. After the lucky break she had with the Lancaster case, she was looking forward to having the day off on Thursday.

The second note threw her hopes of a free afternoon out of the window. She would be meeting Alma Quinlin for lunch at 11:30 tomorrow.

Lunch was at Ellis' Soda Shoppe, located across from the Martha Washington Inn in downtown Abingdon, Virginia. Originally it had been a pharmacy with glass doors covering large oak cabinets filled with apothecary jars. Like most drug stores of the 1940's and 50's there was a small counter where people could get hamburgers, root beer floats, and ice cream sundaes. Had it remained a pharmacy it would have needed extensive renovations; but as a Soda Shoppe the old shelves and counter-top were a part of its nostalgic charm.

Alma was sitting outside talking to the waitress as Nattie walked up to the table.

"Here she is," Alma said.

The waitress stepped back so Nattie could sit across from Alma. "Do you know what you want to drink?"

"Just water with lemon please"

"I'll be back in a minute with your drinks." The waitress left.

"I almost ordered water with lemon for you myself, but I wasn't sure." Alma rearranged her silverware. "You do know why I called, don't you?" she asked, without looking up.

Nattie waited until Alma made eye contact before answering, "Your husband lied to me yesterday. And you know I know it.

"It was not all lies, but you are right; he did lie to you." She held Nattie's gaze. "And you lied to us as well. James doesn't know you lied--but I do. And so do you, Ms. Moreland."

One of Nattie's first impressions of James Quinlin was that he severely underestimated the depth of his wife. That was yesterday. Today was different. Today Nattie realized that Addie's patronizing, authoritarian father was not the only one to severely underestimate the depth of Alma Quinlin.

The waitress came back with their waters and took their order. Alma ordered a tuna-melt because she "heard it was great"; Nattie, a grilled pimento cheese sandwich because she had never seen it on a menu before. They split a basket of sweet potato fries because the waitress said, "It's what we are known for."

Alma was pleasant and demure while they ordered. But her expression turned serious again as soon as the waitress left. She leaned forward, but did not speak.

Nattie leaned forward as well, "What is on your mind Mrs. Quinlin?"

"Did you really mean it yesterday when you said you would protect Addie's whereabouts?"

"I did."

"From anyone?" Alma's voice trembled slightly.

"Even you."

Their eyes locked. "You can trust me with yours daughter's secret, Mrs. Quinlin."

Alma looked from one eye to the other, searching. Then, looking away, she pursed her lips. "Trusting you is no longer a choice for me."

"I'm sorry?" Nattie was not sure what she had just heard.

"I think I must trust you," Alma explained, "now that you have that letter."

It was a pivotal moment. Nattie had feared being discovered. She knew she was guilty of theft. The laws were blurry about what trash was considered private property and what was not once it was placed at the street or mixed in with the other trash at the dump or in a garbage truck. But taking trash from under someone's kitchen sink was clearly theft. Nattie had to choose her words very carefully.

"What do you propose to do now, Mrs. Quinlin?"

"Like I already said, Miss Moreland, I'm going to trust you. You already know that Addie wrote me from that town in Italy. And I'm sure you noticed that the letter was postmarked two weeks ago." She paused and waited for a man in a suit to walk by. "But she did not go to Italy because she was afraid that Oliver would follow her."

"No?" Nattie asked.

Putting her hands flat on the table, Alma took a deep breath. "I'm getting ahead of myself. I need to slow down and tell you everything I know from the beginning."

Nattie patted her hand.

"About seven weeks ago Addie came home unexpectedly. She said she had quit her job and broken her engagement."

"Did she say why?" Nattie asked.

"She just said she had found something that broke her world apart," answered Alma. "Those were her exact words too, 'broke my world apart.'" She paused to get a drink and collect herself. While she did the waitress brought their food and refilled their water glasses.

Alma's tuna melt was open-faced and bulging with tuna. She ate it with a knife and fork while Nattie ate her sandwich with her fingers. After they each had taken a few healthy bites, Alma laid her knife and fork down and wiped her mouth with her napkin.

"Was Addie frightened by what she found?" Nattie asked.

Alma thought a moment. "I don't think she was. It seemed to me like she was more hurt than anything. She also used the word 'confused.'"

"So you don't think she is afraid of Mr. Ruggaliano?"

"She is in love with him. I'd stake my life on that. I had talked to her a few days before she came home. She talked about his big plans for changing the menu of those restaurants his family owns."

Nattie waited as Alma took a drink of water.

"She was proud of him," Alma continued. "I've never heard Addie talk about anything the way she talked about him. And she was just delighted about the way he treated her. He was gentle, sensitive, and genuinely interested in the same things she was interested in. She was proud of him," she repeated.

Alma took another small bite of her tuna melt while Nattie sampled some of the sweet potato fries.

"Addie was our middle child. Her older sister was a daddy's girl."

"Tomboy?"

"No, more like a princess." Alma smiled. "God love her, but she made flattering the man in her life her life's work."

That's a tough thing to say about your own daughter, Nattie thought.

"She married a man just like her Daddy. Hard working, loyal, honest..." she looked at Nattie, aware that Nattie probably formed a negative opinion of her husband when they first met. "I know he can be opinionated and overbearing too. But he was raised to believe that it is the man's job to take care of the women in his life. He would do anything he could to give any of us what he thought we wanted."

"Including asking her what she wants?" Nattie regretted the question as soon as it left her mouth. It was too much, too soon.

The question seemed to catch Alma off guard. "It sounds like you have experience with that kind of man yourself?"

"Stepfather."

Alma nodded and took another bite. "Annie, that's Addie's sister's name. She was more equipped to handle her father than Addie was."

"How do you mean?"

Alma took a drink and glanced at the fries but did not take one. "Annie was a good kid. Her daddy liked her hair long so she kept it long. He likes sports and she was a cheerleader. She even married a baseball player named Jimmy. She's Annie Smith now and her husband works for her father."

"On the farm?"

"No, the trucking business. James has five trucks. Mostly they haul coal. But the important thing is that she brought a husband home James could understand."

"School?"

"Math came easy to her, but she never applied herself. Enough to get by was all her father expected and it was all she gave." Alma shook her head. "The real problem was that she was too pretty and charming for her own good. I tried to make her work harder but it was impossible when her grades were mostly B's with a few A's. She could have been an accountant or an engineer if she had been pushed harder."

"And Addie?"

"Addie lived in Annie's shadow. Everyone knew Annie--head cheerleader, homecoming queen. Addie was like me when it came to sports, uncoordinated. Nice looking, especially when she smiled, but not a cover girl like her sister. She liked to read; she liked theater, art, music, ballet. She was not interested in what her father was interested in. And he could not understand what she was interested in."

"That's tough," Nattie said, "I don't think many fathers realize how important they are to their daughters, especially after the pigtail stage is over." She paused, "I'm sorry," she said, "that was more about me than Addie."

"That's okay. You're with me. James never believed he mattered to her. As far as he was concerned, he would offer advice and she would never take it."

"Did he feel betrayed when she wanted her life to be different than his?"

"I never thought of it that way, but that might be true. He felt betrayed by her," agreed Alma. "Giving her the approval she craved was just too close to giving her permission to be different."

"You sound like a psychology book."

"I got a bachelor's in Social Work from Radford," Alma explained. "I was a caseworker in Washington County for fifteen years."

"Not anymore?"

"No. Managed care took all the fun out of it and replaced it with paperwork."

Nattie nodded.

"Is everything all right with your food?" asked the waitress, startling both of them.

Nattie and Alma looked at their plates. Nattie had half a sandwich left and so did Alma.

"We've just been talking instead of eating," explained Nattie.

"The food is fine, thank you," Alma added.

After the waitress refilled their water glasses and left, Nattie asked, "Do you have any idea about what Addie found?"

Alma shook her head. "Whatever it was, I think it was in her bag."

"Did you see something?"

"No, but when we were carrying her luggage upstairs, she overreacted when I picked up her handbag."

"How much luggage did she bring with her?"

"She had one of those huge bags you use for international flights and maybe another dozen bags, totes, and small boxes. The back end of her Honda was full."

"Would you say she packed with the idea that she wasn't going back anytime soon?"

"Absolutely." Alma answered without hesitation. "She brought everything she cared about, her books, CD's, art pieces, and that sort of stuff. She had a crock pot and some everyday silverware that were my mother's and she brought all of that home with her."

"Furniture?"

"She left a bed and a television that we paid for, but all the rest of her furniture was older pieces from Oliver's family. Her father was pretty unhappy about the bed and the television, though."

Alma picked up a sweet potato fry and studied it. "This is the part of the story that's going to get harder to tell."

"You can trust me, Alma. Honest."

She looked at Nattie again, "Yes," she said, "I believe I can." Alma put the fry down without a taste. "As I said, James couldn't understand Addie. He disagreed with nearly every decision she ever made. He wanted her to major in something practical, like education or accounting. She majored in languages. He wanted her to get married, settle down and have kids."

"Like her sister?"

"Like Annie did." Alma agreed, "But Addie wasn't interested in that. She wanted to travel. He wanted her to begin a career. He even offered her a job as a book-keeper. But Addie didn't care about that either. She went to Italy, traveled around until she ran out of money and then got herself a waitressing job."

"Good for her," said Nattie.

Alma smiled, "It was the life she wanted. But her father hated it."

"How did she end up in Chicago?"

"She came home from Italy when her father had a heart attack. We thought we were going to lose him."

"When was that?"

"November 3rd 2002. Addie was home before Thanksgiving. She began working for her father that January."

"He was happy about that I'm guessing?"

"He was. It was what he wanted when she graduated. But she was miserable," Another sip of water. "He was back at work by March and she was ready to go soon after that."

"Chicago?"

Alma nodded.

"Why there?"

"She couldn't afford to go back to Italy, but a friend she waitressed with in Florence was working in Chicago and told her about a job there. James was furious. He felt like she was turning her back on her family again. Turning her back on him again."

"But she went anyway."

"She did. And I agreed with her. And I talked James into giving her some money to start out with."

"He agreed?" Nattie said, surprised.

"He agreed. But he sent her off with a curse. She felt she had to listen." Alma took a deep breath, "he told her that she'd get there and enjoy herself for a while; but as she got older, she'd latch on to a city man and he'd use her up."

"Oh my."

"It was awful enough when he first said it; but when she came home after breaking off her engagement, he threw it up at her." Looking down Alma shook her head.

Nattie grit her teeth, "Talk about kicking someone when they're down."

"He gloated a bit when she first got here, but he was mostly glad she was home again. I think he hoped she'd stay this time."

"But that wasn't her plan?" asked Nattie.

"No. Addie said she had something to do in Italy." Raising her eyebrows, Alma continued, "she told us that the day after she got home. James went wild. He took her cell phone and broke it into two pieces with his hands and then he told her to leave that night."

"Really."

"That was the worst night of my life. I never thought I could hate him so much, but I did. I must say that I thought Addie's plan was crazy myself. I don't see why she could not have stayed longer."

"I'm sure she had her reasons."

"I'm sure she did, but she didn't share them with me. When she left the next morning James told her never to come back, or call, or write."

"Did he mean that?" asked Nattie.

"He thought he did, but that was just his anger talking."

"And now?"

"Now--he's still hurt--but now there's guilt and embarrassment in the stew. I'm sure she could come home. He'd blow off some smoke, to save face, but she's still his daughter."

"So she found something in Chicago that upset her, and coming here was just part of the route to Italy for some purpose she did not share with you. Is that right?" asked Nattie.

"Yes."

"And she's in Italy now. And sending you letters, which you hide from your husband because of the friction between them?"

"Not exactly," Alma answered. "She only sent one letter."

"You do know where Addie is, though, don't you, Alma?" Nattie asked with the hope of an easy investigation slipping from her grasp.

"I know where she was, Montepulciano. It's where she sent the letter from. And that's where I want you to start."

This was the moment when, in a cartoon, Nattie's eyes would have shot out of her face. "Excuse me?" was all she could manage.

"I want you to go to Italy and find my daughter and give her this." Alma placed a sealed envelope on the table. The initials "A.Q." were printed on it. "Will you do it?"

Nattie looked down at the half of a grilled pimento-cheese sandwich. It was not exactly a conflict of interest with her contract with Ollie, but it could become one pretty easy. Going to Italy was always a dream; but with the possibility of actually going so imminent, it hit her as more frightening than she had expected. She had never traveled that far before. Her honeymoon in Cancun was the only time she had ever needed a passport.

"Traveling to Italy would be a fairly expensive proposition," observed Nattie.

Alma nodded, "I talked to Kevin at your office and I know your fees. If you have already read that letter you know she was saying goodbye. So I'm asking you, Nattie--I'm trusting you--will you do it?"

Nattie grinned. "You drive a hard bargain, Alma. I think you're tougher than you look."

Alma grinned. "I'd almost have to be, don't you think?"

Nattie extended her hand across the table. As Alma grasped it, Nattie said, "Since we're going to trust each other, would you answer a question?"

Alma squeezed her hand, "I will if you will."

"It's a deal. You first."

"Ok," said Alma, "you probably need that letter to find my daughter, but I'm going to want it back. As of this moment it is my last link to her."

"I'll make a copy and return the original tomorrow."

Alma nodded.

"My turn now," said Nattie. "When did you first realize I had taken the letter?"

"I wasn't sure about the letter but I knew you were lying when you told James you had washed your hands."

Nattie looked at her hands.

"Your hands were not wet," said Alma.

"I could have dried them--"

Alma interrupted her. "You could not have dried them with that bathroom towel--it was on my lap."

CHAPTER 10

JUNE

The wedding had been as pleasant as could be expected considering it was her father's family and she was the divorced daughter of the missing alcoholic. It did not matter that more than half of the guests were also either divorced or alcoholic--because whatever her father did, was always worse than the same offense committed by one of his siblings. At least in their minds. That attitude extended to his children, especially if he was absent. The bride was her cousin, Peggy Sue, who, when she gave Nattie the job of registering the gifts said, "It's a job for a detective, so bring your gun."

It's a good thing the bridesmaids did not come armed, thought Nattie when she saw the lime green dresses they were forced to buy.

The questions were all predictable, but being predictable did not keep them from being painful: Why aren't you married anymore? Where is Nathan now and how did you screw that up? Why isn't your brother here? When is your father going to straighten his life out? Why would a woman want to be a private detective? Are you gay? Are you butch?

The only question that Nattie really wanted to answer was the one that continued to pop up in her mind: *Why in the world did I come here for this?* The invitation was from family; it was a family obligation. Nattie never considered not going. The sense of responsibility, or whatever it was that forced her to accept the invitation without question did not seem to plague either her father or her brother. She vowed to remember this and never repeat it. And she meant it too. At least she would never repeat it again with the Benjamin's, her father's side of her family tree.

Sharing the hotel's complimentary breakfast with the family on Monday morning was the last of the family obligations. Nattie sat at an empty table and was joined by her Uncle Pete and Aunt Gladys. When Pete discovered that she was a private investigator, he took it upon himself to tell her everything he knew about detective work, which was nothing. Uncle Pete had little to say, but he could always take a long time to say it. With Uncle Pete there is never any room for anyone else in the conversation. Even when he chatted, he lectured.

Aunt Gladys was as offensive as Uncle Pete was tedious. If she was not telling Nattie endless stories of her father's failures and missed opportunities, then she would tell the same story about Kevin endlessly. Kevin was the target *du jour*.

"I don't know if you remember this, Natalie, but Kevin always had those skinny little arms."

"I remember Aunt Gladys. He was a little kid."

Gladys laughed and touched Nattie on the forearm, acknowledging that Nattie had said something; but she continued without acknowledging what was said. "He was so cute when he'd hold up his arms like he was flexing his muscles."

"I remember," Nattie said, "and I remember what you told him."

"Well he did look like he was doing an imitation of a coat-hanger." The line was clever, and it might have been marginally funny if it had not been aimed at a child. Nattie always wondered if Gladys kept bringing it up because it was the only clever thing she had ever said.

"He was just eight years old."

"Oh, but it was so funny."

"And it is just as funny each and every single time you tell it again." Nattie said with no attempt to hide the sarcasm.

Oblivious, Gladys replied sweetly, "Thank you, dear."

That was Nattie's cue to look at her watch and say, "I had better be on my way." She leaned over, pecked Pete on the cheek and backed away before he began to grope her. She gave Gladys only a slightly longer peck.

"It was very nice to see you again, Natalie." Gladys said as she amused herself with her own imitation of a coat-hanger.

"I can't tell you how delighted I am that we could have breakfast together," Nattie responded; and as she turned, she quietly added, "I really can't."

It took an hour and a half to get from Libertyville, where the wedding was, to the doctor's office in Countryside, where her friend June Marma worked. Staying with June for a few days after the wedding was Nattie's reward to herself for doing her family duty over the weekend.

June had been Nattie's freshman year resident assistant at Freedom University in Kingsport, Tennessee. June was a junior nursing major at the time. June gave up the RA job for her senior year as she would be busy enough with the clinical practicum required of senior nursing majors. Nattie and June decided to room together for Nattie's sophomore and June's senior year.

Nattie's mother, or more accurately her stepfather, disapproved of the psychology major Nattie had decided on, and they withdrew financial support. Rather than beg or choose a more palatable major for them, Nattie decided to leave school. It was June who encouraged her to apply for an RA job. The people who got such positions tended to be the best and the brightest students, so Nattie had not expected to get it. But she did, and it meant she could return to school the next fall and finish her degree.

The bond between Nattie and June solidified even more during exam week at the end of the year. Nattie had gone out to Taco Bell with her brother, Kevin, who was still in high school at the time. In plain sight on the floor of the back seat of his Civic, she found a bottle of Coors beer. He was under-aged at the time and could have lost his drivers license if a policeman had just looked through the window while writing him a parking ticket. So, of course, Nattie took the beer and put it in her backpack. It would be safer out of sight in her backpack than in the back seat of his car. She could just throw it away when she passed a garbage can.

But Nattie did not throw Kevin's beer away. She forgot. And when she came back to her dorm room with her backpack, she unwittingly violated school policy. It was an innocent mistake and would have easily been rectified if June had not found it first. June had grown up in a family that never drank; it was not considered a sin or a weakness, it was just not considered at all. She never gave alcohol much consideration either, but soon June would be on a mission staff that required abstinence. She was simply curious, so June opened the Coors and after taking a healthy drink of the warm beer she promptly spit it out into a plastic waste basket by her desk. She dropped the nearly full bottle of beer in as well. Her curiosity was satisfied.

Had June been more experienced with alcohol she would have known better. She had no idea how rapidly the room would begin to reek of beer. Soon the smell was in the hall and shortly thereafter attracted the attention of the dorm staff. The RA called the resident director, who came to their room. Nattie returned from studying in the library right before the RD arrived. She had just enough time to make a quick assessment of what was happening.

"I am the one who brought the beer to the room," confessed Nattie. "It is my fault."

"But I am the one who opened it," argued June.

"Who drank it?" asked the RD.

The question struck Nattie as strange. "No one drank it," she explained. "Look at it. It is all still there in the trash can."

The RD left with the evidence after she made appointments with each of the roommates for the next day. As soon as they were alone Nattie convinced June to "let me take the heat on this. You leave for Uganda in less than a week. You cannot afford to get bogged down with this."

"But it is not your fault," pleaded June. "I can't believe how stupid I am."

"I'm going to say it was mine, that I left it open and you spilled it. That's ninety-nine percent the truth."

"And then what?"

Nattie shrugged, "They'll make me go to the honor council and then make me do a few hours of community service. It won't be worse than that I promise. I can do it easily because I'm here. If you had to do it, it would mess up the timing of everything you have been working for. Please, June, let me take care of this. It's not a big deal at all."

June finally agreed and assumed that everything had gone exactly as Nattie had described because after Nattie met with the RD, June received a call telling her that her appointment had been cancelled. June's loyalty to and admiration for Nattie was fixed.

A week later, June was in Uganda, serving a four-year tour of duty with a medical mission group. She wrote Nattie regularly and even flew back to be in her wedding. June never knew what really happened in that meeting with the RD because Nattie never told her.

The RD had lectured Nattie about being a moral and ethical example for her classmates, questioning her commitment and her faith and her values. All of which surprised Nattie, but listened quietly. After all, she was guilty of bringing the beer on campus. The rebuke did, however, feel very much like one of her stepfather's browbeating sessions. The greater surprise came when she was told that she was no longer fit to be an RA.

Nattie never told anyone what had happened in that interview. The loss of the RA job reactivated the decision to leave school. She went to talk to Dr. McDonald, the King College professor she had first gotten close to during the summer study trip to Britain. She had already sought him out twice during that semester to get advice about classes and about what to consider in a graduate school. This time she confided in him that she would be withdrawing from school. She did not tell him why the decision was so "abrupt," as he called it.

Nattie waited until she was working at the Hiram Moreland Detective Agency and then wrote June that she was working her dream job and school would have to wait. June believed her. After five years in Uganda, June returned to the United States where she got a job as a nurse for a family practice doctor in Countryside, Illinois.

"You can sit here for now." June told her as they walked past all the examination rooms toward an open area in the back of the office. Nattie sat in a chair with extendable armrests. It was where the patients donated blood for lab tests.

"I've got tonsillitis!" exclaimed a woman sitting to Nattie's left. The woman wore her gray hair in a bun and sat with her back toward them. By the way she leaned forward and moved her arms Nattie assumed that there was a computer on the other side of her.

"That's Debbie," explained June. "She is learning to look up symptoms and diagnosis codes on a new ICD-9 program."

Nattie nodded as if she knew what an ICD-9 program was. "Go ahead and do what you need to do. I know I'm a little early for lunch." She shooed June away with her hand. "I brought a new Robert Parker novel, so I'll be fine until you are ready to go."

Robert Parker was Nattie's favorite writer of detective novels. She liked Alex Cross, James Patterson's detective, and Kay Scarpetta, Patricia Cornwell's detective, also, but Robert Parker's Spencer was her favorite. She liked that Spencer, the former boxer and current tough guy, could cook and was well versed in English literature. But the real joy of following Spencer was that he was the consummate smart-ass. Nattie was an accomplished smart-ass too, but she lived vicariously through Spencer because his comments were spoken out loud and directed toward whoever deserved them. *That's why Spencer is a main character in a detective novel and I register gifts at weddings I don't even want to go to.*

Nattie was quite content to entertain herself with her novel, but the wait was even more entertaining as Debbie continued to shout out various medical maladies as she found them.

"Are you ready to go?" June asked, startling Nattie.

"Absolutely," answered Nattie. "Say, June, do you know of a restaurant called Ruggs?"

"Sure. There's one in Yorktown and another one over by the College of DuPage. Is that where you want to go for lunch?"

"I would, if that works for you."

"Oh yeah." June answered, "I go there a couple of times a month. I love their Italian sausage sandwiches."

They left the office through the back door where June parked her car. Just before the door closed shut behind them Nattie heard Debbie cry out excitedly, "I've got diarrhea!"

CHAPTER 11

RUGGS

It was just before noon when June and Nattie got to the Ruggs located along the outer perimeter of the Yorktown Mall. In Bristol they would have beaten the lunch crowd, but that was not the case here. The patrons, which seemed split in half between shoppers and tradesmen, were already here at 11:45. The presence of the shoppers meant that it would be clean and safe. The presence of the tradesmen meant the food would be good and the portions generous. The presence of June along beside her at lunchtime meant the service would be quick.

Service was cafeteria style, which was a surprise to Nattie. After eating the gourmet quality slice of cake Ollie had prepared for her, she had pictured a restaurant with menus and waitresses. What she got was a menu mounted on the wall and trays sliding along a ledge with servers handing you the food you pointed at from the other side of a glass partition.

At the top of the menu, just below the "Welcome to Ruggs" sign, the slogan read, "It's in the Buns." Underneath the slogan was a list of everything that could be ordered with a bun; hot dogs, Italian sausages, bratwursts, and Polish sausages. Under the list of sandwiches was another menu of soups and sides.

"Can I get a salad here?" asked Nattie without looking away from the menu board.

"No one comes in here if they are watching their weight."

Nattie pointed at the "It's in the Buns" slogan and wondered out loud, "Is that a reference to their hot dogs or where they food ends up on your body?"

June giggled and pointed at Nattie like her finger was a gun. "I forgot about your sense of humor, girlfriend."

Nattie enjoyed the remark for a moment, but even small compliments felt awkward. She smiled meekly and turned back toward the menu.

Taking Nattie's arm, June said, "I'm going to order an Italian sausage and onion rings, so I'd appreciate it if you wouldn't mention my buns again."

"It's a deal, but if I think of something really good, all bets are off."

"Of course."

Hot dogs were not a delicacy for Nattie. The only hot dogs she had ever had were the cheap ones found in gas station steamers with thin runny brown stuff that passed for chili. She had never eaten a hot dog bun that was not soggy wet or stale and stiff. But given she was in a hot dog place, she ordered a hot dog as she slid her tray along the rack and stopped at the "buns" station, which was first. Nattie ordered her hot dog with mustard, onions, and tomato wedges. She made a special point of saying, "no celery salt" because she had been told that adding celery salt was a common practice in Chicago. The request got her a frown from the server.

June slid her tray past the soup section and ordered her onion rings under the "sides" sign.

"Soup?" asked the woman holding what looked like a very large coffee cup.

"Please," answered Nattie.

"Tomato Florentine or Ribollita?"

"Tomato please."

A lunch of soup, water, and a hot dog cost Nattie nearly twelve dollars. It was twice as expensive as she had expected. It was, after all, her idea to come to Ruggs so she made the best of it. Her first bite of hot dog was tiny. She held it up and inspected it while she chewed. The next bite was a healthy mouthful.

June just laughed at her. "It's better than you expected, isn't it?"

"I'll say," was all Nattie could utter. The meal was fantastic. The hot dog was meatier than any she had ever tasted, the tomatoes and onions were fresh, and the soup was as good as any she had ever had. All that would have been enough, but the bun was extraordinary. The hot dog buns could have been served as rolls in an elegant restaurant.

Nattie savored her lunch, barely hearing June describe the man she had met on Match.com. Apparently he was a dentist from Des Moines, Iowa. They had only met face to face once and that was only two weeks ago. Before that, their relationship consisted of emails, text messages, and Facebook photos. He mentioned that she was always "dressed up" in her photos. He, on the other hand, was never dressed up in his Facebook photos. When she first saw him as she picked him up at Midway airport, June knew this relationship was special. Just to please him, she had made a point of wearing jeans and a T-shirt. He got off the plane in a three-piece suit. His name was Scott Pinella.

"Did you bring him here?" asked Nattie.

June nodded, "He had three hotdogs," she said as if she was proud of it.

"Marco!" barked a dark haired, slightly heavy woman wearing a nametag that said, "Roz." She was clearing the booth next to Nattie and June.

Marco looked to be seventeen and alarmed by Roz's tone. He was washing the inside of the front window at the moment.

"I know I told you to wash that window every day, but do you really think during the lunch rush is the time to do it?"

But it's apparently the perfect time to call your workers on the carpet, thought Nattie as she watched Marco begin to clear an empty table on the other side of the room.

"How was your lunch?" The question surprised Nattie. She had not noticed Roz approach her table and could not have anticipated the sweetness in Roz's tone now that she was making nice with a customer.

"Mine was great," answered June.

"So was mine," agreed Nattie. "Say, you don't give out the recipe for that bread do you?"

Roz smiled, "You like it then?"

"Enough to want that recipe."

"That's sort of a family secret. But you can come back and have more anytime you want."

Nattie looked at her, "You wouldn't, by any chance, know Ollie Ruggaliano would you?"

Roz paused and stiffened her back. "I'm Roselind Ruggaliano. Ollie is my brother."

CHAPTER 12

ROZ

Nattie returned to the doctor's office with June where she retrieved her rented Mustang and drove back to Ruggs. The lunch hour had passed so she could sit at an empty table with a diet coke and read her Robert Parker book. Roz had agreed to talk to her, "as soon as things slow down."

When Nattie returned from her second trip to the ladies room (diet coke had that effect on her), the dining room had slowed down considerably. Roz was nowhere in sight. Nattie decided to sit back down and wait. Waiting was a big part of a private investigator's life.

Fifteen minutes later Roz plopped down across from Nattie. She took a sip of coffee and pointed at the book Nattie was reading, "Is that a murder mystery?"

"Detective novel." Nattie corrected her. "There's no murder in this one."

Roz frowned. "You said you were a private investigator hired to find my brother's fiancée right?"

Nattie nodded yes.

Pointing again at the book, Roz asked, "So is that technical reading for you?"

Nattie smiled politely. When confronted with unexplained venom, it was her practice to find something positive to say to whomever she was speaking. It was just something she did for her own amusement, but the compliment had to pertain to the person's head, like "the way you comb your hair," or "the way you apply your eye makeup."

"I like the way you part your hair to one side." Nattie decided to say.

Roz looked back at her suspiciously.

It's amazing you can fix your hair at all with your head shoved so far up your--buns, thought Nattie as she smiled and held eye contact across the table.

Looking at her watch, Roz said," I've got about half an hour before I get busy again; so if you have some things you want to ask me, you'd better get to it."

"Ok." Nattie leaned forward. "Tell me whatever you think might help me find Adelle Quinlin."

"Wow." Roz shook her head slowly. "You call that a probing question?"

"No. I call it a respectful question." The term 'respectful' question was what Hiram had called her questioning style when he first noticed her skills in getting information from people. "I don't know what you know. Before I ask something specific, I'll let you tell me what you think I should know. So, Roz, what do you think I should know?"

"Ok. Here's what I think you should know. My brother, Ollie, is a flake. He is charming and talented in the kitchen, but he is a flake. His first wife was a certified whacko and that Addie-do-right was as phony as a three dollar bill."

"Phony?"

"She was just too--too--nice or sweet or something. I know that doesn't sound bad, but it was too much."

"Was she on her best behavior, trying to win her fiancé's family over? Or do you think there was a malicious motive?"

"Now that was a better question."

Nattie waited for her to answer.

"I think she was a mousy little waitress who stumbled upon a golden opportunity."

Nattie knit her eyebrows, but did not say anything.

"My brother was vulnerable. His first marriage was a complete disaster. His wife disappeared, and he had to wait seven years before she was pronounced dead." She rolled her eyes. "Then he spent another two years at yet another culinary school studying to be a pastry chef."

"He's pretty good," observed Nattie. "I had a piece of lemon cake he made and--"

"Yeah, I know," interrupted Roz. "He's good, but it's a hobby. We aren't in that kind of food business. He went to school while the rest of us worked."

"Us?"

"The rest of the family. We all work in the business. Everyone except him-- and, Olivia, but she's a nun so she's not in the business anyway."

"I see."

"Ollie was never required to be responsible. Mom called him 'sensitive' and pampered him. After the ordeal around his wife and all the years he avoided women, he was vulnerable to any woman who showed any interest in him at all." Roz's expression transformed from exasperation to a scowl. "And that sweet little Addie knew exactly how to hook him and reel him in."

"Do you know what her motive was?"

"Some women will do anything to get a man, and this was a man who was about to inherit a lucrative business."

"That all fits together nicely," observed Nattie, "except for the primary question."

"What's that?" Roz asked.

"Why did Addie Quinlin leave and where is she now? If she is the gold-digger you say she is, then why would she leave now?"

Roz spread her hands in a gesture that meant "isn't it obvious?"

"Do you think something frightened her?" Nattie asked.

"No, I think she got another offer."

"Offer? What kind of offer?"

"Money."

"Who would pay her, and what would they pay her for?"

"Well--" Roz' tone was condescending. "--what she did was disappear. So if you want to know who would pay her to disappear, then I suppose you would need to ask the question a good detective would ask."

"Who benefits from her disappearance?"

"You see," Roz said, "you can come up with a quality detective question when you try."

"Why thank you Roz," smiled Nattie, "And might I say how much I admire how you apply your lipstick."

CHAPTER 13

IRMA

As Roz stood and left the table she took a folded piece of paper from her shirt pocket and slid it across the table. It was the phone number of Irma Ruggaliano.

The woman who answered the phone had a pleasant voice and just a trace of an Italian accent. "Are you the detective helping my Ollie?"

"I am," Nattie answered. "And you are?"

"His mother," Irma explained. "Ollie is my son."

An hour later Nattie was sitting in Irma's kitchen in Melrose Park. The Ruggaliano home was in an old neighborhood. The homes were large, with high ceilings with crown molding and oversized trim around the doors and along the floor. Most of the rooms were dimly lit and each was decorated with a different floral wallpaper, muted by age. Nattie got the tour of the front room where framed family photos were crowded together covering every flat surface in the room.

Unlike the other rooms, the kitchen was brightly lit, and its walls were covered in a linoleum pattern simulating small white bricks. The large oven in the back corner looked like an antique. The pot of whatever was cooking on the stove smelled delicious. The only furniture in the room was a wooden table with six chairs around it. The table was covered with a yellow checkered plastic table cloth. On the table was a single bottle of olive oil.

"Do you drink coffee?" Irma ushered Nattie to the table.

"I do. Thank you."

Irma took a small plate of small fancy cookies from the counter and placed it on the table as she removed the olive oil. At the back of the counter were two different-sized silver coffee pots shaped like hourglasses. Irma placed the smaller one on the stove and lit the flame under it with a kitchen match.

"May I call you 'Natasha'?"

Nattie had not expected to hear that name. Irma had surely heard it from her son. "You certainly may," she said, "but my friends call me 'Nattie,' and I'd prefer that."

"Well, Nattie, thank you for coming to see me. I just wanted to meet you."

"Do you mind if I ask you a few questions? As long as I'm here."

Irma extended her open hand and said, "*Prego.*"

Assuming that Irma meant "please go ahead" Nattie proceeded, "Roz told me that Ollie was about to inherit the business. Is that right?"

"My husband, Oliver, and his brother, Carlo, own the business. They talk about retirement sometimes, but that is between them. Roselind is concerned that Carlo is going to take more than his share of the business. She thinks that with Ollie away, no one but she can protect Oliver's children."

"Is there a reason for her to be concerned?"

The silver hourglass shaped coffee pot began to gurgle. Irma excused herself and turned the burner off. When she returned to the table, she carried two saucers, each containing a tiny cup of coffee and a tiny spoon.

"It's Italian coffee," explained Irma as she placed a saucer in front of Nattie.

Nattie could smell the rich aroma without leaning forward. "Espresso?" she guessed.

"*Sí.*" Irma went back to the counter and returned with a bowl of sugar cubes. "Do you like milk with your coffee?"

"No, this is fine."

Irma sat down. After putting one sugar cube in her cup she began to stir it.

The sugar cube looked huge compared to the cup of Italian coffee. Nattie preferred Splenda, but if she did have to use the sugar cubes she would have put one cube in a full cup. This cup was one third the size of a full cup of coffee. She tentatively dropped in the cube and began stirring as Irma did.

"The kids, ours and Carlo's, grew up together. Our Olivia was the oldest. Our Roz and their Laura were just a year apart. Then Ollie and Alberto, the two babies, are the same age. The kids have always known that each family was going to get half the business one day." Irma stopped stirring and pulled the spoon through her lips. "It was Roz who first realized that Carlo's two kids would each get more than our three kids. She was in the sixth grade, but she wrote up a business proposal trying to convince her father that since his father had five grandchildren they should each get twenty percent."

"That's pretty industrious for a sixth grader."

"Oh that's my Roz. She did make a pretty good argument; but after her father told her 'no,' she just wouldn't let it go."

"What was her argument?" asked Nattie.

"She knew that before the brothers began Ruggs restaurants, their father, Joseph, had the bakery. He really started everything off and he has five grandchildren."

"They should each get twenty percent," Nattie echoed.

"Yes."

"Very clever."

"Yes." Irma nodded. "But her father told her that if he used her argument then Carlo would just go have two more kids and she then would only have one seventh instead of one fifth."

Irma took a tiny sip of coffee to test the temperature and then took half the contents in one gulp.

"A few years later, Olivia took her vows as a nun and that equaled the inheritance."

"I don't understand." Said Nattie.

"Olivia took a vow of poverty. That means if she inherited a share of the business it would go to her order, the Sisters of Mercy."

"So the inheritance will be equal now."

"Yes."

"But Roz is still concerned."

"She is very skilled at finding new ways to be upset. Everyone has assured her that she will be fine when that time comes, but she doesn't believe anybody. It got worse when Roz was moved from one store and replaced by Laura."

"Why was that?" Nattie asked.

"Oliver--my husband--said it was a business decision. He said her management style would be a better fit in the other store."

Nattie wanted to ask what Roz's management style was, but thought better of it. "Roz told me she believed Ollie's fiancée disappeared because someone had paid her to go." She watched for Irma's reaction, but seeing none she added, "Does Roz have a reason to suspect that Carlo or his children would do this?"

"None of them would ever do such a thing. And even it they were that kind of people, it would not change the inheritance because we control the recipe."

"What recipe?"

"The bread recipe for the buns. It is Oliver's recipe. Roz thinks that since Carlo is more involved in the office, he could take advantage of Oliver. Her father prefers the kitchen to the office."

"Like Ollie."

Irma nodded. "And Carlo's son Alberto prefers the office to the kitchen. Roz thinks their control of the office side of the business makes us vulnerable. But she is wrong because the key to our business is that bread recipe and it belongs to Oliver."

Nattie finished her coffee. It was strong. Strong enough for a whole cube of sugar.

"You don't believe Roz's theory then do you?" asked Nattie.

"I don't."

"Do you have an idea about why Adelle left?"

"I am sure she did not leave because she was bribed by Carlo's family. And I am sure that she and Ollie loved each other very much. Something must have scared her."

"What could have scared her so much that she did not even leave a note?"

"I don't know. Roz tried to run her off a long time ago so I doubt she had that kind of influence. Edith tried to cause trouble, but I don't think she had any contact with Addie before she left."

"Who is Edith?"

"Edith is Alberto's wife, but they have been separated for months." Irma paused, and looked more deeply into Nattie's eyes. "Edith is also Judith's sister."

"Edith is the sister of Ollie's first wife?"

Irma nodded.

"The sister of the woman who disappeared and was pronounced dead seven years later?"

"Yes."

"Did she blame Ollie?"

"Blame him? She accused him of murdering Judith, but no one took that seriously. She may have wanted to hurt Ollie by scaring Addie off. But she was separated from Alberto well before Addie left."

"Why did Alberto and Edith separate?"

"Frankly," Irma said as she cleared the coffee dishes from the table, "I don't know why he put up with the fuss she made after Judith disappeared. We were all shaken, but she had no call to accuse Ollie of murder. He was devastated by his own grief. She made his life miserable." Sitting back at the table, she continued, "Things settled down until after Judith was declared dead and then she started making a big fuss about some jewelry that belonged to Judith. Edith began making accusations about it when Addie moved into the apartment we own. She accused us of giving Judith's things to Addie."

"Do you think I could look around that apartment where Addie lived?"

"I'm sure you can, but I doubt it would be of much use to you."

"Why is that, Irma?"

"We moved everything Addie left into storage and had the place cleaned and painted from top to bottom."

"You kept everything she left?"

Irma nodded, "We did. Would you like to look though what she left?"

CHAPTER 14

LOU MALNATI'S

"The sauce goes on top of the cheese," June had always told Nattie. "That's what makes the difference between real Chicago-style deep dish pizza and the wannabes." Nattie had heard about it many times at college, but now she would find out for herself. The chance to taste authentic deep-dish and the commitment to have dinner with June were only two of the reasons she was able to bring herself to turn down Irma's invitation for dinner at the Ruggaliano home. The larger reason for visiting the Lou Malnati's restaurant was that this is where Adelle Quinlin had come to work when she left home the second time. According to Alma Quinlin, Addie's friend Maria from Florence had gotten her the job here.

She was standing in front of Lou Malnati's, an old fire station in downtown Naperville, waiting for June when her phone rang. According to June, Lou Malnati's was the pizzeria with the best deep-dish pies in all of Chicagoland.

"Hello," said Nattie into the phone.

"Hey, Sis. How was the wedding?"

"Hello, Kevin. The wedding was nice. Silvia looked beautiful and the guy she married was cute. He walked around with this silly grin all over his face. I thought he was going to start laughing any minute. You should have been here."

"Did you meet him?"

"I introduced myself, but that was all. He seemed nice."

"How about Aunt Trudy?"

"I didn't spend much time with her. She had all that mother-of-the-bride stuff to tend. But Aunt Gladys said to say hello to you."

"Did she mention the coat hanger thing," he asked tentatively.

"No," Nattie lied. "She didn't mention it."

Kevin paused, "She probably got tired of telling that story."

"Probably. What did you end up doing this weekend?"

"I saw mom on Saturday."

"How did that go?"

"Nothing new," Kevin said. "We were in the kitchen and Taffy came bounding in with a ball in her mouth. So I took her in the backyard and played fetch with her."

"Was Attila there?" Nattie asked about her stepfather, Lionel O'Brien. Attila was really more Kevin's name for him than hers.

"He wasn't home when I took Taffy out back." Kevin answered, then his voice got more animated, "Have you ever been playing ball with that idiot dog when it had to go to the bathroom?"

"No," she said slowly.

"It's the funniest thing," Kevin laughed, "Taffy will have the ball in her mouth and then she'll get this look in her eye and you know what will happen next."

Kevin stopped talking. She could hear him take a drink of something.

"And what happens next, Kevin?"

"Taffy gets this real embarrassed look on her face, and then she'll drop the ball, and take a couple of steps directly over the top of it. She'll walk bow-legged because she'll be getting ready to squat at the same time. It's just bizarre. Then she'll do her business close to where she dropped the ball." Kevin laughed out loud at his own story.

"I guess you have to see it for yourself; but after she's done and does that flip-up-some-grass-with-your-back-legs thing, she won't go near the ball."

"What do you mean?"

"The dog won't go near the ball because there's a pile of poop too close to it."

"You're kidding."

"No, seriously. She'll circle around the ball a few times like she's trying to get close to it, but it's just as if it turned into kryptonite."

"So what happens next?"

"Well somebody's got to go get the ball because Taffy's done with it."

"So you got the ball, right?"

"Yep."

"And let me guess. When you brought it inside, Mom said, 'She's sensitive,' in a baby voice."

"She was getting a treat for Taffy. She'd probably have said that, but just then Attila came in from the garage." Kevin forced a weak laugh, "He walked in, glanced at me, looked at Mom, and then said, 'Thanks for running Taffy, honey.'"

"What did she say?"

"She said 'you're welcome,' like she was the one who did it."

"Well she did get the treat." Nattie said sarcastically.

"True enough. And why would he think I had anything to do with it? I was just standing there with the ball in my hand."

"You had the ball in your hand and he didn't say thanks to you?"

"Hello would have been nice," Kevin said, "but who notices a persona-non-grata?" After a moment of silence Kevin added, "I've got a couple of messages for you. Zoe Lancaster called to say you didn't need to do surveillance anymore."

"What did you say?"

"I didn't talk to her. It was a message, but I wouldn't have told her we already knew about Thursday."

"Anything else?"

"Yeah. June called; she got hung up at work and can't make dinner. She didn't have your cell phone number."

"Kevin," Nattie said very slowly, "Do you think you could have told me that first?"

Dining at Lou Malnati's alone did give Nattie the freedom to ask about Adelle Quinlin. She ordered a salad with ranch dressing, water, and a slice of pizza. Kelly, her waitress, said that a single slice would be plenty.

After looking at a picture of Addie, Kelly said, "I was here about a month before she left so I didn't really know her. She worked lunch mostly. But I think she and Maria were pretty close."

"Is Maria here?" asked Nattie.

Scanning the room Kelly's eyes came to rest upon a dark-haired waitress on the other side of the restaurant. "That's Maria. I'll tell her to come over when she gets a chance."

Five minutes later Maria stood across the table from Nattie. "You were asking about Adelle?"

Nattie had seen her coming and left her last bite of salad attached to the end of her fork.

"I did ask about Adelle. I understand you were friends. Is that right?" asked Nattie.

"Who are you and why do you want to know?" Maria looked guarded, almost defiant.

"I'm sorry," Nattie apologized as she handed Maria a business card. "I'm just trying to find her. Can you tell me anything that might help me?"

"You're a private investigator, huh?" snorted Maria, "Who hired you?"

"That I'm afraid I cannot say, but I can tell you that no harm will come to her as a part of my investigation."

The expression on Maria's face did not denote trust. If she did know where Addie was right now, it was unlikely that she was going to share it with a private investigator she just met.

Nattie's instincts led her to say, "I can understand your hesitancy to tell me anything that might betray your friend. You don't know if you can trust me or not."

"Right," Maria agreed pointedly.

"Maybe you could help me understand why she left," offered Nattie. If Maria was concerned about Addie's safety, this would open the door for Maria to reveal something about whoever she assumed had hired Nattie.

"All I know is that she left work on Tuesday and said 'see you tomorrow.'"

"So when she left she expected to return to work?"

"Yes. If something was wrong before that, she would have told me."

"You sound confident," observed Nattie.

"I am. Whatever happened, happened after she left that day."

"Any ideas about what might have happened that night?"

"All I know is she called me and left a message on my machine. I don't know what time that was because I didn't notice it until the next morning." Maria looked over toward her area of the restaurant then rolled her eyes, "My answering machine doesn't tell me what time messages were left because I never figured out how to set the clock."

"What was the message, Maria?"

"I could tell Addie was in her car when she called because I could hear the traffic in the background. Anyway, all she said was, 'I'm leaving. Tell Rocco I won't be back either.'"

"Who's Rocco?"

"He's the manager here," explained Maria, "Rocco does the scheduling of the waitresses."

"Anything else?"

Maria watched Nattie more closely as she answered. "She said, 'Ollie's not the man I thought he was.'"

As Kelly brought Nattie's pizza to the table Maria added, "That's all I know. We haven't talked since, but if you find her tell her I miss her."

"I will," Nattie said.

CHAPTER 15

LAURA

When Nattie woke the next morning she found a note from June on the kitchen table. June got home just before dawn, having spent the night in the emergency room at Central DuPage Hospital with an elderly woman who had a psychotic episode at the doctor's office. Nattie made herself some coffee and toast and read from her Robert Parker book until it was time to leave for the ten o'clock appointment Irma Ruggaliano had arranged for her with Laura Benedict.

Laura Ruggaliano Benedict and her husband Trevor managed the Ruggs on Roosevelt Avenue near College of DuPage, known as 'COD,' for short. She was the oldest child of Carlo and Johanna Ruggaliano, a year younger than her cousin Roselind. According to Irma, Roz has always felt that Laura was the favored child: cute, stylish, and popular. When Laura took her place at the COD location, Roz's jealousy became hostility.

The COD Ruggs was a larger restaurant with its own parking lot in the front and storage building in the back. The upper room of the storage building was where Nattie had to go to see what Addie had left behind. And it was Laura Ruggaliano Benedict who held the keys to the storage building.

It took no more than one interaction with Laura to realize how inaccurate Roz's view of her was. Roz had made her sound like a soap opera diva. Irma's picture was that of a junior high A-girl, a softer image, because those women could, possibly, grow out of it. That wasn't to say that if junior high A-girls didn't grow out of it, they could become soap opera divas. Most women have never been injured by a diva, but the mystique of a diva was based upon painful memories from junior high.

A lifetime of defending the disenfranchised and being misunderstood herself prepared Nattie to balance Roz's experience of Laura with the objective reality of Laura herself. Hiram had noticed this quality in Nattie when he first encouraged her to become a private investigator. "Anyone can conduct a first interview with unbiased curiosity," he had told her, "but you're able to do that in the third and fourth interview."

At 10:00, when Nattie walked through the doors, the Ruggs staff was busy getting ready for the lunch business that would start arriving in an hour. The atmosphere here was noticeably livelier than it had been at the Yorktown Ruggs. The staff, all in the neighborhood of twenty years old, wore jeans, white shirts, and short maroon aprons. The only older person in the room was a short woman with curly dark hair dressed in jeans and a metallic blue shirt. This woman had her back to the door and was making coffee. Next to her was a young man, dressed like the others, who was telling her something that made her laugh.

Laura was the woman in the blue T-shirt. When she noticed Nattie's arrival she stepped away from the coffee maker and said something to the young man next to her. He took her place making coffee as she made her way toward Nattie.

"Are you Natasha?" she asked with a pleasant smile and an extended hand. "I'm Laura Benedict."

"I am." Nattie said as she shook Laura's hand. "Thank you for meeting with me."

"Oh no problem," Laura said with a flip of her hand. "If I can do anything that helps Addie, I'm eager." Then she turned sideways and added, "I just made coffee. Would you like a cup?"

"No thank you," Nattie answered.

"Something else? Soft drink? Water?"

"Thanks, no."

"Well let's go then." Laura headed for the front door.

The storage building behind the restaurant was basically a two-story, two-car garage with a bathroom and an office on the first floor. The garage was organized with industrial shelves neatly filled. The upstairs was a single loft with an odd collection of boxes, furniture, and contraptions scattered along the walls.

"I'm sorry that it is not more organized, but the stuff from Addie's apartment is all of that pile in the middle," Laura said as she turned the lights on. "If you need me, I'll be in the office downstairs."

"Are you sure you don't want to stay here while I look around?" asked Nattie.

Laura's face grew solemn, "Look, I've got a pretty good idea about what you have been told about me, so let me set the record straight about one thing." She paused, then continued. "Addie was not just Ollie's fiancée. She was my friend. And if you are looking for her, then what I want is for you to find her. Even if she never comes back, I just want to know she's ok."

Nattie studied Laura for a moment. Satisfied that she spoke as she felt, Nattie said, "I would like to hear your thoughts, if you don't mind?"

Laura nodded. "I've cleared my morning so take your time. We can talk when you're done."

It took Nattie only forty-five minutes to go through the boxes, thumb through the books, open the CD cases, and feel through the crevices of the stuffed sofa and chair (She did spread CDs out on a table and took pictures). Nattie found nothing of much interest with the singular exception of an empty jewelry box that looked like a small old-fashioned trunk. She set the box aside and took it with her when she went downstairs to Laura's office.

"Did you find anything helpful?" Laura asked, watching Nattie place the jewelry box on her desk.

"Just this. It was in a cardboard box. Did it belong to Addie?"

Laura flinched slightly. "Not exactly. That actually belonged to Ollie's first wife, but Addie found it hidden in the loft here--under some blankets in that big trunk you must have seen in the back corner--when she was gathering furniture for her apartment. I told her who owned it before." Laura shrugged. "But that didn't bother Addie, so we let her have it." Then tilting her head Laura asked, "Has anyone told you about Edith and that box?"

"Irma mentioned something about it, but I'd like to hear your thoughts if you don't mind."

"Edith was my brother, Alberto's, wife. Actually they are separated now. She left him." Pointing at the jewelry box Laura added, "And that box had a lot to do with it."

Nattie looked at the box, then back at Laura.

"When Judith left Ollie, Edith made a big stink about Ollie killing her sister. When no one would listen to that, she went after his sexuality. As if his sexual orientation would explain her disappearance."

"Is Ollie gay?"

"I don't think so. I know Addie heard it from Edith and it concerned her. But I don't think she questioned his sexual orientation for long."

"You and she talked about that?"

"We were friends," Laura explained. "I'm pretty sure I was closer to her than anyone else in the family--except Ollie, of course."

Nattie nodded.

"The Ruggalianos are a close family. We're in business together. We do holidays together. Edith's issues with Ollie made life tough on all of us for several years after Judith died. We made the best of it because she was family and Judith was her sister. But after a couple of years things settled down."

"Did she stop blaming Ollie?" asked Nattie.

"I'd say it was more like she could be civil to him. And then about two years ago, just before Ollie met Addie, Edith started making trouble again. She said she wanted Judith's jewelry box."

"This box?"

"Maybe." Laura shrugged. "Edith looked through that stuff in the attic, but she didn't find whatever she was looking for." Laura flipped her hands over. "No one tried to hide that jewelry box from Edith. She just didn't find it. But Edith started accusing us of keeping jewelry that belonged to her grandmother. Finally Berto told her that enough was enough. Things got worse and worse for them after that."

"Did you consider giving Judith's box back to Edith when Addie found it?"

"We probably should have," confessed Laura, "but it was empty and we had already been accused of stealing the jewelry, so I didn't even want her to know that we found it."

"Did Addie know about all the turmoil around that box?"

"She did. Addie had Edith figured out after she accused Ollie of being gay." Laura leaned back in her chair, "That's pretty much all the drama there was about Judith's jewelry box until that last night."

"The night Addie left?"

"Yes," answered Laura, "Addie was going over that box and found something hidden in it."

"Hidden where?"

Laura stood up, opened the box, removed the tray on top and reached inside. She peeled back the felt lining from the bottom.

"What do you think she found?"

"I know she found a picture of Edith and Judith and a baseball player from the Cubs." Sitting back down across from Nattie, Laura explained, "It was just another thing Edith made a big deal out of. She said it was the last photograph she had of her sister and Berto had it on his office wall because of the Cub player. He is a fan I guess. Anyway, she wanted him to give it to her, so he did."

"And Addie found another copy of it?"

"No, but she thought she did. It was just a picture of Judith and Edith in Cub hats. She knew Edith would want it so she called to talk through what to do about it."

"What did you tell her?"

"I told her it was more thoughtful than Edith deserved. But if she was going to do it she should say she found it in an art book." Laura grinned, "Addie said, if I do that Edith will demand we give her the art book."

"What would say Addie's mood was at that moment?"

"At that moment it was playful. We were laughing and then she said, 'Wait a minute.'"

"Wait a minute?"

"Yes," confirmed Laura, "then she put the phone down and about a minute later she came back on and said she had found an envelope with Edith's name on it. That's when Addie's mood changed. She got real excited and said, 'Laura, this is the recipe.'"

"The bread recipe?"

"I assume, but before I could ask Addie got frantic and said, 'Oh no, I've got to call Edith.'"

"What did she find?"

"I don't know. She hung up then."

"Did she talk to Edith?" asked Nattie.

"I don't know. I never heard from Addie again. I asked Edith if Addie had called her and Edith said 'no,' but I don't know if she'd tell me the truth."

"Did you try to call Addie?"

"Of course, several times, but her phone was no longer in service."

"Could she have found something that really rocked her world?"

"I don't know what it could have been, but something big happened when she found that envelope."

"Do you have any ideas about what that might be?"

Laura shook her head, "None."

"Do you have anything else to tell me that might help me find out why she left or where she went?"

"I think I've told you everything I know."

"How about Ollie?" asked Nattie.

"Ollie?"

"What were your impressions of Ollie and Addie's relationship?"

"They were perfect together. They had similar interests with art, movies, music, and they were very compatible. Gentle, not shy, but a little introverted. They argued sometimes, usually about Roz, but they were civilized about that."

"Why do you think Ollie went to find her himself--you know, instead of hiring someone?"

"I think it was embarrassment. This is the second time the love of his life has vanished on him. I think he just wanted to do something about it himself."

"And now that he's hired me why doesn't he come on home?"

"Berto says Ollie just needs the time away."

Nattie wondered what Alberto might know that Roz, Irma, and Laura did not know. "Do you think I could meet your brother?"

"He's at the bakery. I talked to him last night after Aunt Irma called me. He told me to tell you that he would be available all afternoon."

"Thanks." As Nattie stood to leave, Laura tipped the jewelry box on its side to make it easier to reach inside and replace the felt bottom. "What's this?" Nattie asked out loud as she ran her index finger over a seam on the bottom of the box. Someone had attempted to pry open the wooden bottom. Laura moved around the desk and watched as Nattie felt around the outside edge until she found a rivet she could push in. The bottom of the jewelry box sprung open and they both looked inside. It was empty.

CHAPTER 16

ALBERTO

Ruggaliano's bakery in downtown Melrose Park was much smaller than Nattie had expected. It was little more than a doughnut shop. Two glass cases filled with doughnuts and pastries lined the middle of the small front area. In front of the glass cases was an open area large enough to accommodate seven or eight customers. Behind the glass cases was a counter with a cash register, shelves filled different kinds of breads, and a door leading to the bakery in back. It hardly looked like it could contain central offices of a successful chain of restaurants. And, in fact, it didn't. Alberto's office, according to Rose, the cashier, was next door.

The offices next door to the bakery might have housed an insurance agency or a lawyer's office in the past. Now the pre-Depression era architecture masked a more modern interior with earth tones and oak trim.

"Mr. Ruggaliano is expecting you," said the receptionist as Nattie entered the lobby through the glass door. "His office is at the top of the stairs."

Stepping forward Nattie asked, "How did you know I was here to see Alberto Ruggaliano?"

The young woman smiled and pointed toward the bakery, "My mom just called and said you were on your way. You just met her at the bakery. Her name is Rose."

A man who could have been a celebrity look-a-like for Alec Baldwin stood at the top of the stairs.

"Ms. McMorales, I'm Alberto Ruggaliano," he said warmly offering her his hand.

Nattie took the outstretched hand in her own and shook it firmly. "Please call me Nattie."

"Ok, Nattie," he said gesturing toward an office, "and please, call me 'Berto.'"

Berto's office was large enough to contain two large desks separated by a conversational cluster of two couches and a coffee table. He ushered Nattie to one couch and, once she was seated, sat down across from her.

"That's my desk." He pointed to his right. Behind his desk was a large window overlooking the street in front of the building.

"And that's Ollie's desk," he said of the desk at the other end of the room. Behind Ollie's desk was a large poster of Raphael's "School of Athens."

"You have a very interesting office, Mr. Ruggaliano."

"Call me 'Berto,'--please. And thank you." Berto then leaned back, put a foot on the edge of the coffee table and asked, "After the conversation you had yesterday, I suppose you're surprised to see that Ollie and I share an office."

"What conversation are you referring to?" asked Nattie.

"I'm not referring to the afternoon you spent with Aunt Irma. I'm talking about Roselind."

Nattie paused.

Grinning, Berto added, "I know about your visit with my sister this morning. We are a very close family, Nattie. Ollie and I are more like brothers than cousins. He talked to his mother last night and she told him about your visits with her and Roz yesterday."

"And Irma told Laura and she told you?"

"No," responded Berto. "I heard about it from Ollie this morning. He thought you'd want to check me out after you heard from Roz."

"He did?"

"We both have a pretty good idea what Roz told you. That's why I wanted you to see our office." He spread his arms out in both directions to illustrate which room he was referring to. "My father and Ollie's father share an office across the hall. It's just like ours. My father got an MBA and was working in the Chicago Stock Exchange while Ollie's father worked in the family business and developed the creative ideas that expanded the bakery business into Ruggs." Lowering his arms he continued, "My father is a great businessman and he made Ruggs into the profitable enterprise that it is. But Ollie's father is the creative one who brought Ruggs into existence in the first place." He raised the index finger on his right hand, "A good businessman knows how to squeeze the last drop from the olive--but a great businessman knows how to make the drops last. This is the most important business principle I learned from my father. The way he made it work was by being partners with his brother and by placing great value on what the creative one brings to the business."

"That sounds very nice." Nattie said, although it sounded suspiciously rehearsed.

"I know it sounds a little corny, but Ollie and I are like brothers and we complement each other's strengths the same way our fathers did. Ollie is the creative one. It was his idea to serve Ribollita."

"What is that?" asked Nattie, "I saw it on the menu, but didn't know what it was."

"It is a very common soup for Italians. Basically, it is a vegetable soup with day-old bread in it."

"Day-old bread?"

Alberto smiled, "You see. It is a simple idea. We specialize in making bread for buns--it is the one thing we cannot run out of in a day, so we make a lot of it and have a lot of it left over."

"Ribollita gives you something to do with stale bread."

"Exactly." Raising his index finger he added, "And it was Ollie's idea--.have you tasted any of his desserts?"

"I have."

"He has been creative that way all of his life. When we were little, Ollie would mix chocolate pudding, crushed graham crackers, banana pieces, and broken up bits of chocolate together."

"That sounds great."

"It was--we were seven--he called it 'dirty diaper in a bowl.'"

'That sure sounds like a seven-year-old,' thought Nattie.

"Ollie doesn't want you to get bogged down with Roz's paranoia." Then Berto sat up straight, "You know, Nattie, Ollie didn't know that you'd be coming to Chicago to check out his family."

"He didn't know about my trip to Chicago. I came to a wedding this weekend and I'm staying with an old friend now." She decided that this was enough explanation for her client's cousin. If Ollie needed a detailed justification of her expenses then he would get more when that time came.

Alberto put his hands up defensively. "Please, you don't have to explain yourself to me. Ollie's not complaining about you checking us out. He's glad you are on the job. He just doesn't want you to get bogged down with Roz's paranoia."

"Ok."

"So how can I help you?" he asked.

"I'm not sure. Do you have any idea why Adelle Quinlin left or where she is?"

"I don't know why she left. I would never have predicted she would have left the way she did."

"How did she leave?"

"Without a note." Berto explained, "She knew he had already been left once that way. Judith was a whacko from the beginning. When she disappeared, no one was surprised." He sighed. "When Addie left, it broke his heart."

"Do you have any ideas about why Judith left?"

"She was never happy. I think she was mental."

"Do you mean she had a mental illness?"

Pointing at his left arm he said, "She had a bunch of scars, like cut marks, on her left wrist."

"Were those suicide attempts?"

"I thought so. Edith, my ex-wife, said it was cries for attention--Judith was Edith's younger sister. Edith was always defensive of her."

"What was their relationship like?"

"You mean Edith and her sister?"

"No." Nattie said apologetically, "I meant Ollie and Judith. You introduced them right?"

"Edith and I met when I was finishing my MBA at the University of Chicago. She was a waitress at the House of Blues. We got married when I graduated, and I came to work in the family business. Edith got along great with the family. It seemed like she brought her sister here precisely to hook her up with Ollie."

"Did that concern you?"

"Not at the time. Edith said she wanted her sister to be as happy as she was." He laughed, "It sure concerned Ollie, though."

"Did you tell Ollie of Edith's intention before Judith came?"

"Of course. I wasn't going to let him get ambushed."

"Did he go along with it?"

Berto bit his lower lip, "It made him nervous. He's not exactly a lady-killer or anything. But he was ok to double date with us as long as Edith promised not to tell Judith that he was a potential husband."

"Did Edith promise?"

"Oh sure, but who knows if she kept her promise or not? Anyway Ollie and Judith hit it off right away. They dated for about six months. We all thought she was perfect for him. He's sensitive and creative and she seemed supportive and patient, but that all changed right after they got married. She got moody, controlling, and critical. He drove himself crazy trying to make her happy, but nothing helped. She finally left after about a year and a half."

"What do you think happened to her?"

"I hate to say this," Berto said sheepishly, "But I think she probably went somewhere and slit her wrist."

"Did they ever find a body?"

"No, but after seven years she was declared legally dead."

"If she slit her own wrist you'd expect her body to be discovered, wouldn't you?"

Alberto shrugged. "The insurance company paid out a lot of money. You know their investigators tried hard to find her, but after that amount of time even they said she was dead."

"Who got the insurance money?" asked Nattie.

"Their aunt in Italy. She raised Edith and Judith after their parents died when they were little."

Nattie let a moment pass before she asked, "And what about you and Edith?"

"We got along great until Judith's issues started taking over our lives. Edith blamed Ollie, she accused him of murder, then mental cruelty; finally, she said he was gay. All that craziness quieted down after a couple of years."

He leaned back and folded his hands on top of his head, "It was like I got my wife back. She even stopped taking shots at Ollie, although they still stayed clear of each other." He lowered his hands and leaned forward. "Then it all started up again. She started making a big deal over a missing jewelry box and then that picture." He pointed at a photograph on the wall.

Nattie wondered if he was referring to the same photo Laura had told her about. "Do you mind if I take a closer look?"

"Help yourself."

The framed photograph was of two women wearing Chicago Cubs hats. They looked enough alike to be sisters, but enough different that one was plain and the other a beauty. Between them was a man holding a newspaper with the headline, "Cubs Take Wildcard." All three of them wore T-shirts displaying the phrase "FOOD FOR THOUGHT."

"I found that picture in an oversized art-book of Caravaggio. Edith must have put it there. That's Edith," Berto said as he touched the beauty.

"Is that Judith?" Nattie asked, touching the other woman.

Berto nodded yes. "After Judith died the picture was probably too painful for Edith. I guess that's why she put it away. But I am a big Cub fan, so I wanted to keep it. I was afraid to show it in my office because I didn't want to upset Ollie with Judith's picture, but after Addie came along I asked him if I could put it up and it was ok with him."

"And Edith?"

"She didn't know about it until Adelle said she had seen it." Berto shook his head slowly, "I had to give it to her."

"You gave that picture to her?"

He smiled, "I gave her a copy."

Nodding Nattie asked, "Do you mind if I take a picture of this picture?"

"If it would help Ollie, certainly," he gestured toward the photo, "Is there anything else?"

"Anything?" she asked.

"Anything for Ollie," Berto repeated.

"I'd like Edith's address."

CHAPTER 17

EDITH

Berto was eager to facilitate Nattie's interview of Edith, giving her not only Edith's address, but directions and advice as well. "Just go knock on her door," he said. "If you try to make an appointment she'll either refuse to talk to you or she'll have time to make up something to sabotage Ollie."

As Nattie walked up to the door of Edith's condominium in Hoffman Estates, she heard a voice call from an upstairs window. The woman from the window appeared to keep her eyes on Nattie's rental car, "I told them to send something nice. That really does the trick."

Watching the woman from below Nattie could tell it was Edith Ruggaliano, Edith's hair was pulled back into a loose pony tail and was covered by a light blue bandana, but there was no mistaking who she was.

Edith finally turned her attention to Nattie. Pointing she said, "You are early. Go on in and I'll be down in a moment. There are two bags in the foyer, but don't take them out yet."

Edith never saw the thumbs up signal Nattie gave her. She had already pulled her head in and closed the window. Nattie did as she was told. She entered the foyer where she had to resist the temptation to carry the matching maroon rolling luggage to the car. Since Edith had obviously mistaken her for a limousine driver, Nattie was torn between her eagerness to play along with the mistake and her guilt that the real limo driver would be cheated out of a fare.

Besides the foyer, the first floor held a small open kitchen with a breakfast counter and family room with a sofa, a large flat-screen television, and a fireplace that had never been used. On the breakfast counter sat an open piece of luggage that matched the two in the foyer. Folded neatly on top was a maroon T-shirt that would not have caught Nattie's eye except it looked exactly like the one in the photograph in Alberto's office.

The Jack Nicholson movie *Wolf* was on the television. She had decided that the reason women secretly like Jack is his ability to maneuver seamlessly from polished confidence to spoiled little boy to raving lunatic. On the screen Jack was telling the James Spader character, "I'm coming after you, Stewart." Nattie thought he got all three of his alter-egos into one sentence.

"How stupid." Edith said from behind her. "That's for men."

Nattie turned in time to watch Edith place something in the suitcase on the counter and close it. "What's for men?" Nattie asked.

Edith pointed at the television, "Only a man would warn his enemy like that. It's a testosterone moment with no strategic value whatsoever." She turned back and pulled the oversized suitcase from the counter and put it on the floor with ease.

Edith had looked like a beauty in the photo Nattie saw yesterday. In person, she looked statuesque. Her appearance was particularly impressive to Nattie because two minutes ago she was dressed for chores and now she looked like a model for casual clothing in a Talbot's catalogue.

"I'm glad you're here early. I'd just as soon get to O'Hare early and get my bags through. It's the International Terminal."

"No problem," said Nattie. "Where are you going?"

"Rome." Edith said, "Have you been to Rome?"

"No." answered Nattie sounding woeful. "My brother has been to Rome and Pompeii."

"Pompeii," Edith repeated with a sly expression on her face, "He brought back pornographic figurines didn't he?"

Kevin had brought back a small male figurine whose male apparatus was as large as his torso. He put it on the toilet tank in his bathroom thinking it would intimidate his male guests. It disappeared the next time his mother visited.

"How did you know?" asked Nattie.

Edith put one hand on her hip, "I know Pompeii," she said, "and I know men." Then she pointed at the suitcases in the foyer, "If you will take those I'll get this one and my purse."

The carry-on bag and the middle-sized bag fit into the Mustang's trunk. The largest bag had to go in the back seat. After the luggage was settled Edith strapped herself into the passenger seat and asked, "Would you mind putting the top up for me?"

"Oh sure," Nattie said, "your hair?"

"No," Edith took out a cell phone, "it's the noise."

Nattie typed O'Hare Airport into the GPS and followed the instructions to the curb in front of the International Terminal. Although there had been no conversation between them during the drive Nattie did get to listen to a series of phone calls between Edith and people she was saying goodbye to. It was clear to Nattie that Edith Ruggaliano was not planning on returning from Italy.

At the curb, after turning her luggage over to a porter, Edith handed Nattie a fifty-dollar bill and said, "Thank you, miss. I hope you get to make it to Italy some day."

Nattie held the bill in her fist. "Actually, I need to confess something."

As Edith's eyes tightened, Nattie put her fist in the side pocket of her jacket. "I'm not exactly with the limousine service." She withdrew her fist. It still held a bill.

"Well who are you?" demanded Edith, stepping uncomfortably close.

Without stepping back Nattie introduced herself and for the first time was pleased to have a false name, "My name is Natasha McMorales and I am a private investigator."

"You bitch." Edith said slowly, over pronouncing the "b."

"What can you tell me about the disappearance of Adelle Quinlin?"

Edith pressed her lips together; then, with snake-like quickness, her hand shot out and snatched the bill from Nattie's fist. She walked to the glass doors into the terminal and turned back to face Nattie with a smug look on her face. She held up her fist with the bill still in it and said, "You see. If I had warned you like a man, I would never have gotten this back."

Nattie took the fifty dollar bill from her pocket, held it up, and then gestured with her chin that Edith should look at the bill she held in her hand.

With eyes flashing angrily and without looking at the one-dollar bill, Edith wadded it up. Then she nonchalantly tossed it at Nattie's feet and turned toward the terminal. As the doors opened, she saluted Nattie with a one-digit salute over her shoulder.

Just before Edith disappeared from sight, Nattie yelled, "And might I say how much I admire the way you fix your hair."

CHAPTER 18

RETURN TO BRISTOL

"Did you have a good time with June?' asked Kevin on the way from the airport.

"Oh I did," answered Nattie, "June took Wednesday off and we spent the day together. It was a good thing she did because she got hung up at work Monday night and then I got hung up in traffic Tuesday night."

"But you did have Wednesday together," Kevin noted.

"Yeah. We spent the day in the city at Brookfield Zoo and then we grilled steaks out at her place. It was nice."

"I'm glad." He said.

"Me too. I got a lot done on Monday and Tuesday, but it was good to take the day off yesterday. Did you set up a meeting with Ollie?"

"I did. Three o'clock."

"Did you get me a flight to Italy?"

"I did. You fly out of Tri-Cities early tomorrow morning and then it's Charlotte to London. You'll be in Italy early Friday afternoon."

The thought of a day and a half of continuous travel would have been more discouraging if Nattie had time to let it sink in. As it was, she had to find her passport, and she would be doing laundry most of the evening.

"Oh my," Nattie said, holding her hand to her mouth. "That sneaks up on you."

Ollie's expression did not change as he watched her intently, waiting for reaction to the dark chocolate raspberry torte he had brought her. What made his recipe unusual was the habanera powder he had embedded in the layer of raspberry filling beneath the chocolate layer. If the dessert worked, then the chocolate would be the first taste with every bite. And as the chocolate faded into raspberry, the heat would come.

He was pleased that the sequence of flavors had worked on Nattie, but he wanted more. So he waited, watching.

Taking another healthy bite Nattie asked, "Is this on the menu at Michelangelo's?"

Ollie did not answer. He took a small bite of his own, but he was far more interested in savoring her enjoyment of his creation than in enjoying it himself.

As she took the last bite and licked her fork, he asked, "Did you enjoy that enough to order it?"

"Absolutely," she said enthusiastically. "What's it called?"

"I'm afraid I have not gotten around to naming it yet. But if you have an idea for a name, I'd appreciate it."

"How about Mayan lava torte?" Kevin suggested from just beyond the door to Nattie's office.

Ollie put his plate on Nattie's desk and turned in his chair to look at Kevin, who now stood just inside the door. "Mayan lava torte," he repeated. "I like it. It goes well with the way the raspberry layer oozes out the sides."

"Do you think this could end up on the menu of Ruggs?" asked Nattie as she nodded toward Kevin.

Kevin took the cue and excused himself, shutting the door behind him.

"It could indeed." Ollie replied to Nattie's question. "And tell me, Natasha, how did you enjoy your time in Chicago?"

"I'm glad you mentioned that, Ollie, because I developed a few questions while I visited with your family. By the way, they are delightful and so are the restaurants."

"Thank you. I'm glad you got to try our restaurant."

"I'm interested in hearing your thoughts about Roz's theory," began Nattie.

"Do you mean the idea that Addie left because someone from Berto's side of the family bought her off in order to alter the inheritance?"

"Yes, that's the theory I meant."

"It is a ridiculous theory and I can explain why if you can assure me that what I tell you will go no further."

"I cannot promise you that I can or will maintain your confidentiality if it conceals a criminal act, but beyond that you have my word and my license for assurance."

"Thank you. My father and my uncle are ready to retire now. All they're waiting on is for Berto and me to be ready for what we are planning."

"What are you planning?"

"A chain of coffee shops with gourmet coffee and signature desserts."

Ollie's experimentation with dessert recipes made much more sense now.

"So that's why the Mayan lava torte was not destined to be on the menu of Rugg's." She smiled, "It will be on the menu of the coffee shop."

"Rugg-a-Muffins."

"I'm sorry?"

"The coffee shops," he explained. "They will be called Rugg-A-Muffins."

Nattie nodded, "And this is still a secret, right?"

"Yes."

"So the inheritance issue is secure because you and Alberto have plans?"

"Yes."

"And your fathers know about this plan?"

"Yes."

"Who else knows about it?"

"No one."

The explanation seemed plausible, and Nattie was convinced that Ollie believed everything he had just said. Roz's credibility was suspect because of her overall paranoia. But her personality did not make her theory wrong. If Carlo and Alberto were going to take advantage of Ollie's family, then they would most certainly concoct a plausible story that would be sure to entice Ollie's passions. On the other hand, being a good ploy did not make the story false either.

"Why not let the rest of the family in on the plans?"

"When the time is right, Roz and Laura will have the opportunity to expand with us or to go on their own with their restaurants."

"But Ollie, their restaurants is one of the issues that Roz is alarmed about."

"Do you mean when we moved Roz from the Ruggs near the college?"

"We?" asked Nattie in a startled voice.

"All of us. Me, dad, Berto, Uncle Carlo. You met her. You saw how she is." Ollie shifted forward in his chair, "Let me explain. The restaurant business is labor intensive. That's part of why the coffee shops are a good move for us."

"Less labor?"

"That's right, and less space too. The labor available around a college will be mostly college kids, and you can't treat them like flunkies."

"Which is Roz's management style."

"You noticed." Ollie smiled. "Roz can be more successful in Yorktown. There is much more lunch traffic and her overhead is smaller."

"And Laura?"

"Laura will be successful wherever she is."

Nattie paused and stared at Ollie for a long moment. Then, changing the subject, she asked, "Everything I have heard seems to point to this--Adelle Quinlin's decision to leave came suddenly. Do you agree?"

Ollie nodded his agreement.

"And the decision came sometime after she left work that afternoon."

"I don't know," replied Ollie.

Nattie rubbed her temples lightly, "If Alberto's family did not bribe her then could someone else have done that?"

"I suppose. I would have never believed she could have been tempted with money, but I would never have believed she could leave without a note either."

"Could someone have scared her?"

Ollie shrugged.

"Could she have found something?"

"Something like what?" Frustration laced Ollie's question.

"Could she have found out something about you?" She asked watching his reaction closely.

"I don't know what it could be."

"Could she be hiding something about her past?"

"Like what?"

"I don't know, Ollie," Nattie replied out loud. To herself she said, *but tomorrow I'm going to go to Italy and I'm going to find out something for myself.*

CHAPTER 19

TO THE AIRPORT

"Ok, Sis," Kevin said on the way back to Tri-Cities airport, "it's time for a first-timer's guide to Italy."

"A first-timer's guide to Italy? What is that, another book? I'll read it on the plane." He had already given her the Italian-to-English phrase book he had used when he traveled to Italy.

"Slow down, Nat," he said. "It's not a book--not yet anyway--but it will be."

"Are you the author Kevin?" she asked a little more sarcastically than she meant.

"I am, but I'm not very far into it yet."

"How many pages do you have so far?"

"The pages will come in time. The first part is coming up with the idea. And next it needs a good title. Do you like the title?"

"I do. I'm on the way to the airport to fly to Italy for the first time and I'm going by myself. If I had seen that title on a book in the last two days, I'd have bought it without opening it."

Kevin smiled, "Titles sell books."

"I'd say you have a good one then. Do you have any useful guidance for this first timer?"

He held up one finger, "The first thing is language. What words do you know?"

"*Si--grazie--bonjour--ciao.*"

"Ok, that's a good start. Only it's not 'bonjour.' That's French, it's 'buon giorno.' You can do fine with just those words, but I suggest that you try to pick up a word a day. The experts try to give you too many words all at once; but unless you are one of those 'do everything the teacher tells you students', then you just get overloaded and zone out."

"But Kevin," she said with a syrupy sweet voice, "You were one of those teacher's pets weren't you?"

He ignored her and continued, "You'll be fine with a small vocabulary because there are a lot of Italians who speak English, especially in shops and restaurants where tourists go. But mostly because they make it easy on us. You would probably be fine to say '*bonjour*': I said '*buenos noches*' for 'good evening' for a long time until I saw it written."

"So what is 'good evening'?"

"'*Buona notte.*'" He over pronounced the words so she could hear the difference. "But there is one phrase that you need when you go to restaurants. '*il conte, per favore.*' It means 'check please.'"

"Why is that so important?"

"Eating dinner in Italy is different from eating dinner here. The restaurants here try to get you in quick and out quick so they can serve several meals at the same table. In Italy the evening meal is a social event; it is done more slowly. It is to be savored. When they give you a table, they assume it is yours for the evening."

"I don't see why that means I have to ask for the check."

Kevin smiled. "It is a cultural thing. It is considered rude to bring you the check before you ask for it. You are their guest. You do not try to rush your guests out quickly."

"That makes sense, Kevin. You really are a natural-born teacher. Is that the way you're going to write your book?" Nattie asked.

He grit his teeth slightly and shook his head back and forth. "That's the problem. I want to make is simple, useful, and useable for first-timers; but the more I think about what they need, the more I add and the more complicated it becomes."

Nattie nodded, "And that would make your book more like the other ones."

"*Sí*," he answered. "So now that I think about it, you'll be fine to just say 'check please.'"

"Ok, scratch that phrase. But the lesson on restaurant etiquette is a good one, so don't scratch that."

The little-boy, embarrassed, smile came across his face, "Thanks. I won't lose that story, but it doesn't need to go in the first few lessons."

"There are lessons in your book?"

"The lessons are what make *The First-Timer's Guide to Italy* unique. My plan is to divide it into lessons. Each chapter is one lesson and the directions are that the reader is to develop some mastery over the first lesson before even reading the second lesson."

"How do other tour books do it?"

"Some tour books are laid out like resource manuals," explained Kevin. "When you come up against something you don't know you can look it up in the book."

"That's good isn't it?"

"The problem with those books is that they are so complicated that you have to know the da Vinci Code to find what you're looking for. The other kinds of books are more like college courses on how to actually speak that language well enough to move there."

"Isn't that what you want?"

"It's what some people want, and there are plenty of books for them. But *The First-Timer's Guide* is for whoever wants enough to go for a good first visit."

"Ok, Kevin, let me play devil's advocate for a minute."

"Go for it," he said as if he was responding to a challenge.

"The people you are writing this book for are not the ones who want the more elaborate books right?"

"Yes."

"But do those people buy books anyway?"

"You see, you are making an assumption about their being lazy or illiterate. And you're right that illiterate folks won't buy it, but lazy folks buy books--they just don't read them. But the real market for *The First-Timer's Guide to Italy* is folks who are going soon and need some help right away, or it's people who aren't so academic and need someone to help them get started so they can get their heads around those other books."

Nattie bowed her head humbly. "You're right, Kevin. I was being judgmental. This book is actually a great idea and I hope it works out for you because it could do a lot of people a lot of good. It's really a primer."

Kevin thought a moment and verbalized his thought, "*A First-Timer's Primer to Italy.* That has a ring to it too, but I still like 'Guide' better. Maybe I could use the word 'Primer' in the subtitle."

"I agree." Nattie continued, "So if I had the book in my hand now and I was about to board a flight to Italy what lesson would I be reading?"

"I'm having a hard time deciding what comes first. But probably some basic vocabulary words should be included."

"Like the ones I know."

"Yeah, your four words were a great start. And then I was thinking that a lesson about money, credit cards, and ATM machines would be good."

"Do they use Euros in Italy?"

"Yes. And the ATMs are called '*Bancomats.*'"

"'*Bancomat.*'" She repeated.

"They are easy to find. And if you don't see one you can say 'bancomat?' to any shop keeper and they will know what you are asking."

"Oh that reminds me," Nattie moaned. "I bet I should have told Citi Mastercard that I'd be in Italy for awhile."

"That would be in the 'Before you leave' chapter. You always want to tell them because if you charge something and it looks unusual to them they may deny the charge and leave you stranded." He paused, "I knew you were too busy to think of doing it yourself, so I took care of it yesterday."

She lightly touched his arm as he drove, "Thanks, Kev. What else did you do?"

"You're welcome, Nattie. I tried to think of everything, but I'm sure I missed something." He glanced at her sideways, "That's part of the adventure, right?"

"Right!"

"But I still have a lesson about credit cards," said Kevin.

Nattie waited.

"Shopkeepers can get kind of touchy if you try to use a credit card for a bill that's too small."

"How much is too small?"

Kevin grinned, "I don't remember. As long as you are there anyway would you find out for me?"

"Will I get a mention in the book?"

"Sure."

Nattie's voice got stern, "I mean my real name is not 'Natasha McMorales.'"

He shrugged, "If that's the way you want it to be." Then he added, "Also, I put a new memory card in your camera and I put an old battery in it while I recharged the one that was in it. So when you are sitting on the plane with nothing to do change the batteries and use the old one as a backup."

"What about the pictures I took in Chicago?"

"They're safe. Why?"

Nattie exhaled, "That's fine. I probably won't need them in Italy, but there's a photo of a jewelry box that I may need when I find Adelle."

"I can download them to a computer file, and you can get them from an Internet café."

"I didn't bring my computer."

"That doesn't matter. You can go into one of those places and buy a card for as many minutes as you want on their computers."

Nattie nodded, took the camera from her bag and began changing the battery out.

"I'll tell you something about Italy that I never got used to--the showers."

The look Nattie gave him was very familiar to both of them. It was a look that connoted something between "I can't believe how creative you are" and "I can't believe how old you are."

Kevin didn't acknowledge the look. "The showers are so thin in Italy that you can't bend over without touching the sides."

"Why is that a problem Kevin?"

"Why?" he repeated with a look of disbelief on his face, "The sides are cold." Shaking his head, he added, "I don't see how they ever wash their feet."

CHAPTER 20

SALVATORE

Nattie's Type-A personality meant that under stress her default strategy was to hurry up or push herself harder. Generally, this served her well, but it also made slowing down and relaxing more difficult, if not impossible. She was most comfortable when she was working toward a meaningful goal. It was therefore quite understandable that having no goal to work for was for her one of the most undesirable of all circumstances. Also true, but not as understandable is the undesirability of having a goal, but having to wait for the work to commence. This was what made traveling such a trial for her

And the trial before her now was a huge one. When she entered the terminal, she took off her watch. Although primarily a symbolic gesture, it reminded her to set aside her normal "hurry up and get it done" approach to life.

Making sure she had something to read was another means of slowing down when forced to wait. She always took a book with her to doctor's and dentist's appointments. She even carried a book in her car for those occasions when downtown Bristol was blocked by a train parked across State Street. For a trip this long she carried several books: *Hannah Coulter* by Wendell Berry, *Birth of Venus* by Sarah Dunant, and *An Early Fall*, John McDonald's second novel.

Usually when she read for pleasure it was to relax as she went to sleep. 'I need to learn how to slow down and do more things at this leisurely pace,' she noted to herself and then wrote it down on the To-Do list she always kept close by to ensure that she did not forget anything important.

The slow-down strategy worked well as she traveled from Bristol to London and from London to Rome by plane, then from Rome to Chiusi by bus. The bus from Rome arrived in Chiusi after 10:00 PM, which was after the last bus to Montepulciano had already left. She was in a hurry to get to her apartment in Montepulciano, but forced herself to slow down enough to buy a sandwich and a bottle of water in the bus station terminal.

Nattie got the name and email address for Il Sasso in Montepulciano from Dr. McDonald and had arranged for the apartment through them. Il Sasso was a language school that primarily teaches Italian language and culture. Their clients/students tended to be large groups of college students, or smaller groups, couples, and singles who were older, but wanted to immerse themselves in Italian life rather than simply visiting the sights. Il Sasso's classes are between one and three weeks long, so they kept a list of apartments in the Old City that could be rented by the week. Nattie had Kevin make arrangements for one week. What she had with her at the moment was a confirmation letter, an address, and directions for how to let herself in if she arrived after ten o'clock.

The taxi cost 40 Euros and came with a driver named Salvatore who did not speak English, but nodded when she showed him the address of her apartment in Montepulciano. As Nattie settled into the back seat of the taxi, she could feel herself starting to get excited about finally arriving in Montepulciano. She hardly tasted the sandwich she bought at the Chiusi bus station. She eagerly looked forward to a hot shower and real sleep in a real bed and the opportunity to start working on something tomorrow.

Salvatore left Nattie alone for the first part of the drive. He was busy with someone on a two-way radio. But somewhere well before Montepulciano he became very excited about something they were passing. Nattie did not realize Salvatore was talking to her until she noticed that his radio was silent.

"*Montagna,*" he said as one point.

"Mountain," she repeated in English.

"*Si,*" He said, "*Montagna.*" The fact that she recognized his word and he had recognized hers delighted him so much that he became much more animated and faster as he explained something terribly important.

"*Acqua,*" he said.

"*Aqua,*" she repeated remembering some Spanish words from high school. She remembered what Kevin had told her; if you could say a word correctly in Spanish, Italians would be gracious enough to give you the benefit of the doubt. You were, they would think, saying the right word wrongly.

"The water of the mountain?" she guessed.

"*Si! Si!*" He said and added another excited explanation with gestures pointing in every direction followed by pointing down.

"The people come from all around to drink the mountain water here," she said with more confidence.

"*Si,*" he said and continued his soliloquy.

"The mountain water has magic powers," she said boldly, assuming that he was not merely being polite but understood her. "The Italian women come here and drink the mountain water so they can eat pastry every morning, pasta every evening, and still look like swim suit models."

"*Si! Si!*" said Salvatore less enthusiastically.

Since she had guessed so accurately so far she pressed on, "And they take the magic mountain water home and wash their hair in it--and that's why they all have Andie McDowell hair."

Salvatore looked in the rearview mirror at her. The lively conversation was apparently over.

With much less enthusiasm Nattie tried to explain, "You know, she had long curly black hair." Spreading her fingers out and wiggling them as she drew them away from either side of her head as she tried to gesture curly hair radiating downward.

Salvatore just looked at her silently until the other voice on the two-way radio saved him.

"*Scusi*," he said and began speaking on the radio.

Nattie looked out the window and imagined what Salvatore was telling his friend. "You wouldn't believe the crazy Americana I have in my backseat now. She thinks her head is the sun." She made sure he wasn't looking and repeated the radiating finger gesture. "But I am the sun," she wanted to say in her best Scarlett O'Hara voice.

CHAPTER 21

GETTING STARTED

The apartment was cold the next morning, but the bed was comfortable with a toasty thick blanket. She knew it was morning because sunlight came through slots in the shutters. *The first thing I need to do is open those shutters*, she thought until her feet hit the tile floor. She jumped back in bed--*first socks, then shutters.*

Opening the shutters and leaning out of her kitchen window Nattie got her first non-traveling daylight view of Tuscany. "Wow," she said out loud. The scene before her was familiar because half the calendars in the world showed pictures of Tuscan landscapes: pictures she had assumed were touched up and rare. But seeing what she now looked at, Nattie wondered if all those calendar pictures had been taken from this window, her window. The Tuscany she had imagined when she drove into Bristol and squinted her eyes behind the miniature Saint Francis on her dashboard did not do the real Tuscany justice.

Helga, the woman from Il Sasso with the German accent who had arranged the apartment rental for Nattie had told her there was a spectacular view. She was right. To her left Nattie could see over the top of several levels of burnt red tiled roofs and to a patch work of small farms and vineyards. From this distance looked like a quilt with different shades of green, each one vibrant in its own way. And in the distance was Lake Trasimeno.

"When Hannibal attacked Rome, he marched around Lake Trasimeno," Helga had told Nattie. *That was about 200 years before Christ was born*, Nattie thought to herself, surprised by how impressed she was now that she was actually looking at a land steeped in so much history rather than hearing about it.

"Peace and goodwill!" Nattie said to the earth before her as she left the window and got dressed for the day. It was time to "punch the clock."

Nattie's plan for day one in Montepulciano was to set up camp and explore. She had made peace with the bathroom and bed late last night, although her peace with the shower was tenuous. She had been prepared for a tiny thin shower stall by Kevin, but this shower had no stall whatsoever. This bathroom was all tile and porcelain with a drain in the middle of the floor, and an adjustable shower head mounted on the wall. She had previously seen open showers only outside of beach houses, but it was clear to her what she needed to do. It was no easy task to keep her towel dry when she showered before going to bed, but she managed well enough.

It was not until her early morning routine that she discovered the shower's impact on a roll of toilet paper. It was a lesson learned rudely, but she would not forget it tonight. She added toilet paper to the supply list she would tend to during the day.

A survey of the kitchen followed. The tap water tasted fine so bottled water would not be necessary. She would need matches to light the stove or to burn one of the candles on the kitchen table. Fresh fruit was a must for breakfast and evening snacks, and of course she would need coffee. But aside form the silver, hourglass shaped coffee pot on the stove Nattie found no coffee maker. She remembered that Irma Ruggaliano, Ollie's mother, had made espresso in a similar device, but Nattie had not paid attention to how it worked. She put an asterisk next to coffee on her list. If she could find out how to use the contraption she would buy some coffee; otherwise, it would be time for tea.

Besides, she thought, *I could find Addie today and the coffee would just go to waste.* She hooked her bag over her left shoulder. *And Kevin could be elected President while I'm here too.*

Before she left the apartment Nattie retrieved the envelope Alma Quinlin had sent her. It contained a half dozen photographs of Adelle Quinlin and a copy of the letter she had sent her mother from Montepulciano. Nattie had read and re-read the letter so many times she almost had it memorized. She read it again:

Mom,

This is the third letter I've started to write to you since I left. I just can't seem to find the right words to say goodbye. I've always known that I am a complete disappointment to Dad, but it was not until that last night that I realized how much it costs you to have to defend me. I hope you know that I would never have put you in that position if I had known. Please know that I love you and I will never put you in that position again.

I don't know where my life will lead me, but wherever I go I will carry you in my heart. I am fine and I am doing what I need to do to take care of me and my life right now. I have a safe place to live and I am working as a waitress, which meets my needs right now. In fact, I am writing this while on my evening break. I'd like to write more, but it's getting dark and the street pole doesn't have a lamp on it.

So know that I love you, but it's best for me to stay out of your life. I am sorry.

Love,

Addie

CHAPTER 22

CAFÉ POLIZIANO

Off the mountain, ancient Montepulciano grew into a modern town with a dry cleaner, a grocery store, and a Chinese food restaurant. It did not look unlike Nattie's home of Bristol. But passing through the gates into the "Old City" was very close to turning the clock back a thousand years.

The buildings on either side of the narrow street were all well preserved, but in keeping with the integrity of a Renaissance city. Flower boxes with fresh blooms adorned nearly every second and third story window. Weathered doors with ornate knockers and small gargoyle figures hanging from the upper corners of sporadic buildings all added to a genuine Renaissance atmosphere. The street was paved with large flat stones irregularly worn by foot traffic over an amount of time marked better by centuries than years. It was onto those old streets that Nattie stepped as she left her apartment.

"Wow," she said out loud for the second time that morning. She had seen it all last night when she arrived by cab, but then it looked surreal. Now, in the light of day, it was different. This was one of those times when the real was more magical than the surreal.

Nattie just wandered through the city as she tracked her location with the street map which the folks from Il Sasso had left on her kitchen table. She kept an eye open for Addie Quinlin, but thought it unlikely to be that lucky. She just walked leisurely and learned how to navigate around the city making note of any restaurant where Addie might be employed. After dark she would walk the city again looking for a burned-out street lamp. She knew that the lamp under which Addie wrote the letter to her mother might have been replaced by now, and another street lamp may have burned out in the mean time. Mostly, she wanted to become familiar with the city, hoping that being there would somehow be the inspiration for what to do on day two. According to Robert Parker's detective, Spencer, sometimes you have to just do what you can do.

Nattie continued to meander through the city enjoying the sights, sounds, and surroundings. She probably looked like a tourist at the moment, but she was very much at work. She was collecting data. If she were not deliberate about going slow at this stage, she would be tempted to run around the city showing Addie's picture to everyone in sight. A hurry-up technique like that, which was always a temptation for Nattie, could easily have sent Addie deeper into hiding. So for now, Nattie's pace was leisurely. Tomorrow the plan would be different. *Hopefully.*

The streets around Montepulciano were lined with shops that specialized in leather goods, books, ceramics, or wine and cheese establishments, and, of course, many places to get espresso, pastry, or gelato. Although many places along the street had caught her eye, the Café Poliziano captured it. Café Poliziano looked like an old fashioned sweet shoppe, the kind that might have been fashionable in New York City at the turn of the century. Behind a dark walnut bar, with a marble countertop and a brass foot-rail, stood a middle-aged, red-haired woman making espresso. Along the opposite wall were several glass cases filled with pastries, chocolates, and all sorts of other sweets. The back of the café was three steps up and held ten small marble topped tables surrounded by wooden soda fountain chairs.

Delightful, she thought. It reminded her of the sort of place she dreamt of as a child. Ever since she was a little girl Nattie had a recurring fantasy of going with her father to New York City. In her mind she pictured them going to a play, maybe *Cats,* or even to see the Rockettes, and finishing the evening off at a place just like the Café Poliziano for hot cocoa and a tart. She was not really certain of what a tart was, but believed tarts must be exotic because the Queen of Hearts had them. "Have whatever you want," her father would say. "Today you are the princess." She would sit at a table and sip her drink, feeling pretty in a brand new yellow dress and a big yellow bow in her hair. Her father would ask her how she liked the play, and she would tell him how wonderful it was. They would watch the city through the window and giggle about what they saw outside or at what they remembered from the show.

Her father once asked her what she most wanted and Nattie told him about their fantasy trip to Broadway. He laughed and said she should learn how to dream bigger dreams. Then he hugged her and promised her that someday he would make it happen for her.

The back room of the Café Poliziano looked exactly like the room in her dream. She simply had to sit there so Nattie stepped up to the counter.

"Coffee," she said.

When her espresso came in its tiny ceramic cup, she pointed at a croissant in one of the glass cases.

The red-headed woman nodded expressionlessly and gestured "help yourself" with her left hand.

Nattie found a seat and struggled to make her espresso last. It was very strong coffee, designed to be sipped, savored. She was used to coffee in large mugs. If she weren't careful, she would finish this cup in one go. As it was she managed to make it last for three sips, one more than she had managed at Irma Ruggaliano's.

The croissant was easier to manage. It was light, flakey, almost, buttery. She knew how to eat it, how to savor it. So she ate it slowly and thought of a little yellow dress and a big yellow bow. *It would have been nice*, she sighed, *to have been the princess just once.*

Not until long after she had finished her croissant did she remember that she was working. But while she daydreamed about other things, a plan had formulated in her mind. She had noticed how the tourist traffic moved through town and surmised that this pattern also dictated how the people who worked here moved. The workers of Montepulciano would surely move around the city the same way the tourists did, only an hour or so earlier. If Addie Quinlin was still here she would likely have settled into this same pattern. *If the pattern was predictable then there had to be a few good places to view it from.*

For the rest of the day, she scouted for places to watch the city come and go. She discovered the location of several Bancomats; they were, as foretold, everywhere. She walked by at least three Bancomats before noticing a German woman turning from one with a handful of cash.

She went to the Il Sasso School and Helga told her how to get to the grocery store beyond the front gate and how to make espresso with the equipment in her apartment. Before leaving, Nattie asked Helga, "Have you had a student named Adelle Quinlin?"

Helga typed the name into her computer and turning back said, "Not since we started keeping records seven years ago."

At one thirty, Nattie returned to the Café Poliziano for lunch. This time she sat in a side dining room that looked like a dining room rather than the mezzanine, which looked like an ice cream parlor. Lunch was wonderful. She ordered ribollita soup and a salad with balsamic vinegar for a dressing. She remembered from Ruggs that ribollita soup is basically a vegetable soup made with leftovers and day old bread.

"It is the soup of the peoples," the waiter instructed her.

The waiter treated Nattie like a valued guest. He helped her understand the menu, he explained how gelato was made, and where to go for the best deal on olive oil and vino. He was timely and efficient with every part of the meal with the one exception--the last act of service--bringing her the check.

She remembered that her brother had given her the phrase to use when requesting a dinner check. She just could not remember what that phrase was. It was the first time she thought of Kevin's book, *The First-Timers Guide to Italy*. She did not need the information this time as her waiter spoke English fairly well and had already signaled her that he was getting the check. As she waited, she thought, *Leave it to you Kevin to tease me with a good idea, but when I need it ... where is it?*

As Nattie left through the dining room she peered back into the elevated area that reminded her so much of her fantasy outing with her father. She felt warmth behind her eyes as she once again imagined the little yellow dress. *And when I needed you dad...where were you?* It was the last time she entered Café Poliziano.

CHAPTER 23

ENOCECA PASCICCERIA

Slow and steady Nattie had told herself last night as she ended her first work day in Montepulciano. She enjoyed a cup of decaf espresso at her kitchen table as she reviewed what she had accomplished that day and what she would do the next. It was important to stay focused and not let the absence of large victories discourage her. Large victories, like finding Adelle Quinlin, often appeared to be the result of one significant maneuver; but most often they occur, when supported by a large enough foundation of smaller, sometimes miniscule, victories. She had eliminated a possible connection to Il Sasso, discovered there were no burned-out street lamps, gotten familiar with the city, and established a plan for the next day. And so far she had not done anything that might alert Addie that she was being pursued, which was the reason for not showing photographs of Adelle until later.

Remembering Kevin's book idea Nattie decided to make note of her expanding Italian vocabulary. "*Prego*" she had heard several times. After looking it up and discovering that it meant "you're welcome," she had some confidence with it as well. She decided to look up "please" as well. "*Por favore*" would be easy to remember because it was close enough to the Spanish word she had learned in high school.

The entrance to the Old City of Montepulciano was through the gate at the bottom of the hill. Most every visitor and worker coming from outside the Old City came through that gate and traveled up the inclined street leading to the top of the mountain. The street from the gates fed into the main street of Montepulciano. The street, which traced the eastern edge of the mountain on which Montepulciano was built, then circled the northern edge where the fortress was built. It then opened up in the Piazza Grande at the top. From the Piazza Grande the road continued to follow the edge of the mountain along the western and southern sides of the city and finally returned to where it first encountered the street up from the gate. It was, in essence, a simple circle around the city from which the side streets and alleys could appear complicated and disorienting. In reality every twist and turn would eventually intersect the main street somewhere around the mountain.

The circular feature of this main road, which Nattie discovered the previous day, made the Bar Enoceca Pascicceria an ideal location for her morning coffee and breakfast. It was situated slightly to the left and across from where the street from the gate ended and joined the street that circled the old city. With the exception of workers in the shops along the entry street, Nattie could clearly observe anyone else entering the city from the gate. Her hope was that at least eighty percent of the workers and all of the tourists would walk directly by her. If Addie was still working in Montepulciano, then a seat outside the Bar Enoceca Pascicceria was an inconspicuous place to watch for her.

Nattie arrived at the Enoceca at 7:30 in the morning. She had to point at the pastry she wanted and had expected to order an espresso, but another American who was waited on right before her ordered a Café Americana. Café Americana appeared to be a shot of espresso in a full sized coffee cup topped with enough hot water to fill the cup. It would be a new piece of information for Kevin's book.

Antonio, the man behind the counter, spoke Italian to her after pouring the hot water in her cup. She handed him a ten euro bill, assuming he had just told her how much she owed.

"'Con latte' means 'with milk,'" Antonio gently explained in broken English as he held up a small silver pitcher of steamed milk.

"Thank you, no," she said waving her hand.

"Prego," he said turning toward the cash register and returning with a small sales ticket. She owed two euros ten cents.

Nattie had planned on paying with a ten euro bill which could have enabled her to pay without understanding how much she owed. She was prepared to accept whatever change she got back. This was a strategy that would only work as long as her pocket could handle all the coinage she would get in change.

Antonio made it easy for her as he pointed to the number on the ticket as he said, "Due euros....dieci cents," he repeated.

Nattie nodded, more from seeing that she owed two euros and ten cents than because she understood what Antonio said.

Sweeping the coins from the counter he said, "Prego."

It would be nice to say "grazie," "thank you," before the "prego," "you're welcome," thought Nattie, but timing is everything.

Italians speak like they drive, observed Nattie. What looks like chaos is actually more like a beautiful dance. Each driver takes his steps in time with confidence that other drivers will do the same. They do not wait for you to be completely out of the way, as Americans do, before they begin moving into the space you are leaving. They time their movement into your space on the expectation that you will be out of the way when they get there. And you would be out of the way if you knew the dance. Americans watch them drive and wonder why there are not accidents happening continuously. But, in spite of witnessing dozens of close calls on the bus ride from Rome, Nattie never saw an accident. *They must learn to drive with an acute awareness of the dance, Nattie realized.*

Conversation had its own timing as well. Speaking Italian is a dance much like driving. When Italians speak to one another there are no pauses. There are no gaps as one finishes before another can begin. For Italians the final word of the previous speaker is still hanging in the air as the next speaker begins.

Apparently Antonio knew she was going to say thank you and was teaching her the dance. She doubted she would ever learn the dance, but she was learning to appreciate the music.

CHAPTER 24

PIAZZA GRANDE

The next morning was not so difficult at the Bar Enoceca Pascicceria. Antonio recognized her as she entered, *"Buon giorno,"* he said, *"Café Americana, saus latte?"*

Nattie's confusion must have been obvious.

"'Saus' means 'without,'" he explained, "no milk."

"Si," she said, *"grazie."*

"Prego."

Ok, she thought, *that was better timing.*

Addie made no appearance that day either, but Nattie could be patient. She had told Ollie that she had a lead on a town in Tuscany where Addie might have been a month before, and he had agreed to pay her expenses to check it out.

"As long as you need," Ollie insisted.

"One week," Nattie told him. "If one week does not reveal any leads or clues then I will call you and we can decide what to do next."

"Buono," he said and handed her twenty one-hundred dollar bills. "If you need more, you will tell me and I will send more. No problem. Just find Adelle."

It was day three in Montepulciano. No leads, but it was too early to worry. There was nothing else to do so she watched Montepulciano from her bench in front of Antonio's Enoceca. Before 7:30 the only people on the street were the workers who cleaned up the streets. Nattie never saw them, but she could hear them. She could also see the evidence of their work because the streets were remarkably free of cigarette butts. It was remarkable because there were always people smoking in the street. Instead of smoking inside their shops the shop keepers would stand in their doorways and smoke. The butts were always thrown on the street and they would always disappear in the early morning hours of the next day.

Nattie noticed that nearly every shop owner along the street as far as she could see started his or her day at the Bar Enoceca Pascicceria. Between 7:30 and 8:30 they would trickle in. She enjoyed the music of their conversation without recognizing any of the lyrics. A shot of espresso and a few words with

Antonio and the other patrons appeared to be a start of the workday ritual. None of the Montepulcianians stayed very long. They came in, stood at the four-and-a-half-foot-high counter and Antonio served them shots of espresso.

Between 8:00 and 9:00 the shops would gradually open up. Display panels were hung on the walls outside the shops and tables of samples were set up on the street. By 9:00 the tourists began coming through in small groups. The larger groups, who came in buses, would not arrive until late morning. Until then the street would remain relatively calm. Nattie enjoyed watching a newcomer go into the Enoceca, emerge with an espresso, and stare at it in wonder.

That afternoon Nattie sat at a table outside of the Caffetteria del Duomo in the Piazza Grande. The Piazza Grande was the heart of Montepulciano. She would sit facing the Duomo, the cathedral, and nurse a glass of wine for a good while. The Duomo was very old, dating from the 12th century, according to the guidebook. It was the oldest of four buildings that bordered the piazza, the Renaissance version of a town square. This particular piazza was where the flag-throwing scene in the movie *Under the Tuscan Sun* was filmed.

She imagined herself viewing the piazza from a second-story window behind her because that is where the Diane Lane character would have watched the flag-throwing from. In the movie Diane Lane's character came to Italy to escape after she had been betrayed by her husband. There she found a new life and a new family. Nattie owned a copy of the movie. She did not know why, but she often watched it when she felt blue.

As Antonio's Enoceca Pascicceria was her morning perch, her afternoon perch was here in the Piazza Grande. It was the one spot that every tourist was sure to visit. Since Adelle had been missing for close to three months now, it was doubtful that she was still a tourist, but if Addie was waitressing toward the top of the city then this would be a likely spot for her to walk and maybe even stop for a shot of espresso before work. In addition, Nattie knew that if Italy was like America, then food service workers tended to form their own subcultures because they all worked during what were the normal social times for everyone else. Even if Addie did not work in the Piazza Grande, the waitresses here might have seen her. Making a friendly connection with one of them here might open some lines of information that would otherwise be blocked.

As she waited Nattie watched a battle of wills between a mom and a three-year-old wearing a little yellow dress. A boy, looking to be about five was in charge of his younger sister's empty stroller. The mom left the boy with the stroller in the middle of the Piazza while she pursued the little girl who was making her escape to the left of the Duomo. The mom got no more than four paces from the boy when he lost control of the stroller, which began rolling downhill forcing the mom to divert her attention and retrieve it. Once the stroller was secure the mother turned to face her daughter who had stopped fleeing the moment her mother stopped pursuing.

"That's it!" the mother yelled with an Australian accent. "I'm not chasing you all over creation."

This was the daughter's cue to walk over to the steps in front of the Duomo and casually sit down."

"We're leaving," the mother yelled.

This was the daughter's cue to look nonchalantly to her right, away from her mother.

The mother, with her son in tow, began pushing the empty stroller in the opposite direction of the Duomo. They moved completely out of sight, which was the daughter's cue to fold her hands and rest them in her lap. She was too far away for Nattie to see the little smile on her face, but Nattie could "see" it anyway.

After no more than a moment, the mother reappeared marching briskly toward her daughter. When she got three paces away the little girl hopped up and began climbing the stairs behind her. As she climbed a restrained cheer spread across the tables of spectators.

A French woman clapped and giggled.

A German man raised a fist.

A British woman said, "Look at her go."

An Italian couple clapped softly.

Onlookers from every nation knew the daughter was being naughty, knew the mother was right, knew the mother had to win. Everyone, regardless of nationality, wanted the little girl in the little yellow dress to make the top of the stairs. But alas her legs were too short and her mother too determined. The little girl was caught quickly.

Mother, with an angry look, led her daughter, grinning like a cherub, across the Piazza. With the battle over, all of the interested spectators returned their attention to whatever they were doing before. Had the mother looked toward the tables she might have gotten the impression that no one had noticed. She did not look.

CHAPTER 25

LOREENA

"*Buon giorno*," Nattie said when the auburn-haired waitress came to her table. Nattie had seen this waitress here the day before, but they had not spoken then.

"*Buona sera*," the waitress corrected her. "It's four o'clock. At four o'clock the Italians say 'good evening.'"

"*Buon sierra.*" Nattie tried.

"*Buona,*" the waitress said slowly.

"*Buona.*"

"*Buona...sera...*"

"*Buona sera.*"

"*Molto buona,*" the waitress smiled and patted Nattie on the shoulder. "Very good."

"You speak *molto buono* English," Nattie observed.

"I'm Irish," the waitress grinned. Her nametag said Lorenna. "What can I get you?"

"Is there a beer you'd recommend, Lorenna?"

Lorenna glanced around to see who might hear her answer. "Italy is for wine. This is not where you come for beer."

"I think I'll have a glass of wine then."

"Vino Nobile di Montepulciano?"

"*Si,*" said Nattie. According to the waiter at the Café Poliziano, Vino Nobile di Montepulciano was the signature wine of Montepulciano."

She would have to wait a good while for Lorenna to return because Lorenna was working by herself today whereas yesterday there had been two waitresses. Luckily, there was always plenty to watch in the Piazza.

Lorenna eventually returned with a glass of Vino Nobile, and a little bowl of potato chips. "Enjoy," she said as she placed the bill for 4.50 Euros under the ashtray.

"Lorenna," Nattie called out quickly to keep her from leaving, "would you mind if I ask you a question."

"*Prego*," Lorenna said as she turned. Apparently "*prego*" could also mean "certainly."

Nattie handed a picture of Adelle to Lorenna. "Do you recognize her? I'm trying to find her."

"Americana?" Lorenna asked.

"Yes."

"What makes you think she is here in Montepulciano? Most American tourists stay here for a week or less and move on. Tuscana is filled with attractions."

"She wrote to her parents that she was working here as a waitress."

"Did she say which osteria she was serving at?"

"No, she didn't."

"Did she give a landmark, like this is the Piazza Grande or maybe across from the fortesse?"

"No, she only mentioned a streetlamp being out." Nattie shrugged, "I'm sure they have replaced the light bulb by now."

With just a trace of satisfaction in her smile, Lorenna said, "The girl you are looking for works at a pizzeria across from the marble church down near the front gate."

CHAPTER 26

THE PIZZERIA BY THE GATE

Nattie found the light pole without the lamp exactly where Lorenna said it would be, on the right side of the street, about halfway down the hill toward the front gate. In Montepulciano light poles do not come up from the street like tree trunks, but rather extend from the sides of buildings like branches. This one was about twenty feet high and had a plaque honoring Guiseppe Moreno next to it.

Lorenna had known immediately what Adelle was referring to in her letter. "The pole without the lamp is not a landmark for tourists; it is a landmark for Montpulcianians. This city was not supportive of the fascist regime around the time of World War Two. I'm not sure what they did, but there was underground resistance to the fascists."

"Here?" asked Nattie. It was hard to imagine Hitler or Mussolini giving a town like Montepulciano much consideration either way.

"Yes, here," answered Lorenna. "I know it seems incredible, but it was pretty serious. Giuseppe Moreno was just a young person, but the fascists caught him and made an example of him."

Nattie felt her shoulders tighten in anticipation.

"They hung him from that lamp pole."

It was what Nattie expected to hear.

"And then the bastards wouldn't let his family take his body down." She shook her head, "They just let him hang as a warning."

Nattie was touched by the story when Lorenna told it to her, but it became much more real to her as she stood below the empty lamp pole. It struck her as a fitting tribute and reminder. *They leave it lightless to remind them of a dark moment of their history.*

Nattie also found the pizzeria exactly where Lorenna had said it would be, "just beyond the empty street lamp and across from the white marble church." It was only five o'clock in the afternoon, which was far too early for most Italian restaurants to serve dinner. This pizzeria was closed and would reopen at six o'clock. Nattie "relaxed" on the marble steps of the church pretending to tend to her camera as she familiarized herself with the eatery across the way.

With an hour to kill Nattie took time to study the white marble church for the first time. She had driven by it once, but that was in the back of a cab and in the dark. But she had not noticed it on the first day of exploring when she walked to and from the grocery store beyond the gate. The church was recessed from the street and nestled between two larger buildings at a place where the street bent around it. The effect of the bend in the street was that the church could not be seen unless you were virtually in front of it. If you were not looking for it, it was easy to miss. But once you noticed it, you would remember to look for it.

The white marble gave the church a unique appearance amidst all the other Mediterranean stucco buildings. Nattie wondered if the church had been here when the streets were paved with stones during the Renaissance. The marble steps were level, but the paving stones of the street followed the incline of the mountainside. It appeared as if the paving stones were fitted around the steps rather than the other way around. The impression was that if one were to dig up the street the steps would extend to the full length of the church.

Beautiful, Nattie thought as she took several pictures.

Halfway between the pizzeria and the front gate, Nattie found Pulcinos, a wine and cheese shop that was exceedingly generous with samples. She got to taste a Brunello from Montalcino, a Rosso from Montepulciano, and several vintages of Vino Nobile di Montepulciano. After sampling several types of cheeses, sausages, and spreads, Nattie decided to buy a hot pumpkin spread for Kevin, a bottle of balsamic vinegar for her mother, and a 2004 Vino Nobile di Montepulciano for herself.

The bag of souvenirs from Cantina di Pulcino made Nattie look even more like a tourist than normal as she approached the pizzeria shortly after six o'clock. She chose a table near the door and sat the Pulcino bag on the seat across from her. Her shoulder bag she kept close at hand.

A large canopy awning covered twenty outside tables. A lone waitress, too thin to be Adelle Quinlin, took care of two tables of tourists. A single open doorway led to the inside where there might have been other waitresses. The thin woman was the only waitress working the outside tables.

Nattie ordered a bowl of pasta e fagioli and showed the waitress a picture of Adelle Quinlin. "Do you recognize this woman?"

"*Si*."

"Does she work here?"

The waitress shook her head, "No. Not for three weeks. She went to Firenze."

"Firenze?"

The woman shrugged, "Firenze is what you call Florence."

"Oh," said Nattie, "thank you. You wouldn't have a phone number or an address for her would you?"

"All I know is that she worked here for a few weeks and then went to Firenze to work at the Pizzeria Tuscana. Do you want something to drink?"

"Just water."

The waitress nodded, took the menu from the table, and hurried inside.

Nattie put a twenty euro note on the table, gathered her bags, and left without waiting for her soup.

She was so delighted with the afternoon's progress that she hardly noticed the steep uphill walk back to her apartment. She didn't notice the car that had stopped beside her until the blonde woman in the passenger seat lowered her window.

"*Buon giorno*," the blonde woman said.

It was Nattie's first experience of being mistaken for an Italian and it felt good. "*Buon giorno*," she said confidently with her best Italian accent.

"Oh you won't be any help." The woman sounded more British than before.

"Why do you say that?"

"I can tell you are an American by your accent."

"Well--what did you want to ask?" responded Nattie patiently.

"We're looking for a hotel, the Meuble il Riccio."

Nattie smiled and pointing to the right she answered, "Just stay on this road and it will circle the top of the mountain. When you get to the top you'll be facing the other direction and then you will be in the Piazza Grande. You can't miss it. It's the large open plaza. When you get there all you have to do is go diagonally across the plaza and you'll find your hotel on the right side about twenty-five yards past the Piazza."

The blonde British woman looked forward where Nattie had pointed and sheepishly said, "I guess you knew more than I thought."

"*Prego*." Nattie said, honoring the Italian dance as she anticipated the "*grazie*" that never came.

CHAPTER 27

KEVIN'S JELLY

"What time is it there?" asked Kevin.

Nattie looked at her watch. "Eight o'clock."

"It's two o'clock here," he observed.

"Yes Kevin, there's a six-hour difference between Tuscany and Bristol. Is there anything I need to know?"

"Do you mean here at the office?"

Nattie wanted to point out that it was the office she had called or the office she paid him to manage, but the innocence in his voice stopped her. "Yes, the office. Is everything okay at the office?"

"Oh sure, Sis, everything is fine here. There are a couple of calls for you to return when you get back, but both know you are on a case in Italy. I think they were impressed that you work internationally."

"Of course." Her smile was audible. "I am, after all, Natasha McMorales."

After a pause Kevin grew more serious. "Nathan calls every day."

"What does he want?" asked Nattie more quickly than she intended.

"Oh come on, Nattie. Don't be so suspicious. He's just worried about you."

He wasn't worried about me when it counted, she thought as she asked, "Anything else?" Discussing her ex-husband was not why she had called, and it was not what she was interested in at the moment.

"Mrs. Quinlin has called every day this week, too. She's a real nice lady. Did you know that she was a pitcher on a fast-pitch softball team?"

"No I didn't know that about her," *nor do I know why I'm paying a dollar a minute in overseas phone charges to find it out.* "Is she calling for updates on my progress?"

"Yeah. I told her you had gotten to Rome okay, but I haven't had anything different to tell her since then." His voice deepened. "You know, you haven't called to check in since you left the Rome airport."

"I haven't had anything to report until tonight."

"Does that mean that you found her?" asked Kevin excitedly.

"I wish, but no, I haven't yet. I did find the pizzeria where she worked, and one of the waitresses there gave me a lead on where she might be in Florence."

"When do you leave for Florence?"

"The next bus to Florence leaves at 7:10 tomorrow morning--which brings me to something I need you to do."

"Do you want me to find an apartment in Florence like I did for you in Monte-pul-whatever-it-is?"

"It's probably too late to arrange anything but a hotel tonight, but if you can find me someplace reasonably priced and within an easy walk to the Uffizi Museum you can text me and I'll check it out tomorrow when I get there."

"I'm on it."

"Also," Nattie continued, "I'm, going to be leaving my apartment here too early in the morning to take the keys back to the school --"

"Just leave the keys on the kitchen table and lock up on your way out," Kevin interrupted, "I'll email and let them know you left early."

"Thanks Kevin."

"No problem," said Kevin nonchalantly. "What do you want me to tell Mrs. Quinlin when she calls again?"

"You can tell her everything I told you."

"Gotcha. And Ollie?"

"And Ollie?" Nattie repeated.

"What do you want me to tell Ollie if he asks?"

"With Ollie you can tell him I've been in an Italian city, that I have made contact with someone who worked with Adelle a month ago, and that I am following a lead to another Italian city."

"Gotcha."

"Kevin?"

"Yes."

"Has Ollie been coming to the office and asking questions?"

"Not at all. Really. He hasn't come by once since you left. I had coffee with him yesterday, but I called him – he didn't call me," Kevin said defensively. "Why? What difference does it make if he wants to check on your progress? It's no different than Mrs. Quinlin calling everyday."

"One difference is that Adelle ran away from him, not her mother. And another difference is that my contract with him is that he let me find her and not ask questions about where she is unless she says it's okay."

"I know that. You told me that before you left. He is still worried and he is still the customer, right?"

"Right."

"Well then, as long as he doesn't get specific information about where you are, shouldn't he be entitled to updates as much as Mrs. Quinlin?"

"Please don't be offended, Kevin, but I have to ask--"

"No I haven't told him where you have been. And he hasn't asked either."

She knew that her suspicion bothered him. It would have been easy for her to respond defensively and justify the question, but doing so was not tempting. Instead, she apologized. "I'm sorry, Kevin. I know you are on top of all this. Going over everything more than once is just my way to keep things straight in my head."

"That's okay," Kevin said immediately. "You're a private investigator. You have to be suspicious."

Nattie blanched at hearing herself being described as suspicious.

"So--?" Kevin let the word hang in the air.

"What?" asked Nattie, as if she had just been woken up from a nap.

"So--what do you want me to tell Ollie?"

"Tell him the same information you're going to tell Adelle's mother."

"Everything except for the names of the towns-- Gotcha."

"Great."

"And what about me?" Kevin asked.

Nattie hesitated, "What about you?"

"You didn't ask about me. And I just told you that I'm the one who called Ollie. For someone as suspicious as you are, you sure aren't very curious."

Nattie sighed.

"I had an idea that I wanted to run by him."

You have ideas like other people have gas, thought Nattie.

"I was out at the vegetable market on Route 421. You know, Scotty Wade's? Anyway, I was there on Saturday buying peppers to make up a batch of salsa and I ran into this guy out there who makes all kinds of hot jellies and jams. He's a real nice guy. Anyway, it got me to thinking about a flavor of jelly that I think could be a big seller."

Nattie waited.

"Aren't you going to ask me what flavor?"

"Chocolate." guessed Nattie.

"Ooh--that might be a winner too," Kevin exclaimed, "but my flavor is coffee."

"Coffee!" she felt her mouth pucker as if she had just tasted sour milk, "Coffee jelly? Who would eat that?"

Kevin laughed. "That's going to be everyone's first response. But it's unusual and I'll bet a lot of folks will turn up their noses at it when they first see it, but come back later to try it."

"Maybe so, but when they come back, it will still be coffee jelly."

"Well, Ollie liked the idea, and he's going to think about how it could be served. All I have to do is figure out how to make coffee jelly."

"That's all?" Nattie asked, rolling her eyes.

"That's all there is to it."

CHAPTER 28

FIRENZE

"Navigating around Florence is easy," a helpful tourist on the bus told her. "Just use the Duomo as a beacon to get your bearings."

The woman on the bus also told Nattie to store her luggage in a locker at the bus station until she found a place to stay. "Depending on where your flat is and who owns it, they may even send someone back to get your things." It was advice Nattie followed without being convinced of its necessity, but as she made her way through the crowd she was glad she had. Managing her luggage and her bearings would have been too much. Florence was not Montepulciano and she was glad for the tip.

The text message from Kevin directed her to a piazza near San Lorenzo church where she could arrange for an apartment rentable by the week. The directions to find it started from the Duomo. "It's the only space available," texted Kevin, "so I reserved it with your credit card."

The apartment was a one-room efficiency with a small kitchen area on one side of the room and a couch on the other. Two windows overlooked the Piazza Di Mercato Centrale, a well-trafficked market area selling everything from T-shirts for tourists to vegetables for locals. Her apartment was on the second floor above the Kabrazi bakery. Mr. Kabrazi sent his son, Daniel, back to the bus station for Nattie's bags.

"Mr. Kabrazi, *por favore*." Nattie said tentatively. She had looked up the word "please" in the language book Kevin had given her, but she had no idea if she were using it correctly.

The baker looked at her and smiled. His expression gave her his attention, but no indication about the correctness of her Italian.

"Do you know of a restaurant called the Pizzeria Tuscana?"

"*Si*," he told her and gave her directions faster than she could follow. Noticing her glazed look he walked outside and waved for her to follow him. When she joined him in front of the bakery he held up two fingers and said "Two blocks," as he pointed to their right.

"Two blocks that way?" Nattie pointed.

"*Sì*," he said as he turned his body to the right and mimed a left turn with his hand.

"Two blocks that way and then turn left?"

"*Sì*." He smiled, nodded, and went back into his shop.

The Pizzeria Tuscana was exactly where Mr. Kabrazi said it was but it was closed. Being mid-afternoon meant she had missed the lunch time and she was too early for the dinner time. With nothing to do but wait she decided to satisfy her own curiosity about one thing. She was interested in trying an Italian type of ice cream called "*gelato*." She had seen the dessert featured on the television show *Everybody Loves Raymond*. In the show Robert Barone, after tasting a gelato said, "Oh my goodness; it's like I never tasted a peach before." *We'll see*, Nattie thought when she saw the show--and now she would.

Gelato is an Italian ice cream made with less fat and more flavor. It comes in a much larger variety than ice cream could. For instance, grapefruit would be repulsive as an ice cream, but it is a refreshing flavor of gelato.

Places to get gelato were plentiful. It was generally displayed in refrigerated glass cases facing the street. Each flavor was in its own metal tray and was decorated with something that identified what it was. "*Fragole*" was easy to identify as strawberry because of the brilliant red color and the actual strawberry sitting on top of the heaping red pile. Nattie decided to order chocolate partly because it was her favorite flavor, but also partly because she had less confidence in pronouncing "*fragole*."

"*Cioccolato*," Nattie said pointing to the dark gelato.

The man behind the glass case said something back, but the words went by too quickly for her to catch any of them. It must have been obvious to him that she missed what he had said because he smiled patiently and pointed toward the three sizes of plastic cups stacked on top of the case.

Nattie pointed at the smallest cup.

"*Piccolo*." The man pronounced the word slowly while he took the smallest cup.

"Pee-co-low." repeated Nattie, watching her small cup being filled to overflowing. She handed him a five-euro note trusting that he would give her the appropriate change and she could then know what a *piccolo cioccolato gelato* costs.

He gave her two coins in change which she had to study closely to realize that they were one and two-euro coins. To the confusion of many Americans, paper currency in Italy, and most other countries as well, was reserved for denominations of five euros and above. The gelato cost two euros. It was a bargain at two euros.

As tasty as the gelato was it did fail in one important area. It did not kill much time. For this she decided to sit at the coffee shop across from the pizzeria and have a cup of Café Americana. She knew how to savor her coffee and make it last. Plus it would give her a perfect place to watch the waitresses as they arrived for work.

Nattie waited at the bar to order her Café Americana which allowed her to watch as several Italian patrons were served ahead of her. She had always wondered how drinking espresso would work. She had once practiced sipping hot cocoa out of a shot glass, but could not make it last. As soon as the cocoa was cool enough to chug, she could not help but finish it off. How the Italians made their espresso last was a mystery she could now put to rest. The fact is these Italians did not make their espresso last. The shot of espresso did not last any longer in the hands of an Italian than the cocoa had lasted in hers. It was as if the purpose of espresso was to get a shot of caffeine in the system. *They may get something out of the ritual,* she thought, *but there is no pretense about savoring the drink.*

CHAPTER 29

PIZZERIA TUSCANA

At five o'clock Nattie noticed that a waitress had emerged form the pizzeria and was setting up the twelve tables under the canopy at the front of the restaurant.

"*Buon giorno.*" Nattie said as she approached.

The waitress jumped slightly and turned to face Nattie. "*Buona sera.*"

"*Buona sera,*" Nattie repeated sheepishly knowing that her cover as an Italian was blown. "English?"

"A little."

"It is too early for me to have dinner, but I wondered when you got busy."

The waitress smiled, "*Americana?*"

"How did you know?"

"You want to beat the crowd," she observed. "It is very American."

"Yes," answered Nattie feeling a bit like she should be offended, but guilty as charged as well.

"You can usually get a table before seven o'clock, but at seven people often have to wait."

Nattie glanced at all the empty tables. "Oh my. Do you have to take care of all these tables by yourself when it gets that busy?"

The waitress looked at Nattie suspiciously and asked, "Are you looking for a waitress job?"

"No," Nattie said trying to assure her, "I'm just here on vacation. But I used to waitress at home and I know how hectic it can be."

"By six o'clock there will be four servers here," the woman said matter-of-factly.

"*Grazie,*" Nattie said. It was the information she wanted. She would be back at six o'clock and with any luck Adelle Quinlin would be one of the waitresses.

The waitress' name tag said "Greta." She handed Nattie a menu and disappeared after taking her drink order. Greta appeared to be in her late twenties, a brunette with unnatural looking reddish highlights. She was thin, but not as thin as the waitress Nattie had seen earlier.

A second new waitress emerged through the door carrying a tray of drinks. She, like the thin one, wore no name tag. She was middle-aged and heavier than the other two, but seemed to be livelier as she did her job.

Three down, one to go, thought Nattie, hoping the forth waitress would be Adelle Quinlin.

When Greta came back with her water and a basket of bread, Nattie ordered salad and carbonara, and then asked, "Where is the ladies' room?"

"Inside," Greta said pointing with her pen.

"Grazie."

A trip to the toilette allowed Nattie a view of the inside dining area, which was very small and very dark. It was basically a bar. And the forth waitress, a buxom brunette, was as much a bartender as a waitress. She was not Adelle Quinlin either.

Her meal was wonderful. In fact, when she thought about it, Nattie could not recall any meal in Tuscany that was anything but wonderful. After dinner she ordered a decaf Café Americana, but resisted ordering the tiramisu, which she had seen when the thin waitress walked by with two pieces for another table. It looked huge and it held its shape on the dessert plate rather than collapsing into a glob.

"Do you mind if I ask you a quick question?" asked Nattie as Greta delivered her coffee.

"Prego."

Nattie turned over a photograph of Adelle Quinlin that she had placed face down on the table. She watched for Greta's first reaction.

Greta was expressionless as she looked at the picture. Then she lifted her eyes and tapped on the picture with the back of her pen, "She looks a little like the girl I replaced, but her hair was darker and pulled back. If that is her, then I only worked with her for two nights before she left."

"How long ago was that?"

"Four, maybe five weeks." Greta answered as she scanned the surrounding tables. She was either getting inpatient with the conversation or concerned about her customers.

"Please," pleaded Nattie, "just one more question. Do you know where she is now?"

Greta turned away from the table and called out to the thin waitress, "Catherine."

When Catherine arrived next to her, Greta simply pointed at the picture of Adelle and left.

Catherine picked up the photograph and held it up for a closer look.

"Do you recognize her?" asked Nattie.

"A little." The thin waitress shrugged. "We worked here together for a couple of months. She was nice." Then Catherine looked more closely at Nattie, "Why? Is she in some kind of trouble?"

"No, not at all." Nattie answered reassuringly. "I am a private investigator and I am trying to find her for her mother."

Catherine tensed up and drew back slightly. Nattie tried to reassure her. "Her mother does not know why she left America. Did she tell you she was in trouble?"

"Not really." Catherine gritted her teeth. "It was more like she was—"She searched for the right words. "Distracted--or heartsick." After removing Nattie's bag from her chair, Catherine sat down and continued. "She was very quiet and kept to herself, but she worked hard and was always helpful to me. I don't want to see anything bad happen to her, but I worried about her too."

Nattie leaned forward against the table and spoke softly, "I assure you, Catherine, that I have her best interests at heart. She blamed herself for causing problems between her mother and her father, and her mother just wants to reassure her that it was not her fault."

Nattie hoped it was an explanation Catherine could accept. The waitress seemed to relax her shoulders as she considered what she had just heard, so Nattie pressed her luck a little. "Did she tell you about why she left home?"

Catherine shook her head, "All I know was that she was working here until another job opened up. I'm pretty sure it was a job she had once before."

"A waitress job?" asked Nattie knowing that she would be headed for Florence soon.

"*Sì.*"

Fighting off her renewed excitement, Nattie took a deep breath. "Do you know the name of the restaurant?"

Catherine flinched, "I'm sorry. I don't remember. She told me the name-- I think it had 'Boar' in it. 'Boar's Head' or something like that." Then sitting up straighter, she added, "I think it's on the other side of the Duomo. Does that help?"

"Yes Catherine, that helps a lot. Thank you. I will make sure nothing bad will happen to Adelle."

Catherine's eyebrows tightened in a look of confusion.

"What is it, Catherine?"

"Did you say 'Adelle'?"

"Yes. 'Adelle Quinlin.'"

Pointing at the picture, Catherine said, "That's Judith Ruggaliano."

CHAPTER 30

AT THE DUOMO

After an evening of strolling around the Duomo looking for the Boar's Head without success, Nattie decided to call it an early evening and start the next day off more systematically. For breakfast she ordered a decadent looking pastry from the bakery downstairs and hoped it would be served with a side of information.

"Mr. Kabrazi por favore, do you know of a restaurant called 'The Boar's Head'?"

"Please," he said, "call me 'Lou.'"

"Lou," she repeated.

His smile broadened, "Is this a *ristorante* here in Firenze?"

"I think it's near the Uffizi museum," answered Nattie, making note of how he pronounced both "restaurant" and "Florence."

Lou Kabrazi turned from her and spoke Italian to his wife, who was at the cash register waiting on an elderly couple. The four of them conferred in Italian for several minutes. Their conversation was very animated with a wide range of facial expressions, hand gestures, and tones of voice. It continued until each of the four had expressed something and expressed it passionately. Finally they turned simultaneously toward Nattie.

"The Boar's Head?" Lou asked doubtfully.

"*Sì.*"

He shrugged apologetically, "I don't think that's a *ristorante* in Firenze. We don't know about Rome or Naples, but we are certain that it is not anywhere in Toscana. I am sorry."

"*Grazie,*" she said as she nodded toward each contributor.

Nattie made her way back to the area of the front of the Duomo. When she had walked by it earlier, she noticed several souvenir kiosks that had tourist guides written in multiple languages including English. She thumbed through the thickest book and after finding a large section listing restaurants in Florence she paid seven Euros for it. The man running the kiosk was very nice, but did not speak English well enough to help her with locating The Boar's Head.

Sitting on the steps of the Duomo gave Nattie a shady spot to sit while she carefully read through the list of eateries. The names of the restaurants were printed in bold so it was easy to scan through the list just reading the names. She found no "Boar's Head" on the first pass through the list; a second pass required that she read the full descriptions of each establishment, hoping to find something, anything that could relate to a boar or wild pig. The second pass through the list took much longer, so long that she had to move twice to stay out of the afternoon sun.

Standing brought to her attention how stiff she had become sitting on the marble steps. It was then that she also noticed another effect of sitting on marble steps for so long. *It adds new meaning to the phrase sticky buns,* she thought trying to keep her spirits high as her search for the restaurant was still fruitless.

Nattie feared that Lou and the gang back at the bakery were right about "The Boar's Head". *Addie had no reason to tell the truth about where she was going to the waitress in Montepulciano when she was lying to her about who she was.*

In her discouragement, Nattie had become oblivious to everything else. She then realized that she had been unconsciously digging at the seat of her pants to get them unstuck. When she realized what she was doing, she looked around to see who had noticed. *Get your head in the game,* she told herself after finding no one staring at her dance with her pants. *There's nothing to do, but play the Boar's Head lead all the way out.*

Although her tourist's guide had no Boar's Head listing, it did have a good street map of Firenze. The map showed another large piazza near the Uffizi museum. According to the map it was only five blocks to the west. Maybe she could find another kiosk with other guides containing different lists. *Who knows, another kiosk owner might even speak English.*

While walking to the Piazza Della Signoria, Nattie passed several gelato shops. It was something in the third gelato shop that caught her eye. Pineapple gelato. *It is the best Lifesaver flavor; it could be the best gelato flavor.*

"English?" Nattie asked the woman behind the glass counter.

"*Si,*" the woman said. "Cup or cone?"

"Cup," answered Nattie, "*por favore.*"

"What size?"

"*Piccolo.*"

The woman smiled at Nattie as she dug deep into the tray of pineapple gelato and piled it high above the small cup.

Nattie took a small taste and moaned. She added pineapple to her ever-growing list of favorites: *melone, fragole,* and *cioccolato.* She had yet to find peach.

"Can I ask you about a *ristorante*?" Nattie asked between bites.

"*Si.*"

"The Boar's Head?"

"I don't know about a *ristorante*," the cashier said as she played with a metal loop that pierced the lower left corner of her mouth, "but there is a square that has a small bronze statue of a boar in a fountain. Tourists rub its nose and make wishes as they throw coins into the fountain."

"Are there places to eat around there?"

"It's mostly vendors in the square, but there are several *ristorantes* close by."

Feeling her energy and enthusiasm surge back, Nattie asked, "Can you show me where it is on my map?"

"You won't need the map." She pointed. "Just go to the next street and turn right. You will run right into the square."

"*Grazie.*"

"*Prego.*" Suddenly she shouted "Talia" at a woman in a waitress uniform walking by.

Hearing her name called, the waitress stopped and stepped toward them. After nodding at Nattie, she turned toward the gelato cashier and said, "*Prego.*"

They spoke Italian to each other quickly. The gelato lady said, "She will show you where the Boar fountain is."

"*Grazie.*"

"*Prego.*"

"English?" Nattie asked Talia.

Talia smiled. "A little," she answered with a heavy Italian accent. She looked to be in her late thirties, pale, with hair an unnaturally bright red.

"Do you know of a *ristorante* in Florence called 'The Boar's Head? My brother ate there when he was here, but no one seems to know where it is."

Talia grinned, "I'll bet he had a steak."

"He probably did." Nattie was surprised at how easily the lie came. Kevin had not visited Florence when he came to Italy.

"The osteria where I waitress is near the fountain and we sell spouts for bottles of olive oil and balsamic vinegar shaped like a boar's head. If he had a great steak then he is probably thinking of us. Steak is our specialty."

"Can you take me there?" pleaded Nattie, "My brother would kill me if I was this close and didn't eat there."

Talia looked at her watch. It was five o'clock, "They won't seat you until six thirty, but I'll show you where it is. We can get you a reservation."

As they came to the small market area Nattie could see the merchants packing up their goods for the day. Talia led them around the edge of the square to the bronze statue. She threw a coin in the fountain, placed her hand on the snout of the boar, and closed her eyes as she rubbed.

"Make a wish," Talia said. "The Italians say that if you rub its snout you will return to Firenze."

Nattie took two coins from her pocket and without looking to see how much was in her hand, she threw them into the fountain. Then she placed her right hand on the boar's head and with her eyes open said, "I wish that everyone finds what they are looking for."

Talia chuckled. "I'm not sure it will work like that. Do you think that everyone else has rubbed the luck off its nose?"

"I don't believe in luck."

Talia hesitated and eyed her a moment before cocking her head. "My osteria is this way." She had only taken two steps when something Nattie said stopped her cold.

"Your mother sent me to find you, Adelle."

CHAPTER 31

AN EARLY TRUCE

"You know my mother?"

"I do," said Nattie, "I had lunch with Alma in Abingdon."

The two women let life proceed around them as they searched out each other's eyes. Nattie assumed Adelle was trying to decide whether or not to trust her while she herself was deciding how much she should reveal.

"My name is Nattie Moreland," she said breaking the silence as she handed Adelle a business card, "I'm a private investigator from Bristol, Tennessee. Your mother hired me to find you and make sure that you are safe."

"Is she okay?" Addie asked sheepishly.

"Well I think she is pretty worried about her daughter."

Nibbling at her lower lip, Adelle turned away. Nattie wondered if she was trying not to cry until she turned back with a solemn expression on her face and her jaw line clearly clinched.

Anger or resolve? wondered Nattie.

"Look Nattie," Adelle said, "I don't know who you are, but I have to go to work right now. So if you want the whole story, if you want to find out if I'm safe or not, then meet me tomorrow. I will explain everything that my mother will want to know." Then she definitively repeated the word, "Everything."

"No offense, Adelle, but you left Chicago suddenly and then you did it again from Meadowview. As far as I know you left Montepulciano suddenly too."

Adelle's eyes narrowed, "Would **you** try to stop me?"

Putting her hands up in an I-mean-no-harm gesture, Nattie said, "That's not what I'm about. Really. I'm here to help you, Addie." She put her hands down, "Can I call you 'Addie'?"

Adelle ignored the question. "How did you know it was me?"

"I wasn't sure you were Italian when you walked in the gelato shop and nodded at me without knowing me first," answered Nattie. "That kind of familiarity is an American thing."

Adelle nodded expressionlessly.

"I didn't really recognize your face at first either. All I have are a couple of photographs that your mother gave me. And that red hair really changes your look. But when you said, 'The Italians believe that rubbing that boar's snout ensures that you will return to Florence' I knew for sure that you weren't Italian. After that I started looking closer and I could recognize you through your disguise."

"And you are a detective, right?"

"A private investigator."

"Okay," Adelle said, "If you meet me tomorrow I'll explain everything to you--" she paused momentarily, "including how you can do what you said."

"What did I say?"

"You said you were here to help me. And I need the help of a private detective."

"But you won't explain until tomorrow."

"Look, Miss, you already know that I left Chicago suddenly."

Nattie nodded.

"Did you also know that I was engaged?"

Nattie nodded. The question rattled her. It reminded her that she had chosen to withhold her relationship with Oliver Ruggaliano, which could eventually be problematic as Adelle considered whether or not to ask her for help.

"The reason that I won't be leaving Florence suddenly," Addie explained, "is the same reason that I need your help. I came to Florence to find something out and now I'm stuck. I'm not leaving until I finish what I came here to do."

Nattie took a half step closer and looked deeply into Adelle's eyes. "And you promise--I mean promise--that you'll meet me tomorrow?"

Adelle smiled and gently reached out to hold Nattie's forearm, "I promise. Please call me Addie. And thank you." She turned to go.

"Uh, where are we meeting?"

Turning back Addie rolled her eyes as if to say, "silly me," "How about six o'clock at the Savonarola plaque."

Again Addie turned to go causing Nattie to blurt out, "I don't know where-"

"Ask anyone," Addie called back over her shoulder without slowing down.

CHAPTER 32

THE ACADEMIA

Having made contact with Addie Quinlin and assuming she would show at six o'clock meant Nattie had the next day off. She could just be a tourist. In Florence being a tourist means going to the Galleria dell' Academia where Michelangelo's statue of *David* was housed. She remembered from her art history class at Freedom University that the *David* was one of the most famous pieces of art in the world.

"How many pieces of art can you name?" Nattie's art professor had said on the first day of class. "Not artists, but the piece itself." The *David* came in third behind the *Last Supper* and the *Mona Lisa*, both by Leonardo da Vinci

"Those da Vinci paintings are just more famous now because of the 'da Vinci Code' craze." One of Nattie's classmates had said. He was a bit of a suck-up, trying to score points with the professor who obviously preferred Michelangelo.

"It is not da Vinci." The art professor replied. "It is Leonardo of the town of Vinci." He is not Mr. of Vinci." The suck-up got no points.

"Is this the first time for you?"

The woman's voice startled Nattie. "I'm sorry?"

"Is this the first time for you to see the *David*?" the woman repeated. She was older, but not elderly, nicely dressed, but clearly a tourist with her sensible walking shoes and totes. She stood several inches taller than Nattie and compared to Nattie's athletic frame, this woman was slender. Her accent was southern.

"Why do you ask?"

"Because you are standing in the entrance staring at it, dear."

Nattie looked around quickly. She had entered the dimly lit exhibition hall and turned right, which was the only option. The *David* was at the other end of the long thin room, the only piece illuminated from above. It was breath taking-magical.

"It's--bigger than I had imagined," Nattie said, moving to the side of the hall away from the flow of tourists.

The woman smiled, "That is everyone's first reaction." Then taking Nattie by the arm she added, "come with me. If you will keep me steady, I'll show the *David* to you down there. It is even more impressive up close."

Nattie bent her arm and offered her elbow as a grip. "It's a deal. I am Natalie Moreland, but my friends call me 'Nattie.'"

"Nattie," the woman said as she stepped closer. "That should be easy to remember. My name is London Southerland. I don't think I've ever had a nickname. My name is just not conducive to nicknames. My maiden name was Ayers but no one ever asked me if my middle name was Derry until I was in College."

"Londonderry Air," repeated Nattie, "Isn't that a song?"

London nodded, "An Irish song."

"Why did you say my name would be easy to remember?" Nattie asked.

"My mother's mother was named 'Natasha.' She was from Bulgaria. When they moved to Tennessee she became Nattie," London explained, "And when our daughter was born we were surprised. She was supposed to be Nathaniel after my husband's grandfather, but that wouldn't do so she is Nattie."

"After your grandmother," Nattie observed.

London leaned closer and in a low voice said, "yes dear, but don't tell my husband."

Chuckling quietly, Nattie said, "I think I like your spirit, London. You have a real zest."

"Why thank you dear. That's very nice for you to say." Then touching her finger to her lips she added, "But let's not tell my husband that either."

Nattie held one finger across her lips and winked.

For the next half hour they circled the *David* in silence starting by looking at his face, then working slowly counter clockwise until they finished in front of his face again.

"What did you like best about the *David*, dear?" London asked as they exited the Academia.

"Oh that's hard London. His hand is amazing and that is what I knew to look for from my Art History class." Nattie paused and tilting her head slightly to the left she committed to David's face. "The expression on him was so--"

"Focused?" offered London.

"Yes, focused. It's like he had a job to do and he was too focused on it to be frightened."

"Michelangelo gave him the look of quiet, but confident determination."

Nattie agreed, "And how about you London? What's your favorite part?

"Oh his butt, dear, his butt." London's eyes twinkled, "You will never see another one like it."

CHAPTER 33

LUNCH WITH LONDON

Lunch for Nattie was vegetable soup, faccocia bread, and bottled water. London had a Coca-Cola and some kind of flat bread sandwich with prosciutto and cheese. As a side dish she ordered fried potatoes.

"I cannot resist the fries here," confessed London, "They fry them in olive oil. Can you imagine? They don't need condiments. Would you like to try one?" she asked, holding out the plate of golden brown fried potatoes. "I've been accused of being a witch because I can eat just about anything without gaining weight."

"Thanks," Nattie said, taking one fry and eating it. "You are right, the olive oil makes it amazing."

"Help yourself to more."

"Thank you, but unfortunately I have never been accused of being a witch. At least not for that reason."

Nattie held up her water bottle, "To Italy."

"To Italy." London said tapping the water bottle with her coke." So Nattie,-- don't you think we've talked about me enough."

"Not at all, I'm having a marvelous time."

"But I want to hear about you now."

"There's nothing really to tell. What would you like to know?"

"Is there a man in your life?"

"I was married for a few years."

"Was?"

"Yes, was. He was charming, good looking, and lots of fun, but there was just one thing we could never agree on."

"And that one thing was--?" London asked.

"I thought he should grow up." Nattie laughed as if he had just delivered the punch line.

London did not laugh, but rather reached across the table and squeezed Nattie's hand. "I'm so sorry to have touched a nerve dear."

Nattie was tempted to say something funny again, but looking into London's clear blue eyes she changed her mind. "We're still friends. His name is Nathan and he's trying to keep the door open between us."

"Is that what you want?"

"It depends on the day. I'm just not sure if he isn't going to end up being a day late and a dollar short," lamented Nattie, "I guess that part of my life is on hold for now."

London leaned back. "So why not tell me about where you are investing your life these days?"

"Well, London," Nattie proudly said, "you are sitting across from the lead investigator and owner of a detective agency."

"Impressive," London beamed, "I see the pope next week--it will be anti-climatic."

They both laughed, drawing the attention of the counter attendant, which made them both crouch slightly with their shoulders and say "Americans" at the same time. This brought another water bottle to coke can toast.

"Tell me about operating a detective agency, Nattie. It must be fascinating. I want to hear everything," London said. "How you got to the top and how many detectives answer to you. I just love the idea of a young woman taking charge of all those men."

"First things first," Nattie said. "I must confess something."

"Do tell."

"I am the only detective and the agency is less than a month old. We've solved exactly one case and that one virtually solved itself."

"I'll bet there is more to it than that."

"Not really," Nattie said, "My client thought her husband was having an affair with a woman who was actually teaching him how to ride horses which he was learning as an anniversary surprise for her."

"That wouldn't make for a very interesting story in a book or a movie, but I think it's sweet."

"I think so too," agreed Nattie, "but it's hardly a great investigative accomplishment."

London smiled. "But you are one for one on the scoreboard."

Nattie thought for a moment and remembered that the first mystery the Natasha McMorales Agency faced was to discover the identity of the man who knocked her out in the parking lot. "Actually we are two for two, but I'm not the one who solved that one either."

"Who did?"

"My brother actually solved it," she said, without adding, "he solved it by reading an article in our local newspaper."

"Does he have his own agency?"

"No, he's my receptionist."

"A win is a win."

"A win is a win," Nattie agreed. "And now I'm here working on a missing person case, which could be resolved at--," she looked at her watch, "It could be resolved at 6:00."

"Today?"

"Yes, today."

"You could be three for three by dinner time today."

"We could."

Extending her coke, London said, "Here's to success in business."

"Thank you."

After they toasted and each had a sip of their respective beverages, London asked, "If you want me to, I could take one of your business cards to my husband. He's a banker and he occasionally needs a detective. He prefers using agencies from outside of Franklin."

"That would be great. Thank you." Nattie looked through her wallet, but none of the old cards were to be found. Then she remembered that when Kevin had taken her to Tri-Cities airport, he had given her a cheap plastic card caddy with some new cards in it. She found them in her bag and handed several to London.

London read the name out loud, "Natasha McMorales."

Nattie could not keep herself from lunging across the table and snatching the card from London's hand. She was nearly in shock as she looked at the card. It was just as she feared: Kevin had not only re-named the agency; he had re-named her.

She handed the card back to London. "I'm sorry. You must think I'm terribly rude."

"Nothing of the kind, dear. Is there something wrong?"

Nattie explained the whole story of how Kevin had come to give her the name 'Natasha McMorales.' She was tiring quickly of the why Natasha question.

"Is this the right phone number?" London asked when Nattie finished.

Nattie had to look at another card before she could answer. She nodded. "Well, it seems he got one thing right."

"I think he got two things right."

"Really? What else?"

"People will remember the name 'Natasha McMorales,' that is why I think it works rather nicely."

"As a business?"

"As a name. If you will remember, 'Natasha' was my grandmother's name." Looking down London surveyed the empty dishes, "If you don't have plans for after lunch I'd love for you to join me."

For most tourists after seeing the *David* the second stop would be the Uffizi Museum. It housed, among many great early Renaissance pieces, the real *Birth of Venus* by Botticelli, a print of which was hanging in her waiting room. She often told anyone who lingered in front of the print, "That's not the real one." It was a stale joke, but telling it over and over again made seeing the real one that much more valued.

But the Uffizi would have to wait, London "needed" her. Nattie had become attached to London and London was headed to San Marco.

"When the Dominican monks moved to Florence, the Medicis restored San Marco as a home for them."

"The Medicis?" Nattie asked.

"The Medici family financed the early Renaissance. They were bankers and ruled Florence with their money."

Nattie nodded attentively.

"The Medicis financed works by Michelangelo, Leonardo, Raphael, and Donatello."

"The Ninja Turtles," observed Nattie.

"And more than the Turtles too," London smiled. "There are supposed to be frescos by Fra Angelico in every monk's bedroom, cell. Fra Angelico would be more famous today if a cartoon had been named after him," London said.

"I guess Sponge Angelico Square Pants doesn't have the right sound to it."

"I supposed not. Where are you from, Nattie? You sound a bit southern."

"Bristol--Tennessee."

"Nascar! Right?"

Bristol Motor Speedway, the world's fastest half mile, was how many people knew of Bristol. The two races each year, one in the spring and the other in late summer, brought thousands of tourists and millions of dollars to town, but they did not treat Bristol the way Bristolians treat Bristol.

"Yes, Nascar--and Nascar fans. Bristol would go broke without the fans so they get special treatment; but when they leave, we are happy to have our town back."

"I suspect that is how the Florentines feel about us as well," observed London. "But Nascar is not how I know Bristol."

Nattie turned her head to look directly at London.

"Do you remember me mentioning that my daughter's name is Nattie too?"

Nattie nodded.

"Well, my Nattie lives in Johnson City with her husband. He's a professor at East Tennessee State University."

With lunch over London re-applied some lipstick and then said, "San Marco was closed when I was here three years ago. Every time I come to Florence, something is closed for repairs."

"How often do you come?" Nattie asked.

"I come to Italy once a year. Not always Florence. Last year I was in Assisi and the year before that Positano on the Amalifi coast. I'll be heading back there tomorrow. It's going to be my last time."

"Really? I have always heard it's beautiful there."

"Oh I love it. I just can't take the stairs any more." She glanced down at her right ankle. "When I was young I ran in a race across the Charleston, South Carolina, bridge."

"And that hurt your foot?"

"Not exactly the run," London confessed, "my friend and I got tangled up and fell pretty early in the race. I think I broke it." She shrugged. "The adventures of youth become the arthritis of the elderly."

Nattie smiled.

"You were right about Positano being beautiful. I'm going to stay in a lovely hotel called the Meramare. I'll be able to see the Mediterranean Sea from my bathtub."

"Really!"

"And I'll have breakfast on my balcony every morning. Coffee, croissants, little packs of Nutello, and fresh orange juice while I look at the beach below and the city on the other side of the slice."

"The slice?"

London laughed. "I'm sorry. The cliffs and mountains along there are like a giant cake," she explained. "And to make Positano, God took a slice out of the cake. The people built their city on the inside edges of the missing slice." She smiled, "At least that is the story I was told by a waiter when I was there three years ago."

"So if your balcony is on one side of the missing slice you are looking at the other side."

"And you are looking at the sea as well. No one in Positano has a back window. Every window, every balcony has a view of part of the city and the sea."

"What did God do with the slice He took out of the mountain?"

"He put it on top of Capri."

"Ah, the Isle of Capri. Have you gone there as well?"

"Not me. I get seasick too easily, but there are boats to Capri that leave from Positano all day long. I remember one night I was in a lovely *ristorante* in the Piazzo Murat hotel. You would have loved it there. The food was marvelous, with a complimentary strawberry sparkling wine drink before dinner. The dining area was outside, but under canopies. It was lit by candlelight, and soft jazz was piped in through speakers hidden in the plants. Bougainville was everywhere."

Nattie pictured the scene, "It sounds like Fairyland."

"Yes--Galadriel could have walked in any moment."

Nattie smiled.

"Actually that was not my line. There was a large table of Americans at the next table and I overheard them comparing the place to scenes from *Lord of the Rings*. They had been to Capri that day, but could not get back to Positano because the sea was so rough."

"What happened?"

"They had to go to Amalfi and then take a bus to Positano from there. Amalfi has a harbor. I listened to them talk about it all evening. We Americans can be so much louder than anyone else." London raised her eyebrows before continuing. "Apparently the crew of the boat passed out plastic bags and half the passengers wanted them. One of the ladies at the table next to me used three bags."

"Oh my."

"They made a big fuss over the bill because they wanted separate checks and the cashier mixed up who got what."

"How did that turn out?"

"A young man, too young to be the manager and not dressed right to be the head waiter, came out and explained that it was impossible to get everything right." She stopped them at the entrance to San Marco. "But they did get it sorted out and afterwards one of the ladies came to my table to apologize for the disturbance and the "three-bag" woman apologized for wearing white shoes out of season."

"What could you say to that?"

London smiled the kind of subtle smile only elderly women can manage, "I just pretended I was British and said, 'you yanks make a fuss wherever you go."

CHAPTER 34

SAVONAROLA

In spite of the Fra Angelico frescoes in each of the cells and the entombments of several members of the Medici family, the main attraction of the San Marco monastery was the cells of Savonarola. Visitors had to make a large half circle around a courtyard on the lower level to get to the stairs going up to the second level where the cells of the monks were. Once upstairs, they walked through the long hallway that circled the other two sides of the courtyard. The monks' cells, each with its own Fra Angelico fresco, lined each side of the narrow hallway. Each cell could be viewed from its own doorway, but a rope prevented entry into the room itself. Visitors stood in most of the doorways, but Nattie and London only paused to look into the cells that happened to be open as they passed.

"The cells seem very small," Nattie remarked. "And the windows, too. You'd think they would want to get some air through here."

"That might not have been much of a priority for them then."

"Why not?" asked Nattie.

"They may have considered that concern for the comforts of this world were beneath the calling of a monk."

Nattie looked into the cell again, "Then how do you explain the famous artwork on the walls?"

"A very good question," London said. "One answer is that back then they were probably as hypocritical as we are today. A second answer has to do with vanity."

"Vanity?"

"Yes," answered London. "Have you ever heard of the Bonfire of the Vanities?"

"I remember a John Cusack movie with that name."

"I think it was Tom Hanks, dear, but that movie wasn't about the real Bonfire of the Vanities. The movie just used the reference as a catchy title." She took Nattie's arm again and steered her further down the hallway. "The real Bonfire of the Vanities goes back to Savonarola. He was the monk who came to great power here in Florence just after the Renaissance had been well established. Do you remember me telling you about the Medici family at lunch?"

"Yes."

"Well it was Lorenzo D'Medici who financed all the frescos in these cells, which was initially received as a blessing by the Dominican monks who lived here. But when Savonarola took over, he considered the Renaissance to be an abomination because it brought glory to Greek philosophy, mythology, and art. He began to preach against anything that he thought opposed or overshadowed the Bible."

I know the type, Nattie thought to herself as she remembered her stepfather's attitude toward her decision to major in psychology, his diatribes about the Democratic party, his disapproval of "liberal" churches and pretty much anyone who thought differently than he. It was his incessant badgering that led her mother, Ingrid, to abandon her lifelong fascination with Saint Francis.

"He was a real hell fire and brimstone preacher and he developed quite a following. He was against books, fashion, art--anything he could label as godless."

They came to the end of the hallway, where a uniformed guard stopped them from going further until two people who were already viewing Savonarola's area came back out. Maybe it was the presence of the guard or it might have been the history within these particular walls, but whatever it was, it demanded silence from all that entered.

Nattie walked through the three rooms allotted to the fiery monk, but primarily thought about the impassioned lecture she had received from her hell fire and brimstone stepfather. "Do not conform to the pattern of this world," he would say, "but be transformed by the renewing of you mind." She had always taken him to mean, "listen to me and me alone." She once observed that everyone at his church seemed to use the same phrases and sounded the same when they talked. "Isn't sounding how each other sounds conforming? Why do you think that your church is immune to conforming to the pattern of this world?" she had asked him. He told her, "May God have mercy on your soul if you can't hear the difference." Nattie never asked about his church again, but regretted not asking him if his response to her question conformed to the pattern as well.

"If Savonarola was so against vanity," asked Nattie when they began their return trip down the hallway toward the stairs, "then how did he justify his three cells when each of the other monks had only one small cell?"

"Oh, he had enough vanity for three cells. His self-righteousness did not mix well with the power and influence he came to have over Florence. In the end he was invited to another bonfire in his honor."

"Good," said Nattie. "I hope they ran him out of town. Sanctimonious tyrants should get a taste of their own judgementalism."

"They burned him alive, dear," London answered. "The burned him on the same spot as his bonfire of the vanities." She pointed toward the Duomo, "It happened right over there by the Uffizi museum. There's even a plaque marking the spot. It's in the Piazza Della Senoria, which is on the other side of the Duomo."

Nattie looked in the direction London had pointed. She shuddered and grew thoughtful. Then she brightened. "Thank you. I needed to know where that plaque is. It's where I will be meeting someone later."

They remained mostly quiet as they retraced their steps down the stairs and back out of the front door. Feelings of guilt for delighting in Savonarola's death mingled with her bitterness at her mother's second husband as they walked.

Once they got outside she turned to London. "I'm afraid I must go. I have to meet someone at that plaque," Nattie explained looking at her watch, "but thank you for the lovely day and all the insights into Florence. I had a marvelous time."

"Let's not say goodbye."

"No?"

"No. I'm sure our paths will cross again."

"Really?" Nattie asked.

London looked at the card in her hand, "I'm certain of it."

"Well--until then, London," Nattie said as she hugged the older woman.

"Until then, Natasha."

CHAPTER 35

THE PIAZZA DELLA SENORIA

Nattie found the Savonarola memorial at 5:30. It was exactly where London had described. Coming early was mostly to make sure she found it, but the desire to actually see the plaque was more of a motive for her than she realized. She was curious about the spot where the monk had been burned, but seeing it made her sick.

It was not too many minutes ago that Nattie had been rather cavalier about Savonarola's death. Sanctimonious tyrants did deserve to be put in their place, but being burned alive was no fate for anyone. And being in the spot where he had been burned made his death more real to her. Her guilt had become palpable. She had wished for something and it had come true. It mattered little that her wish had come true centuries before her birth.

Nobody deserves that, she thought, staring at the plaque embedded in the piazza floor. She could read the name, "Girolamo Savonarola," across the eighth line of the eleven lines of brass letters. She had no idea what the other words were, but she knew as much as she could tolerate for now. Standing on it was out of the question.

"Do you know the story?" The voice came from very close behind her.

"I do," answered Nattie as she turned to face the now blonde Adelle Quinlin.

"You came early," observed Adelle.

"I just wanted to make sure that I wasn't late because I couldn't find the spot. You came early too."

Adelle smiled, "I wanted to make sure you were alone."

"I'm glad I'm alone then," Nattie said, confused by the change in Adelle since the night before.

Adelle registered no amusement at Nattie's response.

"Adelle," Nattie said softly, "is there a reason you are so guarded? I mean, if you are being threatened we can--"

"I'm not being threatened." Rolling her eyes, Adelle added, "I'm probably just being silly. I think my nerves are shot."

"How can I help you?"

Adelle flinched. The sternness was back. "You can start by telling me who you are."

"Excuse me," Nattie said through a tightening throat.

"I Googled your name last night." Adelle raised one eyebrow and waited for a response.

It was Nattie's turn to roll her eyes. "Actually that is easy to explain. The office manager of that detective agency is my brother, who is a charming, well-meaning lunatic. He changed my professional name to Natasha McMorales because he didn't think my real name was exotic enough for marketing purposes. There has yet to be an opportunity for that new name to make the internet."

"What is your real name?"

"Natalie Miriam Moreland."

Adelle eyed her expressionlessly.

Holding out a letter from Alma Quinlin addressed to AQ, Nattie said, "Maybe this will help you decide whether or not to trust me."

Adelle looked at her mother's handwriting on the front of the envelope Nattie had handed her. Turning it over, she traced the edge of the sealed flap with her fingertip. "Have you read this?" she asked.

"No – but I've got a pretty good idea about what it says."

"Then you'll understand why I'm going to wait until later to open it."

"I have to say," Nattie admitted, "I don't understand. You need help from someone like me, but you're still trying to decide whether or not to trust me. And I offer you proof of my connection to your mother and you don't open it. No, Adelle--" she said deliberately. "I don't understand."

"If I open that letter," Adelle said as she placed it in the bag hanging over her left shoulder, "the rest of our conversation is going to be about my mother." She closed her bag and folded her hands over it, "What we need to talk about is my fiancé."

"Okay," Nattie said slowly.

Adelle's eyes scanned the piazza. Tourists were crowded around them trying to take pictures of the Savonarola plaque. "I think we need to get out of the way here. Can we just go get some coffee? I'll tell you my story."

The short walk to the pizzeria on the edge of the piazza was in silence. The quiet gave Nattie the opportunity to decide how she was going to tell Adelle that she had been hired by Ollie as well as Alma. Ollie and Alma each knew that Nattie was also working for the other. Although purists would consider that arrangement a conflict of interest, Nattie was comfortable that this was not the case. Each wanted Adelle to be found, her safety accessed, and respective letters delivered. Each wanted progress reports and would have wanted to know that Adelle had been found yesterday. Nattie was sure they would both understand if she did not give them another progress report until after her meeting with Adelle today.

Nattie's comfort at having contracts with both Ollie and Alma was primarily based upon her honesty with both of them. Either of them would have objected vigorously if it were not for Nattie's disclosure of the focus and limits of each contract. The immediate dilemma was that Nattie's contract with Ollie had not yet been disclosed to Adelle, and the longer she waited the more of a problem it could become.

As Adelle ordered their coffee, Nattie placed the envelope from Ollie on the table in front of her.

"What's this?" Adelle asked as she picked up the envelope and examined it. Her eyes tightened and she tilted her head as if she were struggling to recognize the handwriting. "Is this--" she paused before raising her head to look squarely into Nattie's face, "--from Ollie?"

"It is."

Staring across the piazza Adelle's eyes teared up as she tapped the fingertips of her left hand with the envelope. After several moments of tapping she examined the sealed flap of this letter as she had the one from her mother.

"Did Ollie find my mother?" asked Adelle without looking at Nattie.

"No, he gave that to me himself."

Adelle turned to face Nattie, "I don't understand."

"Your mother did hire me--but Mr. Ruggaliano hired me first."

Before Adelle could respond, Nattie leaned forward against the table and said, "Let me make my contract with Oliver perfectly clear. He wants me to give you that envelope and he wants me to bring back your response." Nattie paused to watch Adelle listen, but Adelle's face hid whatever she was thinking. "I have no idea about why you left Chicago so I insisted that my contract with him did not require me to divulge your location if you did not want me to. Here's a copy of that agreement," she said as she handed a folded sheet of paper across the table.

Adelle took the paper, but did not open it.

"Oliver agreed to that condition without hesitation," Nattie explained.

"He would--" Adelle was interrupted by the waitress bringing their café.

Nattie and the waitress said "*prego*" and "*grazie*" simultaneously.

Adelle was silent until they were once again alone. "I find myself in a position that requires that I trust you whether I want to or not."

I had that exact same effect on your mother, thought Nattie. "I think that if you will read his letter, he will back up what I have told you."

"I don't need to read the letter to believe that, Ms. Morales."

"That's McMorales," Nattie said and immediately regretted it for several reasons, not the least of which was Adelle's obvious annoyance at the interruption. "I'm sorry, go ahead."

Adelle nodded, "I'm not going to read this letter until later either. I'm sure I'm going to sit down and cry when the right time comes, but right now isn't the right time."

"Look Adelle," Nattie pleaded, "I have only met your fiancé a couple of times, but I am convinced that he holds you in high regard and means for no harm to come to you. I think maybe he loves you and if you would just read--"

Adelle slapped the table, causing Nattie to jump. The noise drew the attention of several other customers at the pizzeria.

"Do you think I don't know that?" Adelle asked sternly. "Do you honestly think I don't know that he loves me and would be the most wonderful husband I could have ever hoped for?"

Declaring herself confused was a colossal understatement, but she was in fact confused, "Do you love him?" she asked tentatively.

Eyes watering, Adelle answered, "With all my heart."

"I don't know what is weighing so heavily on you, Adelle, but don't you think Oliver would understand? If you love each other what else could matter?"

Shaking her head and looking down, Adelle weakly said, "Until I find what I came to Florence to find, I don't even want him to know where I am or why I'm here. You must promise me that he will not know until I discover what I came here to find out."

"I promise." Nattie held up both hands. "You have my word, Adelle. He won't hear anything from me that you don't want me to tell him except that I have found you and have given you his letter. I owe him that much, but I can wait a few days to tell him that if it would help."

Adelle remained quiet.

"I want to help you, but I don't know what it is that you came to Florence to find. I don't know what could have been so upsetting that you had to leave your home without saying anything to anyone. I think that is what is so distressing to Ollie because of the disappearance and death of his first wife."

"That's just it," said Adelle emphatically, "I don't think she's dead."

"What?" blurted Nattie in disbelief.

"Judith Ruggiliano is still alive."

"I think Ollie is still married."

Nattie stared at her speechlessly.

Returning the stare, Adelle spoke what Nattie was coming to realize, "Ollie is still married."

CHAPTER 36

ANOTHER LETTER

Time seemed to stop as the phrase 'Ollie is still married' swirled around her thoughts. Nattie's general psychology professor had taught her that when a new piece of information makes its way into short-term memory, it is held for a brief time while long-term memory considers where, how, and if it is meaningful. If it is meaningful, then it must be fit into long-term memory accordingly. She had asked him, "What happens when you realize that something is meaningful, but you don't know where to fit it into your memory?" "You get dizzy," was his answer, but she thought he was trying to be funny rather than answer her question. He was right.

"Are you okay?" asked Adelle.

"Of course," Nattie said automatically. "Why do you ask?"

"Because you just sat there with your eyes glazing over."

Nattie nodded. Her breathing had gotten deeper and her shoulders had tightened. "I think I was a bit thrown by what you just said. Did you say--?"

"Ollie is still married," Adelle said crisply, finishing Nattie's sentence.

"That is what I thought you said." Nattie sat back. "I'm going to need a moment to get my head around that."

"I understand."

Adelle's emphasis on the word "I" was not lost on Nattie. As his private investigator Nattie thought she had a fairly clear understanding of Ollie, so the knowledge that Ollie might be married was difficult for Nattie to incorporate into her long-term memory. Her own struggle to process this information momentarily blinded her to how difficult it would be for his fiancée to process it. The moment was over.

"Is this why you left Chicago so suddenly?" Nattie asked sheepishly as a way to acknowledge Adelle's superior right to be effected.

Adelle bobbed her head forward slightly and widened her eyes in the universal sign for, 'that statement is too obvious for me to respond to.'

"Of course it is," noted Nattie as she read Adelle's face. "I'm sorry for being so slow. It is just hard to picture Ollie being a two-timer."

"He's not a two-timer," Adelle said. "He doesn't know."

Again Nattie hesitated. The information in this conversation was changing too fast. For her own clarification she repeated, "He's married--but he doesn't know he's married."

"Right."

"So that means Judith is still alive."

Adelle nodded yes.

"Do you know where she is?"

"Not yet," Adelle said as her shoulders drooped. "That's what I came to Florence to find out--but I haven't done so well so far--that's why I need your help."

"You want me to help you find out if Judith Ruggaliano is in fact still alive and if she is in Florence?"

"That's exactly what I want. Will you help me?"

Nattie looked away from Adelle and noticed the Piazza Della Signoria was getting more crowded. There was a sea of tour guides holding up sticks with different colored flags or small stuffed animals that identified one group from another, making it easy for them to re-gather at the end of the day. For the first time Nattie noticed the large number of groups that wore matching colored T-shirts.

"I can pay you if that's what your concern is," said Adelle.

Nattie was jolted from her trance. The implication that she was concerned only about the money felt insulting to her. As a professional private investigator she did work for money, but doing so fit uneasily with the caretaker role she had accepted as a child. Normally she handled the tension between these two positions by limiting her conversation about expenses and fees to the early stages of a contract, and even then she had to prepare herself for it by quieting the dragon of guilt that stalked her. She was not prepared for it now, and the dragon bit her.

It took a moment for Nattie to fight the dragon off; and Adelle, who was desperate, noticed the hesitancy. Nattie saw the worry in her eyes and tried to relax. There was no reason for Adelle to understand Nattie's hesitancy, so the comment about money was innocent; it was not an attempt to make Nattie feel guilt.

"I do expect to get paid when I work, so thank you for the offer. But collecting a fee is not why I didn't answer you right away. The problem for me is that I have a contract with Ollie and now that I have found you and delivered his letter to you I owe it to him to tell him what is happening."

"Certainly." Adelle nodded. "That makes perfect sense. But if I could I'd like to make a case for you to bend the rules this time."

"I'm all ears, Adelle."

"Call me 'Addie.'"

"Okay, Addie, what do you want me to know?"

Addie took a slow deep breath and began her story. "If I am right, then Ollie's first wife's death was faked which means she is still alive and he is still married."

"I got that, but why would she do that?"

"I don't know for sure, but I have a hunch. What I do know for sure is what it would do to Ollie if he even suspected Judith was still alive."

"What do you think he would do?"

"First, he would be crushed again. Then would feel responsible to make sure she was okay before he could marry me."

Nattie squinted. "I don't see why he would be responsible for her after she left him like that."

"He would not be responsible; he would feel responsible. In his mind, as long as he is still her husband, he still has a husband's responsibility toward her."

Nattie could not believe that any man was as conscientious as Adelle described Ollie. At least Nattie had never met one. But Adelle seemed to believe Ollie was this different from other men, so Nattie kept her opinion to herself. "So you decided you had to handle this yourself without telling anyone else about it."

"I had to do it this way. If I had told anyone else, then it would either get back to Ollie or it would change their opinion of him."

"And you intend to find her yourself, right?"

"With your help," answered Adelle.

"Okay, you intend to find her with my help, right?"

"Yes."

"And then what happens when we find her?"

"Then I'll at least know what kind of person we're up against," explained Addie. "Judith left him high and dry."

So did you, thought Nattie.

"And she let him take the heat for her disappearance."

So did you, Nattie repeated to herself.

"And that bitch--excuse my language--of a sister of hers was in on it."

"Edith?" Nattie asked, sitting up straighter.

"You know about Edith?"

Nattie nodded. "Edith and I have had words." *Calling her a bitch was kind.*

Addie paused, apparently taking in Nattie's comment, but then proceeded with her story, "Well I'm convinced that Judith and Edith were in on it together. They may have even had it planned from the beginning."

"Wait a moment," said Nattie. "Give me a minute to catch up. They had what planned? From the beginning of what?"

"They planned Judith's disappearance--together."

"You're saying Judith's disappearance was planned."

Addie nodded.

"That she was not abducted or frightened or killed," continued Nattie.

"Right."

"But she made it look like she was abducted and killed."

"Yes."

"And you are saying that Edith knew all this."

Addie leaned forward. "I'm saying that Edith was at least in on the plan. And from what I know about them, it was most likely Edith who came up with the plan in the first place."

"What makes you say that, Addie?"

"You said you had words with Edith," Addie recounted. "Can you picture her following anyone else's lead?"

"Good point," conceded Nattie, "but neither of us knew Judith."

"True, I never met her myself, but I do know that Judith was dominated by her sister."

"Did Ollie tell you that?"

"I found a strange sort of journal in an old jewelry box of Judith's. All of the entries were written to Edith." Addie shuddered slightly. "At first it really creeped me out. The journal entries looked more like prayers than anecdotes."

"Prayers?"

"Yeah. It was like Judith was worshipping her sister. You know, like telling her what she wanted. But according to Ollie it was just Judith's way to rehearse conversations with Edith. Because if she did not prepare herself well she would get overrun by Edith."

"I can picture that," observed Nattie, "but why would they have done this to Ollie?"

"Money," answered Addie. "They did it for insurance money."

"Insurance fraud. If Judith is still alive, all we have to do is follow the money trail. That should lead us right to her."

Relaxing her shoulders and breathing more deeply, Addie asked, "So you will help me?"

Nattie hesitated. Through clinched teeth she said, "Everything you have just told me about Judith and Edith makes sense. And I certainly agree with your opinion of Edith. But right now, all you have is a theory. There's really no evidence that Judith is still alive or that there was a plot to defraud an insurance company."

Addie's voice became deeper as she opened her bag and withdrew a weathered sheet of paper. "The jewelry box where I found the weird journal had a false bottom in it. On the night I left I found this." She handed the paper across the table, "It had been torn out of the journal and hidden."

Nattie took the paper. It had obviously been wadded up and re-straightened more than once. It had also been torn into four relatively equal pieces and re-assembled with tape. The writing along the fold seams was fading, as if worn from repeated examination. Nattie read the letter silently.

E-- Everything is set now. Word came from the lawyer in Rome that Food For Thought is ours if we still want it. I'll need to send 150 Euros to set it up, but I don't have it. I know you get upset when I need money, but I can't ask O for it. The last thing we need now is to arouse suspicion...It's getting harder to play the good wife so now that everything is set I want to go ahead with it. O has been good to me so don't be too convincing after I'm gone--I know I will feel better once I get to Firenza --J

When Nattie finally looked up again, Addie repeated her question, "Will you help me?"

"I will," agreed Nattie as she extended her hand across the table.

As they shook hands to seal their new contract, Nattie thought, *Insurance work was not what I wanted to do, but how can I say no?*

CHAPTER 37

KEVIN'S BOOK

"What the hell have you been doing, Kevin?" demanded Nattie. It was 12:30 and she had expected him to call her back by 10:30 at the latest. She had called him shortly after 9:00, which was 3:00 Bristol time, giving him just two hours of the business day to find out all he could about the insurance payout on the declared death of Judith Ruggaliano.

"Well for one thing I got my book back," Kevin said defensively. His backpack had been stolen out of the back seat of his car the day before. In his backpack were his checkbook, a cell phone, an assortment of snacks, and a Catbird Seat CD. The only irreplaceable item taken was his "book." His book, as he called it, was a moleskin journal in which he had written every idea and scheme that came to him.

Nattie's silent assessment of his book: *He's got enough manure in him to germinate the seeds of any of the bright ideas he has planted in that book--if he'd just get around to cultivating any of them.*

"I'm glad, Kevin, I really am; but right now I'm really more interested in some information about insurance payoffs. Remember?" she asked, rolling her eyes.

"You just rolled your eyes, didn't you?"

Nattie rolled her eyes again.

"Federation Fidelity is the insurance company that sold the policy to Judith Ruggaliano. It's based in Chicago."

"Okay," Nattie said, as she wrote down the information. "Who was the beneficiary?"

"I expect to get that information any minute now."

"What are you talking about Kevin? It's 6:30 there. Businesses have been closed for an hour and a half."

"Bristol businesses have been closed for an hour and a half, but there are more time zones in the States than this one."

'Of course,' Nattie felt like whacking her forehead with the heal of her hand, "Chicago is an hour earlier."

"Yes, and San Francisco is three hours earlier."

"San Francisco?"

"Federation Fidelity is in Chicago, but they are a small insurance company and they handle their larger claims out of San Francisco. It's only 4:30 there. I'm waiting for an email from them right now."

"Thanks, Kevin; nice work."

"No problem, sis," said Kevin before he changed the subject. "I saw Nathan the other day."

"How is he?" Nattie asked out of habit. She was not interested in casual conversations about her ex-husband. Nathan Moreland was not a comfortable subject. Entertaining positive thoughts about her ex-husband was dangerous, like the allure of the sirens tempting sailors to their destruction in the treacherous waters around the Isle of Capri.

"He's working now," explained Kevin. "He bought into a bar on State Street."

That sounds like him, Nattie thought to herself. *One good deed to suck me in and then it's off to play with the boys at the bar.*

"I've been there twice so far. He's doing real well."

He should, she thought. *He knows enough about bars.*

"And both of the times I was in his place he drank nothing but coffee all night."

"Oh crap," blurted Nattie out loud.

"What's the matter?" asked Kevin.

"Oh it's nothing, I just heard some sirens." Sighing, she changed the subject, "So you got your book back."

"I did," Kevin said eagerly. "It was cool how it happened. It was about 5:00 here and I was going to run down to Shanghai and get some Governors Chicken and when I got outside there was a cop next to my car talking to a kid. Apparently he caught the kid opening my car door."

"Wait a minute, Kevin. You say you left you car unlocked yesterday and you were robbed and then you left it unlocked again today."

"There was nothing in it today."

"Then what was the kid trying to get?"

"He wasn't trying to get anything," explained Kevin. "He was returning something. He told the cop he had seen this paper bag fall off of my trunk and he was putting it in my backseat."

"He was lying."

"I know. But I figured that he took what he wanted, which was the backpack and when he realized that everything else was personal to me he tried to return it. The cop handed me the paper bag and asked me if everything was there."

"What did you say?"

"I said everything was there and I thanked the kid for thinking of me."

"But he's a thief, Kevin, and everything wasn't there. He took the backpack."

"That was yesterday. Today he thought of me and he took a risk trying to get that stuff back to me. I think it was pretty cool. If I had the backpack in my hand I would have gladly given it to him as a reward."

"So he steals, and when he returns what he doesn't want, he gets a reward."

"You could say that."

"How would you say it?"

"I would say that the world would be a better place if when people did their jobs they also thought of the people who were affected by their jobs."

"And his job is--stealing?"

"Evidently."

"And he was thoughtful enough to consider how his job affected you?"

"Exactly," answered Kevin. "If a pickpocket steals your wallet, wouldn't it be nice to get your photos back."

"Yes. That would be nice," Nattie said, more as an act of surrender than agreement.

"Here we go," Kevin said. "Something came in."

"From San Francisco?"

"Give me a minute--ummm--I'm not sure where it's from, but there's an attachment."

Nattie waited impatiently.

"Nope, it's a picture of some vacation property in Florida. Are you interested?"

"That reminds me. Did you get those pictures I took in Chicago processed?"

"Oh yeah, I went over to the Walmart at exit seven and put them on a disc. I did that the day after you left."

"Great. I'm going to need a picture of Judith Ruggaliano. If you'll email that photo to me I'll find an internet café tomorrow?"

"Hold on a second."

She listened to him opening and closing something and typing on the keyboard.

"Here it is," he said. "Is she a real cute brunette with a pony tail?"

"No, that's probably Laura. The only picture of Judith I took is of another photo where she and her sister are together and they are wearing matching T-shirts."

"Food For Thought?"

"Excuse me?"

"That's what the T-shirts say, 'Food For Thought.'" repeated Kevin.

"I'm sorry, I forgot about that slogan. Yes, that's the picture," apologized Nattie. "Email that to me please." Then she remembered, 'Food For Thought' was also the slogan Judith had mentioned in the note Addie had found.

"It's already done."

"Thank you."

"Say sis, did you look closely at this picture?"

"What do you mean?"

"Do you know who the man in the picture is?"

"Should I?"

"It's Jim Riggleman."

"Oh really? Jim Riggleman? I haven't thought of him since high school."

"You don't know who he is, do you?"

"Not a clue," she admitted.

"He was the manager of the Chicago Cubs when they won their division in 1998." Kevin had been a Cub fan as long as Nattie could remember. Papabear, their grandfather on their father's side, had taken them to see a Cub's game at Wrigley Field at least once every summer when they were young and their vacations were always visits to family. Papabear had been a die-hard Cub fan all his life and had infected Kevin with the same fruitless passion.

"I can't believe I didn't recognize him. And 1998 was the 90-year anniversary of the last World Series victory wasn't it?" she laughed.

"That was cruel, Sarge."

Nattie gasped, "Wait a minute," she said. "Wait just one minute," she repeated louder. "Did you say 1998?"

"Very funny."

"No I mean it. If it was really 1998--oh I can't believe I didn't see it right away. I could kiss you."

"What are you talking about?"

"I'm talking about proof that Judith Ruggaliano was alive in the fall of 1998."

"When did she disappear?" asked Kevin.

"In the spring of--"

"1998," they said together.

CHAPTER 38

BREAKFAST

"I brought breakfast." Nattie held up the paper bag full of pastries from the Kabratzi bakery as Addie opened her door.

Addie waved her in. "Are you always this cheerful in the morning?" Her eyes looked swollen as she took the bag from Nattie.

"Not usually, but I have good news this morning."

"Already?"

Nattie could not contain her smile. "Do I smell coffee?" she asked without actually smelling coffee.

"Come with me," Addie said, heading farther into her flat. "I'll start the espresso and you can tell me your good news."

Nattie followed her into the small kitchen at the end of the hallway. Addie's kitchen was small, but very neat and clean. The only evidence in the kitchen that anyone lived there at all was spread out on top of the small table in the corner.

"What's this?" asked Nattie holding up a phone book. The phonebook was open to the letter "D" and starting in the middle of the left page the listings for DeVitos were systematically crossed off. At a glance it appeared that two thirds of the DeVito listings had been eliminated.

"I've been visiting every DeVito family in Florence," explained Addie as she prepared their espresso. "That's Judith's maiden name."

Nattie looked at her. "Very good. You're beginning to think like a detective."

"Beginning," noted Addie. "You mean this is how a beginner would do it?"

"I didn't mean to say that. In the absence of any other plan you have to resort to legwork and waiting. That's what I did in Montepulciano for several days. Besides it looks like you have eliminated a significant number of places where Judith could have been."

"Thank you for that," said Addie as she lit the flame under the stovetop espresso maker. "But now I have a professional helping me." Turning away from the stove, she added, "So tell me, how would a professional do it?"

Nattie shrugged, "I'd check in with the insurance company and find out the name of the beneficiary."

"But isn't it going to be DeVito?"

"Possibly."

"But you doubt it."

"Didn't you tell me last night that you believed Edith had planned all this from the beginning?"

"Yes."

"Then it's unlikely that they used their real names."

Bowing slightly, Addie said, "That is why you are the professional Natalie McMorales. I am just glad to be part of the team."

"That's Natasha McMorales, if you don't mind."

They bowed toward each other and laughed.

"What's your good news, Natasha? Do you have a way to check in with the insurance company?"

"Oh better than that, I think. My brother was able to track down the company that sold the policy and traced it to an insurance broker that we think handled the payout."

Addie laid a plate with two croissants and two muffins on the table. "So we know who the beneficiary is already." In her excitement she set the plate unevenly on the edge of an open phonebook.

Nattie caught a lemon poppy seed muffin just as it rolled off the table. "Not quite yet, but my brother was waiting for it when I went to sleep last night, and if you will take me to an internet cafe after breakfast I can get his email. If we are lucky, we may even have a name and an address."

Addie, who had moments before joked about being a novice detective, was now overcome by emotion. She sat in the kitchen chair adjacent to the one Nattie sat in and held her face with both her hands.

Nattie placed her left hand on Addie and gently stroked her right shoulder.

Addie quickly composed herself, then, looking up with reddened eyes, meekly said, "I'm sorry. I guess I was getting more discouraged than I realized."

The gurgling sound from the espresso maker drew Addie's attention. She quickly stood, wiped her eyes, and turned the burner off as she removed the coffee from the stove.

"That is great news." Addie poured Nattie's coffee. She moved a bowl of sweetener packets from the edge to the middle of the table.

Nattie added sugar to her espresso while Addie fixed her own cup. When Addie returned to the table, Nattie said, "Actually, the good news I was referring to is that we have a photograph of Judith in the fall of 1998."

"I told you she is still alive."

"This picture does not prove that she's alive now, but it does prove that she was still alive six months after she disappeared."

"Can I see the picture?"

"As soon as we get my brother's email we'll have it."

"Well, let's go," Addie said, standing up. Then after looking at her watch she sat back down, "We've got a half hour before they open at 10:00."

Nattie unwrapped her muffin. "Just enough time for breakfast."

CHAPTER 39

MAXINE BARBONE

Nattie and Addie looked at each other in disbelief. They had read and reread Kevin's email several times. They were clearly at the address from Kevin's email; but it was hard to believe that Maxine Barbone, the beneficiary of a one-million-dollar insurance payoff, would still live in the dingy run-down hovel before them. The outside was desperately in need of paint, and the windows were filmed with grease and smoke, obscuring whatever light there might be on the inside.

They approached the front door cautiously. Nattie took the lead and tapped gently on the frame of the front door with her knuckle. Loose flakes of dried paint fell as she knocked. As she shook a large flake from the back of her hand a muffled voice said something unintelligible from inside. She looked to Addie to translate hoping that the voice was speaking Italian.

Addie answered Nattie's silent appeal by stepping closer to the door and leaning forward such that her left ear was just a few inches from the front door, she listened intently.

"*Buon giorno,*" Addie said. She waited in silence, then launched into a steam of Italian words that moved too quickly for Nattie to follow. Addie was having to take the lead with Maxine, or with whoever was inside. Finally, a few more muffled words.

"She says to come in," whispered Addie as she opened the front door.

They entered a small dark room. The smell of mildew and urine not only offended their noses, but burned their eyes as well. Music, an opera, came from somewhere to the right. Their eyes had not adjusted to the darkness enough to tell if the music came from a radio or a cassette player. It was hard to imagine anything more high-tech, like a CD player, in a place like this.

A small lamp clicked on, washing the corner of the room directly in front of them in a yellow glow. A grossly overweight woman sat in an upholstered chair next to a small table on which the lamp sat. The woman pointed to her left and mumbled something.

"She wants me to turn off her music," said Addie as she crossed the room.

The woman turned her gaze toward Nattie and pointed again. Nattie had to look for Addie's help.

Addie pointed at Nattie and spoke to the woman in the chair before explaining, "I told her that you don't speak Italian."

"What did you tell her about why we're here?"

"I didn't tell her anything. She didn't ask. I think she's just glad to have some company."

Nattie smiled at the woman, "*Buon giorno.*"

The old woman grinned and shook her finger at a small sofa covered with an old blanket. Nattie sat without being told. "Don't worry about me," she told Addie, "just see what you can find out."

"What should I say if she asks me why we're here?"

"Tell her we are from the insurance company and this is a courtesy call to see how she is."

Nattie sat patiently, understanding very little of the conversation occurring next to her. She was, however, able to follow it enough to understand when Addie asked if she was Maxine Barbone and when Maxine replied, "*Si.*" After several minutes Nattie shifted forward to the edge of the sofa. She signaled to Maxine her desire to look at a wall of pictures to her left, by pointing first at the pictures and than at herself and then quickly back toward the pictures.

"*Si, si,*" Maxine said as she waved Nattie toward the pictures.

While Adelle and Maxine conversed, Nattie inspected the photographs Maxine had on her wall. The photos were displayed in an odd mismatch of frames. Nattie moved one of the pictures with her fingertip and discovered that it had been there long enough for the color of the wall behind it to be noticeably lighter than the wall around it. She rubbed her thumb and fingertip together, creating a tiny gummy ball of the grime that had stuck to her finger from merely touching the wall. Although there was no apparent aesthetic organization to their arrangement the photos did appear to be organized in four lines from right to left. Each line of pictures seemed to be of the same person at various stages of childhood. The line at the top was of a red-headed girl and below her of a red-headed boy. The bottom two lines of pictures were of brunette girls. None of the children looked like they could have been Judith, but the subject of the third line down from the top could have been Edith.

Nattie examined third line more closely. It was a series of photos of a slender girl, the first of which had been taken when she was about age five. The series ended when she was around age thirteen. They were all taken at various holidays, but they did have one common characteristic: the slender brunette never smiled.

"Nattie," called Adelle.

Nattie returned to the sofa as Adelle explained, "Maxine has lived here all her life. Her father was a textile worker and so was her husband. She had no siblings and no children. The pictures on the wall over there were children from the neighborhood that she took care of for extra money. She doesn't know anyone named Judith or Judy."

"How about Edith?"

Adelle asked about Edith DeVito and got an enthusiastic response as Maxine pointed toward her collection of photographs on the wall. The subject in line three was apparently Edith, and Maxine had plenty to say about the stoic young girl. When Maxine finally stopped, Nattie instructed Adelle to ask her about Edith's sister.

"According to Maxine, Edith is an only child," answered Adelle without consulting further with Maxine. "Her parents died when she was twelve and the government took her to an orphanage. She was Maxine's favorite because she was the neediest."

Nattie took the photo of Edith, Judith, and Jim Riggleman from her bag and folded it so that Judith was not visible. She stood next to Maxine and showed her the picture, "Edith?"

"*Si*," laughed Maxine.

Nattie turned the picture over and showed it to Maxine. "Ask her if she knows who this is," Nattie said to Adelle.

Maxine took the picture from Nattie's hand as Adelle spoke to her. It was clear that she had much to say about Judith as well. From her position next to Maxine's chair, Nattie could see Adelle's reaction to what she was hearing. Whatever Maxine was saying about Judith was causing Adelle to repeatedly widen her eyes.

Adelle stared at Maxine well after she had stopped talking and had handed the picture back to Nattie. She remained transfixed in that position as Nattie sat back down next to her.

Nattie whispered, "Addie--are you okay?"

Addie nodded very slowly. "I think so. I think I understand what she just told me."

"What did she tell you?"

"She hadn't seen Edith since she was a little girl. Then, about three years ago she showed up and they spent several days together. Edith--Maxine calls her 'Angel,' by the way--brought her food and that cassette player and took her out to eat and to buy those opera tapes. But Edith wasn't alone; she brought--" Adelle stumbled over the words and finally pointed at the picture in Nattie's hand. "--she brought that woman with her."

"So Judith was here," noted Nattie.

"She was here all right," said Adelle, "but she isn't Judith."

"Okay--then who is she?"

Adelle looked long and hard at Nattie before answering, "According to this Maxine Barbone, Judith's real name is also Maxine Barbone."

CHAPTER 40

FOOD FOR THOUGHT

"I wish I could take tonight off," lamented Addie. "Half of the waitresses in Florence have gone to Montepulciano to watch them film a scene from that new *Twilight* movie. I think it's called '*New Moon*,' or something like that. The books have been a real craze around here. Anyway, I feel like I owe it to the Boar's Head to help them out. They have been very good to me."

"That's fine," Nattie replied. "I'm not really sure about our next move anyway, so I could use the downtime to sort out where we are and what we know."

"Explain what we know to me again, please," requested Addie. She had been in a fog of disbelief since they had left Maxine Barbone's home the day before.

"This is an educated guess, but it is still a guess," explained Nattie, "but I think the woman we know as Judith came to Florence and established herself as Maxine Barbone."

"So that's not really her name either?" asked a frustrated Adelle.

"Who knows? There's no reason to believe anything she said at this point. We did find a phone record for a Judith Barbone in Florence from 2004 to 2006. It was a cell phone and it was registered to the same address we visited yesterday."

Adelle shook her head.

"Once the declaration of Judith's death was official, they knew it would just be a matter of time before Maxine received a visit from the insurance company. Arranging to be there to receive the check would have been a fairly simple deception to get by Maxine and then it would have been easy for Judith to masquerade as Maxine while the real Maxine was out on the town with her Angel."

"Some angel," sneered Adelle.

"We could call her the Angel of Death if you prefer."

Addie just raised her eyebrows, "So what do we do now?"

"I'm open to any ideas you might have."

Addie smiled for the first time in the last 24 hours, "Do you mean 'what would a beginner do?'"

"Sure."

"A beginner would realize that she was in over her head and would enlist a professional as fast as possible."

"That's going to be your answer whenever we get stuck now, isn't it?"

"You know what they say, 'go with your strength.'"

"Good plan," said Nattie giving her a thumb's up with her right hand. "At the moment the strength is to track the money, and my staff will start that this morning. A sum of money that large will generally leave a trail, but if they are careful they can cover themselves easy enough."

"Edith is pretty conniving," observed Addie. "Wouldn't she be just as careful?"

"Perhaps, but she's pretty arrogant, too, and that could translate into careless."

"So we wait to hear from your staff?"

Referring to Kevin as her staff sounded odder to her when someone else said it. "No, there are some leads we could track down here as long as we have a day to kill anyway."

"Just tell me what to do."

"We could always try to find the orphanage where Edith went as an eleven-year-old and see if she met Judith there."

"Assuming that is her name," offered Addie.

"And assuming we could get at those records anyway--which is doubtful--we aren't likely to find out anything incriminating. Or we could track down any Barbone named Judith or Maxine."

"But that is still assuming that we know her name."

"Right, which brings me to option number three. It's a long shot, but may be a lead that they don't bother covering." Placing the picture of Edith, Judith, and Jim Riggleman on the table, Nattie pointed at the shirt and said, "I think we should look for a business called 'Food For Thought.'"

Looking closer at the photograph Addie said, "Really?"

"It's just a hunch, but the letter you found made a reference to paying fifty euros for that name. That probably means it is a business name they wanted to reserve."

Addie looked confused as she lifted her head up from the picture.

"You said that they may have planned it from the beginning. Well, this might be the business that they were planning on financing from the beginning. Those shirts are ten years old and last month I saw Edith pack a couple of them when she left Chicago."

"What kind of business is it?"

"If I were going to name a business Food For Thought, it would be a bookstore. How about you?"

"That is a good name for a bookstore," agreed Addie. "Or how about one of those coffee shop reading rooms."

"That's a good idea too. Kevin thinks it could be a health food store."

"Who's Kevin?"

I usually refer to him as my staff, thought Nattie. "My brother," she said out loud. "He's the one on the money trail."

"I sure hope your brother is having better luck than we are," complained Addie in the middle of the afternoon. A trip to the Internet café generated fifty-seven pages of Food For Thought websites, but none in Italy. They had combed through every tourist guide and phonebook. They had checked with the phone company and the municipal office where businesses had to register. They even consulted Lou Kabratzi and his wife at the bakery. They found no trace of a business called Food For Thought.

"It's only 10:00 at home. I'll give him another hour and a half and then we can call to see if he is doing better than we are."

Nattie's phone rang, as if on cue, as soon as she finished speaking. "Hello."

"Nattie?"

"No, Kevin, this is Natasha. Remember."

"I've got some information for you."

"Did you find the money?"

"Most of it. In 2006 $650,000 was put in the hands of a management firm in Rome. That was a couple of years before this depression hit, so it did pretty well for a while. It's still there and it's worth about $700,000 now."

"And the other $350,000?"

"That was cashed out, so there was no tracking it, but--are you ready for this?"

"What is it, Kevin?"

"Three months after the $350,000 was cashed out, a business called '*Argomento di Meditazione*' opened."

"Okay--" Nattie dragged the word out.

"'*Argomento di Meditazione*' is Italian for 'Food For Thought,'" explained Kevin. "It's a restaurant."

Nattie threw her head back and laughed heartily. "You, my beautiful baby brother, are a genius. A stark raving madman genius."

"Tell me more," Kevin begged playfully.

"No sir, you're the one with all the information. You tell me more."

"What do you want to know, sis?"

"Do you know who owns it?"

"Not yet. There's no website for it. But I know where it is."

"Come on. Don't make me beg."

"Positano. It's in Positano on the Amalfi coast."

"Hang on a minute," she said to Kevin. Taking the phone away from her ear she looked at Adelle, "We have a very solid lead on a restaurant in Positano; how far is that from here?"

"Half a day by train. Are we going there to check it out?" asked Addie as she looked at her watch. It was time for her to head to work so she pumped her arms up and down quickly, which, if done by a child meant 'someone take me to the bathroom quickly, but for an adult it means, 'I want time to slow down.'

"Absolutely," Nattie replied. Then speaking back into the phone, she asked, "Can you find us a place to stay in Positano tomorrow?"

"Slow down, Sis. Have you checked your email today?"

"My email? No, why?"

"You may not need to go to Positano yourself. It seems you have a friend there already."

"What are you talking about, Kevin?"

"You got an email from somebody in Positano yesterday. There's an attachment with a picture of Saint Francis."

"Really? Who is it from?" asked Nattie.

"Some guy named London."

CHAPTER 41

LONDON

Buying another sixty minutes on the Internet Café's access card cost $25. Their earlier visit to Google Food For Thought had used up all of the minutes on Adelle's card.

The seven current customers were scattered across the four rows of computer stations such that Nattie and Adelle had to go all the way to the back to find one they could both sit at. The computers in the back looked older. Their speed confirmed their appearance. Nattie opened London's email;

Natasha--

I told you that you would hear from me again. I arrived in Positano early this afternoon and I came across this statue of St. Francis as I walked down to the Hotel Miremare (the view of the Mediterranean Sea from my balcony is still breathtaking). I had to take this picture when I saw it because it reminded me of your story about looking at Bristol around the statue of Francis on your dashboard. I thoroughly enjoyed being with you in Florence. You were most kind to give so much of your time to an old lady you didn't know. I hope your business in Florence went well after I left. Your delay was my good fortune.

Peace and goodwill until our paths cross again,
London

Nattie tried to open the attachment of the St. Francis photograph, but the computer took too long. *It will be there when I get back home*, she told herself as she returned to London's email to get the name of the hotel again. She and Addie quickly found the phone number for the Hotel Miremare and called to leave a message for London.

"I am sorry," said the woman who answered the phone. "She only stayed one day with us before she went to the Isle of Capri. She will be back in two days and I will make sure she gets your message. May I have your name please?"

"My name is Natasha," answered Nattie, "and I will call back. I was thinking of coming to Positano myself."

"Oh you really must come visit us." The speaker identified herself as "Lolita," the manager of the hotel. "Positano is one of the most beautiful places in the world. You must bring your husband."

"I'm not married."

"It doesn't matter. Positano is for everyone. Bring whomever you wish or come by yourself to relax. We have the best *ristorantes* in all of Italy."

"Now that you mention it," Nattie cleared her throat, "do you mind if I ask you about a restaurant that I think is in Positano?"

"Certainly, I know all the *ristorantes* here."

"How about the Argomento di Meditazione?"

Lolita paused. "I know this *ristorante*," she said slowly.

Nattie noticed Lolita's hesitation and took it to mean that her opinion of the restaurant was not favorable. "Is it a good place to eat?"

The slow inhalation was followed by, "I must be honest. If you come to the Miremare, I will take care of you so that you will know that you can trust me. But, no, it is not good. It is very expensive, but it is not a good place to dine."

"I heard the same thing from a cousin who just traveled through there earlier this year."

"Did she stay at the Miremare?"

"No, she was just passing through. She said it was beautiful in Positano, but that she felt she had made the worst choice about where to eat."

"Oh she must come back and give us another chance. She simply must."

"What makes the Argomento di Meditazione such a bad place?"

"It is run by two women who think they are Italian, but they are not."

"Do you mean that their Italian food tastes like American?"

"No, well, yes, their food is *Americano*. But that's not what I mean when I said they are not Italian. It is their service, the way that they treat us."

"The way they treat who?" asked Nattie.

"The workers. These women--they treat their *ristorante* like it is the most important thing in Positano. They demand that their employees do the same."

"What do you mean?"

"Positano is on the Mediterranean, but it has no harbor. When the sea is rough everyone must come to the dock to get the tourists who take the ferry to Capri safely on and off the dock. Not just the dock workers, but everyone." Lolita shifted into a rapid stream of Italian words before proceeding in English, "My cousin, Marco, was working for them one day. He was sweeping, it was early before people started to come for lunch. When he left to help with the boats, they fired him. They told him, 'we don't pay you to work at that business, if you want to work there then let them pay you.'"

"They fired him for that?"

"Well that, and he stole some wine. But the point is they only think about how they make money."

"Please forgive my asking, but isn't that how a business should think?"

"In Positano we must think of the tourists first. If the tourists don't come, then who will buy their bland food and over-priced *vino*?"

"Of course, tourists are more important than profit."

"Profit is important, but there is no profit without tourists."

"Did you say there were two women who run the Argomento di Meditazione?"

"*Si.*"

"I must tell you that I wasn't exactly honest before," confessed Nattie.

"*Prego,*" said Lolita in a much more serious tone.

"I had to be careful because I represent someone who is interested in that restaurant." It was a deception that happened to be true, "So please do not repeat this conversation, okay?"

"You have my word."

"Now you said that it is being run by two women, but I was wondering if both women have been there all along."

"Both women are there now, but the mean one is usually here once or twice a year. The weak one has been here all along."

"Why do you call the one woman weak?"

"She is mean, too, but we think she is just doing what the mean one tells her to do."

"We?"

Lolita laughed, "Yes, we. The people who live here, who are from here. We think they are bad for business."

"If I sent you a picture of the two women, do you think you could identify them for me."

"I will try."

"I'm sending it now," Nattie said as she hit the send button having already addressed the email and attached the photograph to it in anticipation.

Lolita's computer must have been newer because almost immediately she said, "Oh yes, that's them. No question."

"Thank you, Lolita. I will do everything I can to remove these two women from Positano. But, please do not breathe a word of this."

178

Hearing this, Addie held her hand over her heart and breathed deeply. "Thank you!" she mouthed, then pointed at her watch to signal to Nattie that she was leaving. Nattie, in turn, gave her a thumbs up and waved.

"I will be silent," pledged Lolita. "Just get them out of here. And Natasha, please tell the new owners to change the name, who wants to eat *brain food*?"

CHAPTER 42

ROME

"How did it go?" asked Adelle. They had arrived in Rome just before lunch. After eating and checking into the Marriott, they had gone their separate ways. Nattie had an appointment at the Rome office of Federation Fidelity.

"They gave me a hard time for working in Italy without a license. Can you believe that?" asked Nattie. "Then they were suspicious of my motives until I gave them all the evidence we put together."

"You'd think they would be grateful for recovering a million dollars for them."

"It's not real money to any of them," explained Nattie. "It's that someone, maybe one of them, is going to get blamed for a million-dollar mistake."

"What about Edith and Judith? Will they get arrested?"

"Probably, but these boys will make sure they get all their facts together before they go in to action. No one is going to want to risk a second mistake with this situation. But I'm sure they'll eventually do some jail time. Maybe here, or maybe in the States, but they will be arrested somewhere."

"Good."

"How about you, how did your day go?" Nattie chose her wording carefully. While she visited the boys at the insurance company Adelle was going to call Ollie, a call she had been avoiding since she had gotten final confirmation of Judith's living status the previous day.

"I talked to Ollie," she said softly.

"How did it go?"

"He was a little surprised at first. He was expecting a call from you first, I suppose, but I told him I was with you."

"Did you tell him that you were coming back with me tomorrow?"

"I did."

"How did he respond?"

"He wants to come to the airport to pick us up."

"That's great," Nattie responded and then noticed Addie's somber expression, "It is great isn't it?"

Adelle looked away, eyes glossy. "He is still married to her."

"Only legally, Addie, and legally she is also dead. I'm sure as far as Ollie is concerned now that she isn't dead she is really dead to him."

"That's exactly what he said too."

"You believe him don't you?"

"I believe he means what he says." Looking directly at Nattie she asked. "But do you think that when everything else is settled he will ever forgive me for leaving like I did? He says he understands why I panicked, but he also said I could have told him about the letter and we could have faced it together."

"That sounds good to me," said Nattie.

"It does, it sounds perfect." Addie scowled. "So why didn't I think of that then? Why is it so obvious now? I'll tell you why. It's because I didn't trust him. I didn't trust his commitment to me. He is going to realize that eventually, and then he is going to ask me about it. What am I supposed to tell him then?"

Nattie leaned forward, "You tell him that trust is hard and that you are sorry for not trusting him. You tell him that your not trusting him was never really about him, but it was junk from your past that you hadn't noticed. You tell him that you got scared and ran and you know it hurt him because he didn't know what was going on. You tell him that there was never a moment that you forgot him or loved him less or ever considered giving up on fixing what Judith did."

Addie sat still. After a moment, she said, "You could have been a counselor."

The uninvited, but familiar thought arose, but Nattie pushed it back down. "Thank you" was all she said.

Dinner was more relaxed after that exchange. Nattie had melon wrapped in prosciutto and got it all over her fingers. Addie had the calamari, but could not talk Nattie into trying any. They joked, they laughed, and they shared a bottle of Vino Nobile di Montepulciano with their carbonara. Dessert was profiteroles and café which would have finished the evening off perfectly until a couple was seated next to them.

The man, a tall man with big ears and a bald spot on the crown of his head sat with his back to Nattie and Adelle's table. His wife, a short woman with an outdated hairdo sat across from him. Aunt Bea from the Andy Griffith show wore her hair like this woman did. The man's flirting made the waitress noticeably uncomfortable.

"I don't think she liked that, Carl," said Aunt Bea after the waitress left.

Carl ignored her and took a piece of bread from the basket on the table.

"I mean it, Carl; it's embarrassing."

Carl lifted his right hand and pointing it at his wife he mimicked her talking.

"I hate guys like that," whispered Addie.

"Amen," agreed Nattie.

Carl's wife became quiet and disengaged.

"Are you going to pout now?" taunted Carl. "Look Hazel, the women here are different. They aren't so timid about sex or with their bodies." Laughing he recalled an incident that happened to him on the Rome subway just before he joined Hazel for dinner. "It was so crowded that we were all standing very close to each other. I was near the door and a pregnant woman came to stand next to me. She was very pretty and she smiled at me."

"How nice," replied Hazel.

"Oh it was real nice alright. She got real close and rubbed her chest all over me."

Adelle signaled that it was time to leave with her thumb. Nattie followed, having already paid the bill.

As they passed the adjoining table, Carl added smugly, "And let me tell you that pregnant woman had the chest for the job."

"That's it," Adelle whispered to Nattie. She turned to face Carl. "Excuse me sir, I couldn't help overhearing your story about the subway."

"And?" Carl redirected his smugness from his wife to Adelle.

"And--I was just wondering if you still had your wallet?"

As they left the dining room they heard Carl cry out, "Oh, shit!"

CHAPTER 43

A DEAL IS MADE

While Nattie and Adelle traveled back from Italy Ollie talked to a lawyer who happened to be eating lunch at Michelangelo's at the time. "In the state of Tennessee," the lawyer told him, "if a man's first wife is declared deceased and he remarries and then subsequently his first wife reappears, his marriage to his second wife is still valid."

"What if the first wife was declared dead long before he met the second wife, but just before he marries the second wife he finds out that the first was still alive, but in hiding?"

The lawyer eyed Ollie suspiciously, "That is a very specific question. Are you the man?"

"No," lied Ollie shaking his head. "I was just curious."

"Well, I'm glad to hear that because as an officer of the court I can't advise anyone to do anything illegal. But if I was in love with the second woman and I was afraid that the first wife might show up then I'd quickly get myself married to the one I was in love with. That way it is already done. If I weren't already married when the first wife came back, then she could make a big stink and slow everything down. It would be easier for her to stop the second marriage than it would be for her to undo it."

The lawyer got a big slice of Ollie's lemon cake for his "advice."

Traveling home seemed to go slower and slower as Nattie and Adelle got closer to Bristol. The thirty-minute flight from Atlanta to Bristol seemed to take as long as the delay in Atlanta had taken. The wait to depart the plane seemed longer still. They were both ready to be home. For Addie, the anxiety about seeing Ollie again equaled her readiness to do so.

"Is Ollie or your family picking you up at the airport?" asked Nattie as they descended from the plane.

"I didn't tell anyone what flight I would be on."

Nattie glanced back at her for a moment, but it was windy and walking down the thin rolling stairway from the plane to the tarmac demanded her attention.

"If you could just give me a ride into town I'll stay at a motel tonight and figure out how to get in touch with Ollie tomorrow," yelled Adelle over the wind.

At the foot of the stairs Nattie put her hand through Adelle's arm. Leaning close to be heard over the airport noise Nattie asked, "Why didn't you tell anyone?"

"I wanted to be settled first." She shrugged and looked at Nattie timidly. "I'm not sure who's going to be glad to see me and who isn't."

They entered the passenger area of Tri-Cities airport and made their way across to the escalators. "My brother, Kevin, will be waiting for us at the baggage claim. If you want to, you can stay with me tonight and figure out what to do next tomorrow."

"Thank you Nattie."

"Oh that's no trouble. I've got an empty room with your name on it."

It was Adelle's turn to take Nattie's arm, "No, I mean thank you for *everything.*"

Nattie smiled tenderly and nodded her head.

They were standing next to each other, arm in arm, on the same step as the escalator reached the top. The door way beyond security was another ten feet in front of them and standing just beyond that, oblivious of being in the way of virtually everyone who passed, was Oliver Ruggaliano.

Nattie had to guide Adelle forward as she and Ollie were transfixed in each other's sight.

"Do not speak," Ollie said as he touched Addie's lips with his index finger. When he was sure Addie was not going to speak he took her by the hand and moved out of the way of the other travelers trying to get by. "We will marry on Saturday."

Addie looked at her watch. It was Tuesday, but her watch did not tell her so, "Saturday? This Saturday?"

"*Sí.*"

Addie stepped back away from him, "I can't let you marry me knowing that you haven't had time to forgive me for leaving yet."

Ollie held her head with both his hands and asked, "Forgive you for what? Forgive you for being afraid that we could not marry? Forgive you for solving the mystery of Judith and freeing me from the guilt that I had done something wrong with her? What shall I forgive you for-- for making me love you? Okay, I forgive you for making me love you. Are you satisfied now?"

184

"But I ran away."

"You did--and it hurt when you did--but it does not hurt **now**." Then he laughed and after kissing her forehead he said, "And now you want me to wait? What if I don't want to forgive you for making me wait now?"

"But why do you still want to marry me?"

"So I can kiss you whenever I want," he answered using the line from their favorite movie.

She blushed, "You stole that line from *Sweet Home Alabama*."

"It's a very good line, and I am a very good baker."

Adelle hesitated.

"Okay, how about this?" he offered through a crooked smile. "If you will marry me I will make you bologna cake any time you want it."

In *Sweet Home Alabama*, when Reese Witherspoon returned home from New York, her father offered her some bologna cake from the ice box. The first time Ollie and Addie had watched the movie together, Addie had asked him, "What's a bologna cake?" After Ollie admitted that he did not know, it became a recurring joke between them, 'Do you know how to make bologna cake yet?' she would tease him with an innocent voice.

She bit her lip to keep from grinning, "Do you promise? You will make bologna cake **any** time I want it?"

Ollie crossed his heart. "I promise," he said and they hugged.

And so the deal was made, right there in the Tri-Cities Airport in front of a parade of several scowling travelers and one witness. Nattie let herself feel warm and girly until she realized that Ollie was looking her way. He was waiting for her to make eye contact with him. When their eyes met, he let go of Adelle and threw his arms around Nattie and weeping said, "Thank you. Thank you for bringing me back my life."

"It was nothing," was what she wanted to say, what she would have said when she was younger. But now she realized he needed to be thankful. She would manage her self-consciousness another way. Patting him on the back like he was a nephew she simply said, "You're welcome Ollie. I am glad it's working out."

"I still need your help, Natasha," noted Ollie as he stepped back. "We need a church and a minister." Then, looking at Addie, he added, "I have booked the train station for the reception. I will be the caterer myself."

"Why Bristol?" everyone asked. It was the standard response to invitations to the Adelle Quinlin and Oliver Ruggaliano wedding. Because the wedding was being held with such short notice, invitations had to be conducted by phone. Follow-up questions varied, depending on who it was that was being invited.

"Why are they getting married so fast?"

"I thought she ran away."

"Who is he anyway? We've never met him."

"Why aren't they getting married in Chicago? That's where they will settle down, isn't it?"

"Why not Meadowview? That's where her family is."

Why Bristol? It was actually a silly question. Why not Bristol? Bristol is where they chose. And so they came to Bristol, the Ruggaliano clan from Chicago and the Quinlin family from Meadowview.

CHAPTER 44

A WEDDING IN BRISTOL

One of the phone calls waiting for Nattie's return was from Zoe Lancaster. Nattie had ducked Zoe's initial calls before leaving for Italy because she wanted Zoe to be pleasantly surprised when her husband's suspicious behavior was fully explained. For her part, Zoe had gotten frustrated because she thought Nattie was avoiding her, which was true. After several failed attempts to get Nattie to return her calls, Zoe had left one scathing phone message. It became a source of embarrassment once it became clear why Nattie had not returned her calls.

"I'm so ashamed," Zoe said. "I wish there was some way I could make amends."

"Well now that you mention it, I do need a favor."

"How can I help, dear?"

"Your husband is a pastor, isn't he?"

"Paul? Yes he is. Why?"

"What is he doing on Saturday?"

And so it came to pass that Nattie was able to fulfill all her commitments to the wedding ceremony in one off-handed conversation with Zoe, a pastor's wife. "Leave it to me," Zoe had said. She meant, "leave **all** of it to me."

The wedding was a simple ceremony, elegant in its simplicity. Zoe took the role of wedding director, her husband Paul performed the ceremony; and rather than being held at a church, she arranged for it to be held in a picturesque meadow on the Newsome estate between Abingdon and Bristol.

Ollie wore the suit Adelle and he had picked out the day before she disappeared. His cousin, Alberto, was his best man.

Addie's sister, Annie, was the matron of honor and provided the wedding dress, which needed alterations. For a wedding emergency, Valentina's on 6th Street did everything in one day, Friday. *Ollie will like that*, thought Nattie. *Valentina's Russian roots will please his European sensitivity.*

Nattie was one of the last to arrive to the wedding. As far as she could tell she and Kevin were the only non-family members in attendance. Kevin was sitting on the back row on the groom's side. As he watched her look for a seat, he scolded for being late by furrowing his brow and pointing at his watch. Ignoring him was her response. He invited Nattie to join him by pointing to the empty seat on his right. Nattie waved him off and signaled with her thumb that she would be sitting across the aisle on the bride's side. As she took her seat she noticed the woman to his right slid her arm through his and whispered something to him. She did not recognize the woman, nor did she know he would be bringing a date. *Good for you*, she thought, noting the woman's pleasant demeanor and her attire. Her modest purple dress looked like it came from an Ann Taylor catalogue, which was much more professional than his usual dates would have worn.

From the back row of the crescent arrangement of rented white plastic chairs, Nattie had a great view of Adelle and her father as Zoe gave them final instructions before they walked down the center aisle. As soon as Zoe turned away, James Quinlin leaned over and said something in his daughter's ear that made her smile and playfully punch him in the arm. He looked at her the way a little boy would look at his mom after walking for the first time. *Don't cry*, Nattie told herself.

The ceremony went quickly, which was convenient because the gorgeous setting in the middle of a grove of oak trees was an auditory nightmare. Whatever was being said between Paul Lancaster and the bride and groom might have been heard by those in the front row, but it was a silent film from where Nattie sat. She could see when Ollie stated his vows because he got choked up. Addie wiped a tear from his cheek. When it was her turn, she spoke without hesitation or the slightest movement of her gaze from Ollie. Their kiss brought a standing ovation from the Ruggaliano section. Their cheers and shouts persisted until the newlyweds turned to face their families. Addie looked embarrassed while Ollie beamed.

"It is with great pleasure that I introduce, for the first time, Mr. and Mrs. Oliver Ruggaliano," announced Paul Lancaster.

This time it was the Quinlins' turn to leap to their feet and cheer. The Ruggaliano clan followed suit as Ollie and Adelle ambled through the crowd on their way to a horse drawn carriage on loan from the Martha Washington Inn. Addie shook several hands on her side of the aisle as she walked by while Ollie was slapped repeatedly on the back. Without moving from her spot, Nattie once again found herself in the back row as all the guests watched Ollie and Adelle waving from the carriage as it carried them away.

Nattie felt an arm circle around her waist. "I understand you recognize this place," stated Zoe Lancaster.

"It looks a little like a place I visited once," Nattie replied as she put her arm around Zoe's shoulders. "You did a great job with the wedding, Zoe."

Zoe waved off the compliment. "It was actually quite easy. Nancy Newsome and I have become good friends."

"Really?"

"Yes. Paul and I come riding here nearly every Friday afternoon. We stop right here and enjoy the shade and the breeze through the trees. Paul tells me about the sermon he's working on and I pretend to listen."

"I'm happy for you."

Zoe smiled brightly, "Thank you for that. And thank you for the other, too."

It was Nattie's turn to hold up her hand, "The other--that turned out to be nothing."

Looking more serious, Zoe said, "It might have been nothing to worry about, but I was worried, and I had reason to be worried. You believed me--you took me seriously."

Nattie hugged her. As they let go of each other Nattie added, "I had to take you seriously; after all, there was a man's hoo-hoo at stake."

CHAPTER 45

A RECEIVING LINE

Nattie was late getting to the Train Station, which was primarily due to her conversation with Zoe Lancaster. But the delay was also a convenient way to stall going to the reception. It embarrassed Nattie to admit it, but she always felt awkward anywhere she might be called upon to relate to more than one person at a time. Her preference was to slip in a side door late, find a spot to roost, and let conversations come to her in small increments. It was a good plan as long as there were enough people gathered together to conceal her strategy. Knowing that there were less than sixty people at the wedding and having been at other receptions held in the Train Station, she was sure she was going to be noticed. And being noticed at a reception meant being pressured to socialize, maybe even dance. *I'm such a guy*, she chided herself as she entered.

The music from the far left end of the banquet room was coming from "Wall of Pop." *She sounds more and more like Norah Jones*, thought Nattie as she listened to Mariel and Brandon Story harmonize "Homemade Valentine." She did not recognize the only couple that was dancing, but she did recognize how out of step they were and how little it seemed to bother them. *Oh to be that unconcerned about what you look like to others.*

To her right were several banquet tables filled with food: Italian sandwiches, melon wrapped with prosciutto, battered and fried zucchini flowers, sausage and peppers, glazed pears with bacon bits and gorgonzola, several kinds of torts and assorted pastries. There was a table devoted just to wine, all imported from Italy. Auliki Brandt from Inari Wines stood nearby acting as the wine steward. The wedding cake, a monstrous-sized cake with white icing and white roses scattered all over it, was large enough to dwarf the table it occupied all by itself.

At one table, in a semicircle, sat the Quinlins, with Oliver and Carlos Ruggaliano next to James and their wives on the other side of Alma. *Talk about strange bedfellows*, Nattie thought. The Quinlins, she assumed, would be standoffish and thrown by the Ruggaliano clan which outnumbered them two or three to one. The Ruggalianos would be gregarious to the point of being boisterous, or so she assumed. She enjoyed watching them for a moment. She was right about the Ruggaliano family, but the elder Quinlins surprised her. They sat in the middle with the Ruggaliano brothers next to James sharing something they all thought hilarious and their wives equally engaged in conversation. Edna noticed Nattie's entrance and waved with a big smile and a nudge to Alma who waved heartily as well.

Taking the first step toward the mothers of the bride and groom, Nattie felt a hand on her elbow. "I knew you could do it," said Laura, Ollie's cousin from the Glen Ellyn restaurant. She gave Nattie a hug. "Thank you."

Nattie hugged her back. It was more like they were old friends than two people who had only met once. "I'm just glad it all worked out. I think they were destined to be together one way or another. Don't you think so?"

Laura looked across the room to where Ollie and Addie were standing, oblivious to anything except each other. "I think so too." Then she turned back to Nattie. "Do you know about Rugg-A-Muffins?"

"Do you mean the coffee shops with the gourmet desserts?"

Laura nodded. "It's a great idea."

"I thought they were keeping that a secret for now?"

"It was a secret until earlier this week. But after Berto heard from Ollie, he called us all together and told us all about it."

"What does this mean for the other restaurants?" asked Nattie, remembering Alberto's plan to offer Laura and Roselind the option of separating from the family business and owning their respective restaurants themselves.

"My husband, Trevor, and I have decided to stay with the family business. I wanted to take our time to decide, but Trevor wouldn't hear of leaving my family. We'll probably expand the menu in Glen Ellyn, and Trevor is already making plans to get a Rugg-A-Muffins right on the College of DuPage campus."

"What about Roz?"

"Oh she talked about splitting off right away, and everyone else thought she'd do it, but I knew she'd come around." Laura smiled and leaned forward, "If she's smart, she'll set up a Rugg-A-Muffins in the Yorktown Mall. She would make a fortune."

"Is she here?" asked Nattie. "I didn't see her at the wedding."

Laura pointed to the dance floor where Roselind Ruggaliano was in the arms of a very nice looking man who appeared to be closer to the age of Oliver senior than hers. "She's with the Ken doll over there."

"Is she--smiling?"

Laura laughed, "It looks good on her too, doesn't it?"

A small dessert plate bearing a scone with a dollop of what looked like prune filling in its middle appeared in front of her. "Try this," said Kevin.

"Oh those are good," offered Laura. "It's one of the new Rugg-A-Muffins recipes that Ollie has been working on while he was here. Besides getting Addie back, that's why Bristol was so good for him, for us all really."

Nattie took the plate. "Have you met my brother?"

"I'm Kevin," he said, offering his hand.

"Laura Benedict. Good to meet you."

Nattie took a bite of the scone, It had an orange rind flavor that mixed perfectly with the bitter sweet of the jelly. "Kevin!" she exclaimed. "Is this your coffee jelly?"

Kevin's smile was all the answer needed.

"You're the one who came up with that coffee jelly?" Laura asked pointing at him.

"I am."

Laura grinned. "I would never have imagined coffee jelly being so good, but it really is. You must have the same creative gene Ollie has. And you're going to do the cookbook too, aren't you?"

Nattie choked on the scone. "Cookbook?"

Kevin shrugged, "It was a no-brainer. Ollie has so many great recipes; and when they open the coffee shops, they will have a perfect place to market cookbooks. So you like it, the coffee jelly?"

Looking down at the dessert plate, Nattie confessed, "I do, Kev, I really do. But when you first told me about it I couldn't picture it at all. The orange rind scone goes with it well."

"That was Ollie's idea." He smiled sheepishly. "Actually he's the one who figured out how to make the jelly too."

"But it was your idea, right?"

"That's what Ollie says," said Laura. She excused herself.

Kevin leaned toward Nattie. "Have you seen Nathan yet?"

"He came by the office yesterday. Why?"

Kevin looked at her like she had missed something obvious. "Did he give you an envelope?"

"He did. It was from Federation Fidelity."

Scowling he asked, "You didn't open it, did you?"

Nattie did not answer.

"You beat him up, didn't you?"

"Don't start with me Kevin. Not now."

"When are you going to let him off the hook?"

Narrowing her eyes Nattie said, "Alcohol ruined our marriage and now I'm supposed to pat him on the back after he buys a bar. I don't think so."

Although Kevin usually cowered when she narrowed her eyes at him, he did not flinch this time. "If you weren't so mad, you'd see he's changed."

Nattie was just about to poke Kevin's chest with her index finger when his date from the wedding walked up and joined them. "Hi, I'm Twila Pierce." After handing Kevin a cup of punch, she added, "you must be Kevin's sister, Natasha."

"That's me, Natasha McMorales," smiled Nattie.

"Kevin talks about you quite a lot."

"He does?" asked Nattie, with a trace of sarcasm. "And has he told you the story of how we come to have different last names?"

As Twila turned to look at Kevin, Nattie stuck her tongue out at him. "I assumed it was because it was your married name," Twila said, still looking at Kevin.

As Twila turned back toward Nattie, Kevin returned the favor by sticking out his tongue. "You must be careful with my sister, Twila; she's going to be a black belt in karate."

"Really?"

"Well I'm probably as close to getting my black belt as anyone could be with only one introductory lesson."

Twila smiled the kind of smile that said, "I'm not going to say what I'm thinking." Instead, she announced, "I need to visit the little girls' room."

Nattie's pleasant expression evaporated as soon as Twila was out of earshot, "Is that the reporter from the *Courier* who wrote that article on me?"

"It is."

"Are you serious, Kevin? She wrote that article about me and doesn't know who I am?"

"But that's good, Nat. We need some good publicity. It's better if she doesn't realize that the Natalie Moreland who got knocked out in her own parking lot is not the same detective as the Private Investigator, Natasha McMorales."

"This is a dangerous game, Kevin, and I want no part of it."

Kevin's kiss on her cheek was a 7.5 on a 10-point patronizing scale, "Just read the letter from Nathan, Sis."

CHAPTER 46

BACK AT THE OFFICE

"Peace and good will," Nattie said to the town of Bristol as she once again crested the hill on State Street and surveyed the city below and beyond the Saint Francis statue on her dashboard. At seven-thirty on Monday morning, the traffic was thin enough for her morning ritual. She drove by the Train Station on her right and her office on her left and parked across the street from Manna Bagel where she ordered her usual early-bird special: sausage, egg, and cheese on an onion bagel.

She did not turn on the lights when she arrived at her office. Nor did she sit at her own desk. She opened the blinds letting light through the window above Kevin's desk, her desk from her early days in the agency. *How did it happen that I became the boss and lost the window?* The desk still felt homey to her as she enjoyed her breakfast in peace.

Nathan's letter had been placed in a pile on the corner of Kevin's desk. At least that is what she remembered. But now it was conspicuously placed leaning between the key board and the monitor of the computer. She picked it up, looked at it, and returned it to its original position. *Very subtle Kevin.*

Scrolling through her inbox, she found the email from London and opened the Saint Francis picture again. In London's picture the statue of Saint Francis stood in the foreground; but since it was under the cover of a tree, it appeared as a silhouette with the city of Positano and the rocky cliffs that were the trademark of the Amalfi Coast providing the majority of the background. It was not the knobs of Bristol background she experienced most mornings. Nor was it the background that she envisioned Francis looked at from his home in Assisi, either. But it was the scene that she knew Ollie and Adelle would be enjoying soon. Positano was their honeymoon destination.

Nattie found a real address for London and sent her a hand-written thank-you note. An email reply would have been too impersonal. The thank-you included her plans for blowing the picture up to poster size and framing it. It also included a brief detail of how London's email from Positano had been instrumental in helping solve the case.

The thank-you to London had to be brief because there were plenty of details about the case that Nattie did not know herself. This thought redirected her attention to Nathan's letter. She picked it up. The return address was from Federation Fidelity of San Francisco, California. She felt it. It was thin. No more than one sheet of paper. She opened it. The letterhead matched the return address. The message was simple:

Dear Ms. Natasha McMorales,

Concerning your involvement in file # 968-78-5423-001A please contact our office at your earliest convenience to make arrangements for a distribution of your fee. Currently only a partial recovery has been made, but we are pursuing a speedy resolution. Your contributions to this investigation have been exemplary and are much appreciated. We look forward to future collaborations.

Respectfully,
David Walker

"Federation Fidelity," answered the operator on the first ring.

"May I please speak to David Walker?"

"One moment please."

A voice much younger sounding than Nattie expected answered, "This is David Walker. How can I help you?"

"Mister Walker?"

"Yes."

"This is Nattie Moreland from the Natasha McMorales Detective Agency in Bristol, Tennessee. I am calling in response to a letter you sent me last week."

"Oh yes," David said. "You run the agency that found the zombie in Italy for us, aren't you?"

"The--zombie?"

"I'm sorry, that must have sounded strange. Have you done much insurance fraud work before? Life insurance fraud?" David asked.

"None as a matter of fact," answered Nattie. She considered adding, "I wasn't really trying to do this one, either," but she thought better of it.

"Well, in the insurance industry a 'zombie' is someone who is still walking around even though declared dead," explained David. "Capturing a zombie is a big deal to us. You might say that it is the one thing insurance companies take personally."

"I see."

"At this point we have recovered--" he paused. "I'm sorry I'm on the wrong page--here we go--at this point we have recovered and cleared $500,000 from an account in Rome, so we are prepared to release your finders fee at this time. How would you like that sent to you? We can wire it directly to a bank account if you want."

Nattie's silence was the result of not being able to swallow.

"I can assure you Ms. Moreland that we will keep you abreast of the rest of the recovered monies as they are cleared. This first payout is for the liquid assets recovered initially; the remaining money will be settled with you as all other assets are confiscated and settled."

Finally swallowing, Nattie forced herself to ask, "How much money are we talking about, Mr. Walker?"

"The standard is ten percent, of course, so we have a $50,000 check for you right now. The remainder is yet to be determined. I see that there is a restaurant in Positano, a home in Capri, two automobiles, a boat, and miscellaneous artwork. At this point we don't know what all of that is worth or if that is all there is."

"So it could get as high as the original million dollars?" asked Nattie.

"Oh, it could be even more. We're going to recover the profits she made on our money."

"I guess that's how you drain the life out of a zombie," observed Nattie.

"Exactly."

"Could you shed some light on a few unanswered questions for me?"

"If I can."

"How did they do it?"

"It was very clever, actually." David's tone was almost respectful. "Usually this is done by creating a false name for the beneficiary, but in this case the beneficiary used her real name."

"Do you mean that Judith Ruggaliano's real name is Maxine Barbone?"

"That's the information I have."

"Well, who was the woman in Florence?"

"That's part of the cleverness of this scheme; her name is really Maxine Barbone too. Edith Ruggaliano--she was apparently the mastermind--the one who knew both of these Maxine Barbones. One was her babysitter when she was young, and the other she connected with at an orphanage in Milan. By the way, most of these details come from Maxine herself. Edith has not been cooperative."

'That sounds right.'

"They'll both do some significant jail time."

"This may sound like a strange question, but do you have any idea when Edith came up with this scheme?"

"According to Maxine," answered David, "Edith called her with the plan when she became angry with her husband. It sounds like Edith was quite a gold-digger, and her husband didn't turn out to be as big a cash-cow as she had hoped. She started putting it into motion then; but when she came up with this plan is anybody's guess." David paused before observing, "She must be quite a looker."

"Why do you say that?"

"Because there has to be a reason for some poor guy to overlook a personality that is that cold-hearted."

Or Alberto might just be as soft-hearted as Ollie is, Nattie thought.

"Can I help you with anything else?"

"No, thank you, you've been quite helpful."

"Thank *you*, Ms. Moreland. We weren't even looking into this until we were alerted to it by your office."

"That's nice to hear," said Nattie. "I'll have to give a bonus to Kevin."

"Who's Kevin?"

"The one who called you," Nattie replied, then added, "Isn't he?"

"No, the call came directly to me. I'm pretty sure the caller was someone named 'Nathan,' not 'Kevin.' I can verify that for you if you'll give me a minute."

"That won't be necessary," said Nattie without realizing that she was biting her lip.

CHAPTER 47

THE NATASHA

As was his custom, Kevin did not come to work Monday morning. But Nattie found him having an early lunch at Manna Bagel.

"We have to talk!" Nattie said sternly. She sat across the table from him.

"What do you think of this idea?" he asked, sliding an open magazine across the table to her.

Nattie read the advertisement for a white noise machine circled in red. "What is it?"

"It's a sleep machine," he said. "It makes sounds that relax you so you can go to sleep. Like a bubbling brook or the ocean or a tropical rain."

"Okay?"

"Well it costs thirty-five dollars."

"And people pay that much?"

"Apparently."

Nattie rolled her eyes and took a long slow breath. "Kevin, we have to talk about something important."

Kevin smiled, "Nathan, right?"

"Don't be coy, Kevin. You know very well it's about Nathan."

"Well first let me tell you my idea about the noise machines."

"Okay," she said begrudgingly. Hearing him out would be the shortest route to the conversation she wanted to have with him.

"My idea is to sell white noise machines that sound like a fan." Kevin beamed over the cleverness of his idea.

"I don't get it, Kevin. Why is that different than what is already out there?"

Sitting more upright he explained, "My white noise machine that sounds like a fan also produces a breeze."

Nattie's eyes narrowed as what he was saying dawned on her. "So you're going to actually send these folks--a fan?"

Smiling like a six-year-old, he said, "A fan I buy for fifteen dollars and sell for twenty-five dollars, which is still ten dollars cheaper than the competition."

Leaning forward, he added, "It will include a detailed booklet on how to use it as a white noise machine."

"That sounds like a good way to get beat up Kevin."

He shrugged, "That's just an entrepreneurial risk."

Nattie sighed. "Alright, Kevin, I've heard your idea out; and as long as you don't use my office or phone number in your advertising, you have my blessing." To herself she added, *Especially considering there is about zero likelihood that you'll put any of it into action.*

"Thank you."

"Is it my turn now?"

He nodded.

"I read the letter."

"From the insurance company?"

"Yes," she answered. "Did you know we were going to get a finder's fee?"

"I was pretty sure that we weren't going to get anything if we didn't set it up before we gave them any information."

She pointed her finger at him. "So you set it up, right?"

"Well, I thought that something needed to happen, but I had no idea about what to do--" He let his incomplete sentence hang in the air.

"So you called someone who would have an idea about insurance work."

"That was the logical thing to do."

"The logical thing to do," she sarcastically repeated, "and I assume the fact that it included my ex-husband had nothing to do with it."

"Look, Sarge, whether I want you two to get back together or not has nothing to do with this. Nathan was my only option. Who else do I know that understands that kind of insurance stuff?"

"Well, Hiram for one."

"I don't know him Nattie. Besides, Nathan was here and he got it all set up in a couple of hours. And it worked out great, didn't it?"

After taking several long slow breathes Nattie said, "Sometimes I wish you were twins, Kevin."

"Not enough of me now?" he speculated.

"No, it's because if you had a twin I could clunk your heads together right now."

Chuckling he retorted, "You only feel that way when I'm right."

"Okay, mister wizard, since you are on such a hot streak with great ideas, tell me: what am I supposed to do now about Nathan?"

Making no attempt to hide his what-an-obvious-question expression, he smugly said, "I could see how difficult it would be to remember to say 'thank you' when someone does you a big favor."

Gritting her teeth, Nattie mimicked reaching across the table and grabbing him and his imaginary twin by the collar and banging their heads together.

Matthew arrived with the sandwich and soup Kevin had ordered for his lunch just in time to see Nattie's hand gestures across the table. He stood back to avoid having the soup knocked from his hands.

"Hi, Matthew," she said, with a you-caught-me look on her face.

"Hi Nattie--Is it safe now?" Matthew asked with a straight face.

"Oh yeah." Kevin turned and took the plate. "Thanks Matthew." He took a bite of what looked like a Continental, an open-faced sandwich with a slice of tomato covered with provolone cheese on a plain bagel. "Oooo," he moaned. "Try that, Sis." He offered Nattie a taste.

She looked at it first. "Is that a slice of onion?" Open-faced grilled cheese sandwiches with slices of tomato and onion was something their mother often made for them when they were kids. It was a favorite to go along with soup.

"Yep," he answered. "On a pepperoni bagel."

"That's delicious." Her mouth was still full.

"My idea," he bragged.

After swallowing, Nattie said, "I planned on calling him and thanking him this afternoon. And he should get a portion of this money. But the idea of splitting this reward with him after I worked on it for several weeks and he worked on it for a few hours doesn't sit well with me right now. I want to know what you arranged with him so I can do what is fair without being taken advantage of."

"A hundred and fifty dollars."

"Excuse me?"

"We owe him a hundred and fifty dollars. I hired him as a consultant for fifty dollars an hour and he turned in a time sheet for three hours."

"And you got that in writing?"

"I did." His six-year-old smile returned. "That was a pretty good idea too, hungh?"

"It was."

Kevin leaned as far across the table as he could and said, "That was Nathan's idea."

"Would you please wipe that look of satisfaction off your face?"

He snickered and, after looking to his left hand and then to his right, said, "It's too bad there's never a twin around when you need one."

Nattie just shook her head and stood up.

"You're not going to call Nathan now, are you?"

"I was, why?"

"Oh, I was just thinking that it would mean more to him if you went by his business."

"The bar?"

"Yes, the bar. But it's not just a bar; it's more like a neighborhood tavern. And he doesn't drink. Really, I think you should wait until 9:00 tonight after the dinner crowd is through and it gets slow. That's when you can see him in the best light. Trust me."

Hesitating only a moment to consider Kevin's plan, she agreed, "Nine o'clock it is, then."

"As long as you're up anyway, why don't you get yourself one of these sandwiches."

"That's not a bad idea. What's it called?"

Kevin glanced toward the counter and saw who was behind the cash register, "Just tell Susan you want what I got; she knows what it is."

Nattie did just that and ordered what her brother got. "You know Susan, if this sandwich becomes a hit, you'll have to name it and put it on your menu."

Susan nodded and said, "We'll wait and see about changing the menu, but it already has a name. Didn't Kevin tell you?"

Nattie turned slowly toward Kevin who waved and asked her to get him a bowl of tomato-basil soup. Turning back she asked, "What did he call it Susan?"

"It's the Natasha."

CHAPTER 48

NATHAN'S BAR

As soon as she passed under the "Welcome to Our House" sign Nattie knew that Kevin was right. She had to give him that. Nathan's tavern did have a homey neighborhood feel to it. And at 9:00 on a Monday night it was fairly calm. From where she stood just inside the front door, she could look along the wall behind the bar.

Along the left side of the narrow room were half a dozen wooden tables. The nearest table was occupied by two couples eating dinner out of plastic baskets lined with tissue paper. Two middle-aged women sat at the third table drinking some kind of red wine. Two large steins of beer sat unattended on the last table while two young men in jeans and work shirts played darts in the back corner.

Three men in white shirts and loosened ties sat at the bar with their eyes focused on a television mounted above the entrance as Nattie surveyed the room. Nathan stood behind the bar with a plain white oversized coffee mug in his right hand and a coffee pot in his left. When she made eye contact with him, he put the coffee pot away and came to the front end of the bar.

"What do you think?" He gestured across the room with his coffee cup.

She stepped up to the bar. "Did we come here a couple of times to watch Monday Night Football?"

"Once."

"I remember now; I refused to come back because it smelled awful in here."

"You said it smelled like wet cigarette butts."

"It did."

"And what does it smell like now?" he asked.

Closing her eyes Nattie inhaled deeply through her nose. "Is that--steak on a grill?"

"It's our hamburgers. We just use Angus ground chuck and we make them huge. Look at this," he said handing her a menu.

202

Across the top of the menu, in large print was the brazen claim "Welcome to OUR HOUSE, home of the best burger in Appalachia." At the bottom of the menu was the phrase, "Thank you for not smoking."

"Is this a smoke-free bar, Nathan?"

"It is. What do you think?"

"I think it will cost you some clients."

Nathan lifted his coffee mug in a toast to her, "No doubt. But it will also make us unique."

"And attractive to some folks who don't want that stale smell," she added.

"So do you think you might come here to watch Monday Night Football again?"

"I don't know about that, but I'm definitely going to test out that best burger in Appalachia claim."

"Really?" he said excitedly as he put down his coffee cup. "You know, it was Kevin's idea."

"Buying this bar was Kevin's idea?" she asked sharply.

He held up his hands, "No, Nat, not that. It was his idea to have a signature sandwich, like a burger, and to forget about making a profit on it."

"So it will be such a draw that your customers can't stay away and will tell all their friends."

Nathan nodded. "Even if we lose a little money on each burger, it's still the cheapest form of advertising."

She was not surprised by Kevin's cleverness, "So, is it working?"

"We do make the best burger in town. I can make you one right now if you want."

You are sweet, she thought, and she wanted to reach out and hold his hand; instead, she said, "Not tonight, thanks, but I'd just like to talk a while if that would work."

"How about down there?" asked Nathan as he pointed to an empty spot at the other end of the bar.

"That would be fine, but are you sure you can? I mean, you're all alone here."

He waved his left hand, "Let me just make a round and check on everyone here and I'll be right back. Sam will be back soon and he will take over then."

As Nathan checked on the customers at the two tables, a thin young man with long dark hair pulled back in a ponytail entered from the kitchen door at the back of the bar. After getting himself a cup of coffee he came to the end of the bar. Standing across from Nattie he asked, "What can I get you?"

"I'm fine," she said. "I'm waiting to talk to Nathan."

Mr. Ponytail pointed at her and said, "You're Nattie aren't you?"

"I am."

"He talks about you all the time," he said. Offering his hand, he added, "I'm Sam."

"Can I ask you a question Sam?" Nattie asked as she shook his hand.

"Sure."

"Do all the bartenders here drink coffee?"

Sam lifted his coffee cup and bowed his head., "Only the alcoholics."

"So you're an--" she couldn't find the right word.

"I'm an alcoholic. Three years in recovery, but I'm still an alcoholic."

"Don't you think being here in a bar is a little like tempting fate?"

He grinned. "I suppose it would be for some, but for me my drinking problems weren't when I was drinking with others. My problems with substances were when I got more and more isolated from others. Besides, everyone who works here is in recovery. We watch out for each other pretty closely."

The front door opened and in walked Twila Pierce followed by Kevin. He was wearing a bright yellow Hawaiian shirt that Nattie had given him for high school graduation. 'As long as you are going to be a beach bum you might as well look good,' she wrote on the card.

Kevin waved at Nattie as soon as he saw her at the end of the bar. He then said something to his date. Twila looked toward Nattie and smiled as they made their way around the bar.

After saying hello to Nattie and asking him to get her a Bud Lite, she excused herself and headed for the bathroom down the hall behind the dartboard. Kevin ordered Twila's Bud Lite and a Highlands Oatmeal Porter for himself. As Sam tended their order Kevin leaned toward Nattie and asked, "How's it going?"

"We haven't really talked yet. But it's been nice so far."

Kevin nodded, as if he were saying,"I read you loud and clear," then said out loud, "We'll sit over there and give you plenty of room to talk."

As Kevin took the beers he had ordered from the counter Nattie told him, "You don't have to sit over there Kevin."

At that same exact moment a gigantic baldheaded man walked in the front door. Kevin glanced at the big man and turned back toward Nattie and said, "It will be better if we give you and Nathan space."

While Nathan helped the two couples settle their bill, Sam tended the three gentlemen with loose ties at the bar; and Kevin settled along side of Twila at a table, the baldheaded behemoth slowly made his way toward the back of the bar without ever taking his eyes off of Nattie.

"Are you that detective woman who screwed up my life?" he snarled from half way across the room. The outburst drew the attention of everyone in the room. And now, with everyone watching, the goliath kept moving toward her. As he approached, Nattie considered brandishing the gun holstered at the back of her belt, but decided it was too crowded for that. Instead she stepped down from the stool and squared up her feet and shoulders to face the oncoming threat. Her single karate lesson had given her exactly one self defense strategy so far. She hoped it would be unnecessary.

The big gorilla finally came to a stop towering over her. In a menacing tone he barked, "Just who do you think you are?"

Nattie had just noticed the smell of cigarettes on his breath when he was suddenly jerked completely around. "Who do you think you are?" she heard Nathan say and then she watched gigantor pull his right arm back and punch Nathan with a straight right to the jaw. Nathan fell straight back. When he hit the floor he lay still.

Godzilla turned back toward Nattie. She moved closer and drove the heel of her hand almost straight up into his nose. She knew she had only one chance at this, but she had practiced it on a dummy at least fifty times. She pushed off the floor with her right foot and shifted her hips in order to get maximum power and impact into her punch. She knew she had connected because she could feel his head recoil as she drove her hand upward into his face.

"Holy shit," he screamed as he grabbed his face, "you broke my nose." And he stumbled from the bar chanting, "you broke my nose – you broke my nose."

Nattie dropped to her knees next to Nathan and slid a hand under his head. He just started to open his eyes when Twila leaned over her shoulder and asked, "Is he going to be okay?"

"He'll be pretty sore tomorrow, but he'll be okay," answered Sam as he handed Nattie a wet towel. "And he's gonna feel worse when he comes to and finds out what you did to that guy."

"Yeah, Sis, that was something," piped in Kevin. "Did you see that?" he asked the guys at the bar.

"Unbelievable," one said.

"That was the most amazing thing I've ever seen," said another.

The third man slowly exhaled and lifted his beer glass. "To the weaker sex."

"I have to go back to the office and write this up while it's still fresh in my mind," Twila told Kevin.

"Are you sure?" Kevin asked, but before she could answer, added, "Come on and I'll walk you to your car."

When another five minutes passed Nathan became fully alert. He tried to get up; but Nattie, with the aid of the two women drinking wine who were both nurses, insisted that he remain still for a while. One nurse suggested he go to the emergency room at the hospital to get checked for a concussion. They agreed he had hit the floor very hard with the back of his head. The other nurse had been an ER nurse previously and after examining him said, "If they look at him at the ER they will send him home as long as someone can stay with him for the night."

Nattie, of course, did not consider that this might be a job for someone else. "You keep him here while I go get my car," Nattie ordered Sam.

With her arm around Nathan's waist and his arm around her shoulder, Nattie brought them to the passenger side of her car and opened the door. The open door was a signal for Nathan to take his arm from around her, but he did not. Instead, he leaned a bit more weight on her and whispered, "I guess I'm not much of a protector either."

"You were, though, Nathan. That guy was a truck and you got him off me."

"Yeah," he said weakly, "with my face."

"No, really Nate, it was like you took a bullet for me."

He sat down in the passenger seat of her car, but kept his feet on the sidewalk and slowly lifted his face, "I would you know?"

"You would what, Nathan?"

"I would take a bullet for you, Nattie."

His voice quivered. She knew he was near tears. "I know you would," she said, resting the palm of her left hand on his right cheek. But before she could lean forward and kiss him she heard something behind her and she instinctively placed her right hand by her side.

"Is he okay?" asked a husky voice.

Nattie turned abruptly and caught sight of the gigantic baldheaded man moving toward them. An instant later her gun was pointed directly into the middle of his face, "Back off," she demanded. "Now!"

The big man looked startled and threw his hands up and stepped back. "Hey look," he said frantically, "that wasn't supposed to happen. He grabbed me from behind and I just reacted." He pointed at Nathan, "I just wanted to see if he was okay."

Nattie stepped forward, "Fold your fingers together and put your hands on top of your head."

The big man obeyed.

"Now," she said, "explain what you meant when you said, 'that wasn't supposed to happen'?"

The big man looked confused.

Without restraining her mounting frustration Nattie emphasized her words, "I want to know what was *supposed* to happen?"

"I was supposed to come in and say, 'Who do you think you are – you screwed up my life,' and I know I got the lines different, but I didn't think that mattered."

Nattie encouraged him to continue by waving the gun back and forth.

"Then I was supposed to run out of the bar after you hit me. I added the 'you broke my nose' myself."

"*Why* were you supposed to do all that?"

The confused look reappeared across his face. "Because I got paid to do all that," he answered, as if he were a school child guessing what answer the teacher was looking for.

"*Who* paid you?"

"It was a guy I met in a pottery class over at Virginia Intermont College."

"Have you got a name?"

"I don't remember his name. He paid me in cash just before I came in."

"Could you describe him?"

"Oh sure--He was that guy you were talking to right when I came in. You know, it was that guy in the yellow Hawaiian shirt."

THE END, NOT

CHECK OUT OTHER TITLES AT

csthompsonbooks.com

*AUTHOR'S BLOG

*PHOTOS

*AUTHOR'S BIO

*EXCERPTS OF FUTURE BOOKS

*SHORT VIDEOS OF AUTHOR READING

*MUSIC OF THE MONTH

www.ingramcontent.com/pod-product-compliance
Lightning Source LLC
Chambersburg PA
CBHW060807120626
46557CB00001B/118